A Summer of Second Chances

Suzanne Snow writes contemporary, romantic and up-lifting fiction with a strong sense of setting and community connecting the lives of her characters. Previously, she worked in financial services and was a stay-at-home mum before retraining as a horticulturist and planting re-designed gardens.

Living in Lancashire and appreciating the landscape around her always provides inspiration and when she's not writing or spending time with her family, she can usually be found in a garden or reading.

Also by Suzanne Snow

Welcome to Thorndale

The Cottage of New Beginnings
The Garden of Little Rose
A Summer of Second Chances

SUZANNE SNOW

A Summer of Second Chances

CANELO

First published in the United Kingdom in 2021 by

Canelo
31 Helen Road
Oxford OX2 0DF
United Kingdom

A CIP catalogue record for this book is available from the British Library.

Print ISBN 978 1 80032 499 2
Ebook ISBN 978 1 80032 167 0

Look for more great books at www.canelo.co

Printed and bound in Great Britain by Clays Ltd, Elcograf S.p.A.

1

To Fin, with all the love

And Irene, the very best of mothers-in-law

Chapter One

Daisy Lancaster didn't especially enjoy being an accountant in the summer, a profession that should have been at odds with her merry nature and bohemian style. She didn't mind her job so much in winter, living in the Yorkshire Dales where the weather could be grim and the light always changeable. Then she went about her business much as usual whilst only the hardiest of visitors ventured near in those long, darker days when some cafes closed their doors and hotels reduced their rates.

But today, driving back to her office on a flawless late July afternoon when freedom seemed to be beckoning in every dappled shadow and the sun burning high above the hills, she was battling the desire to abandon work for the day and go home. Routine and dedication were her usual defaults and she tried to push the guilt away, focusing instead on the meeting she had just left, pleased with the new addition to her client list, another family farm to whom she had been recommended.

She had never meant to become an accountant, a career her younger self would have dismissed with ease. Her instinctive eye for colour and style was a gift she had always believed would lead to a career in design until the end of her second year at college, when everything had altered and her life had swerved into a direction she had not anticipated. Giving birth at eighteen to her son Josh had not been part of her plan, but holding that tiny new person for the first time had brought realisation that she already couldn't imagine a life without him.

Independence and job security had become her purpose then and she had eventually achieved the qualifications required to set up her own practice specialising in farm and estate accounting. Living in a rural area meant she now had a steady list of clients, the largest of which was the diversified estate where she was based.

She was still a few miles from Thorndale when she decisively sent her car towards the village, avoiding a group of walkers crossing the road and the left turn that would have led eventually to her office. She didn't often skip work, and already she was smiling at the thought of an afternoon spent in her new sewing room.

Sewing was a skill she had learnt years ago, but it was so much more to Daisy. The method of bringing together different materials, threads and stitching to produce something unique and beautiful was as essential to her as eating or sleeping and soothed her mood more effectively than any other means. Nobody would be at home to mind if supper were beans on toast instead of something a little more nutritious, and a peaceful, uninterrupted few hours beckoned.

She pulled onto the drive, retrieving her laptop and handbag as she got out of her Land Rover, appreciating the warm sun on her face. The house was on a corner where two narrow lanes met and she realised she'd forgotten her keys to the back door and headed around to the front, crossing the courtyard outside the kitchen. She glanced up at the Georgian house, her childhood home.

Set over three floors, it had large sash windows which framed impressive views of the edge of the village from the front and the hills at the back, the light changing with every whim of the weather and altering the appearance of the stone in an instant. This same stone had been used to create a low wall sheltering the tiny front garden and Daisy heard a shout as she reached the front door. She waved at the woman who had appeared from her own house two doors down and turned to meet her neighbour on the lane alongside their homes.

'Hello, Daisy. I didn't expect to catch you until later, I thought you'd still be at work.' Connie Wells sounded cheerful as ever, proffering a parcel to Daisy with one hand and clutching a smart navy handbag in the other. 'There you go. Amazon were here this morning, and this wouldn't fit through the letterbox. I was on my way out when I spotted you.'

Connie had lived in the village for many years, knew everyone and liked most of them, and Daisy had always valued her friendship and unwavering support.

'Thanks, Connie. It's for Josh, as usual.' Daisy tucked the box underneath her arm, her laptop bag in the same hand. 'They're supposed to leave deliveries in the porch if we're not in, but I keep forgetting to leave it unlocked. And I should be at work really, but it's too nice and it is Friday, after all.'

'Don't blame you, no point being your own boss if you can't escape now and again.' Connie smoothed her neat grey bob with a small hand. 'Speaking of Josh, ask him to call in, will you please, when he's got five minutes? My new iPad is still getting the better of me, loath as I am to admit it, and I could do with a quick tutorial from someone who knows what he's doing.'

Connie had resisted all attempts to give up her home and move to her daughter's house in Suffolk, telling

3

people she had everything but the family here and what was FaceTime for, if not trying to pin down busy grand-children who wouldn't have time to see her even if she lived in the same house?

'I could do that for you if you like,' Daisy said. 'I'm not sure how much Josh will be around, he's not home until tomorrow and then he's off again on Monday.'

'I can wait. You know I like to see him and this is as good an excuse as any. How are you both liking being back at your mum and dad's? Josh told me the other day he'd set up that old drum kit again in his attic.'

'It's kind of strange and also really lovely.' Daisy was still getting used to living in her parents' house again after years in town with Josh. 'It was good of them to put us up after our house sold so quickly.'

'No sign of them coming home from Canada yet then?'

'No, I don't think they'll be back until the autumn, after Lucy's had the baby. Now they've both retired they want some time with her and the family first.'

Connie's lift had arrived and she opened the door of the car to get in. 'They'll enjoy that, no doubt. Pass on my love, won't you, when you speak to them? Doesn't seem five minutes since you girls were tiny, and now your sister's about to be a mum too.'

Daisy said she would and promised to ask Josh to call round to Connie's as soon as he could. They said goodbye and Daisy began to make her way back to the house, her attention straying to a family some way off, strolling towards the village.

A young woman was wheeling an empty pushchair, holding the hand of a small boy whilst the man alongside her had a younger girl perched on his shoulders, giggling as she waved a stuffed toy in his face. Daisy guessed from their steady pace and the way they seemed to be admiring their surroundings, that they were visitors to the village.

Her phone buzzed with a notification and she paused as she pulled it from her bag. Her friend Nina's image popped up, radiating vitality even through the small profile picture alongside a typically brief message, asking Daisy to join her at home this evening for Japanese food after a session at the gym. Daisy, who never went near a gym, replied at once, accepting Nina's offer. She knew she would not be expected to arrive much before seven and could sew until then.

Putting her phone back in her bag, she saw a cyclist coming up behind the family, who were nearing her house now. The bike was moving at speed as he pushed on, standing on the pedals. Without warning the little girl on her father's shoulders squealed and flung her toy away, where it landed soundlessly in the middle of the road. In a second the young boy had let go of his mother's hand and raced after it.

Daisy saw it all as though it were occurring in slow motion; she heard the woman's scream as she shoved the pushchair aside to go after him, saw the father lurch sideways, trying not to unbalance the girl on his shoulders. She began to run, her bags and the parcel bumping awkwardly against her side.

But they were still all too slow, and the cyclist had barely a moment to react before he would be upon the boy. She saw him yank the handlebars in his frantic haste, rubber tyres shrieking an angry protest as he shot past the boy on the wrong side of the lane just as the boy's mother snatched him back to safety, lifting the child straight off his feet in her terrified panic.

Too late, the cyclist tried desperately to regain control now that the boy was out of danger, but his course and balance had completely changed. Daisy gasped as he skidded into the low stone wall outside her house, the bike becoming entangled around him as he crashed beneath it. All was silent for a terrible second and then both children began to scream, the mother still clutching the boy tightly in her arms. With a quick look at them, satisfied they were shocked but unharmed, Daisy raced to the cyclist and dropped to her knees, leaving her bags and the parcel nearby.

'Please don't move! Keep still until we can lift the bike clear, you might be seriously hurt. Is there any pain? What about your hips? Can you still feel your arms and legs?'

She blurted out the words, alarmed by the lack of response as he lay sprawled against the stone, half sitting, half lying down, his eyes covered by sunglasses. He didn't seem to be unconscious as he groaned, but she expected him to be winded at least and carefully tried to disentangle the bike without hurting him further. She was concerned about the blood spilling down his left cheek into his beard, noticing that his arms and legs, exposed below his kit, were scraped and covered with bits of gravel and dirt. His tight T-shirt was torn across his left shoulder, revealing another patch of angry, reddened skin.

'Can you hear me? Hello?'

'I'm perfectly fine, you can stop wittering,' he told her shortly, pulling off his polarised glasses and watching her anxious attempts to free him. 'Just leave it alone; you're making it worse. I can manage.'

He tossed the glasses onto the ground beside him in disgust, his head low, and Daisy couldn't tell whether it was the accident or her assistance that was annoying him the most. By this point, the shocked father of the children had joined her and was much more effective than Daisy at lifting the bike clear, so she stepped back, wondering if she ought to call an ambulance.

'I'm really sorry,' the father told the cyclist, shooting her a worried look before turning once again to the man at his feet. 'It all happened so fast. Are you okay?'

'Totally.'

The cyclist seemed to be dividing his dismissive response between the two of them, his helmet disguising his expression. The children were still crying and he looked across, as though he had only just remembered the reason for the accident.

'Are they all right?' He tilted his head and the father nodded, thankful relief beginning to replace adrenalin in the wry twist of his lips.

'Yes, they're fine, thanks. It was such a shock, seeing Isaac running out like that and not being quick enough to stop him. We didn't hear you coming, and I suppose we weren't really thinking about traffic as it's pretty quiet here.'

The cyclist carefully touched each shoulder in turn, presumably to check for dislocations and then slowly climbed to his feet, much to Daisy's concern. She dashed forward again, ready to help if she was needed. He paused, hands on his knees as he caught his breath, blood spattering onto the ground from his cut. She knew he had sensed her nearness when he lifted an arm to halt her, the gesture creating an invisible barrier that lodged between them. Then he was upright, still scowling, and she breathed a sigh of relief as she realised there didn't appear to be any more serious injuries.

'Look, about your bike.' The father was hovering awkwardly but clearly keen to be away with his family, and he drew a wallet and mobile from his jeans pocket. 'We ought to compensate you if it needs repairing. If Isaac hadn't run out like that…'

The cyclist was already waving away the suggestion with a shake of his head, stopping abruptly as the blood began to run more freely down his cheek. 'No need. Thanks for the offer, though.' He lifted a hand to catch the blood and carefully touched the cut, wincing. 'I was probably going too fast anyway. I apologise, I ought to have been able to stop. As everyone appears to be all right, let's put it down to experience and we can all be on our way.'

With a final look of relief at Daisy, the father crossed back to his family and scooped the boy up in his arms as the toddler was settled into her pushchair. They walked away, giving a final wave before crossing the village green.

Daisy was alone with the cyclist and, despite what he said, felt certain he was in no fit state to simply cycle away with gravel rash and a cut cheek at the very least. He straightened the bike, still ignoring her, and she placed a cautious hand on his arm, trying to detain him. His head dropped and she saw him stiffen.

'I think you ought to have those wounds looked at before you leave.' Her hand fell away, and she pointed at the house. 'I live just there, why don't you come in and let me clean them up? It's either that or I'll have to call 999.'

Eventually he gave a reluctant nod in acceptance of her offer, wiping his hands on his ruined shirt. He undid the strap on his helmet with bloodied fingers and carefully lifted it off, looking at Daisy properly for the first time.

All thoughts of A&E slipped from her mind as she stared back, one hand rising to catch the strawberry blonde hair dancing around her face in the warm breeze.

Tall and with an elegance that suited a lean frame, the man wore plain black cycling shorts which clung to his muscular legs still splattered with gravel and mud. Her glance went to his grey top, slashed in the fall, seeing the same injury on the exposed shoulder before she looked up again. She took in his messy hair, a rich chestnut brown tumbling into uneven lengths ending around his collar and darkened with dampness where the helmet had sat.

Clear eyes of a vibrant, mossy green were fringed with lashes so distinctive they appeared almost drawn on, and a slightly wide nose lent his face a strength and simplicity that was striking. It was impossible to judge the shape of his lips as they were pursed together in an impatient line and nearly hidden by the rough beard, a shade darker than his hair and sprinkled with grey.

But it was his eyes and the expression in them that finally held her attention. Exhausted, aloof yet observant, as though he saw everything around him and felt none of it. Daisy immediately wanted to chase the look away, to see that extraordinary gaze lifted with the life she instinctively knew passed him by. None of it, she felt sure, was the result of the crash he had just endured but something far more profound before this day that had brought him to her door.

Appalled to realise she was staring, she reached down to collect her belongings, retrieving his sunglasses too and holding them out to him. He accepted with a shrug she supposed was meant to pass for his thanks, dropping them into the helmet and dragging the bike away from the wall. She spun around, quickly leading the way to the house, sensing his presence behind her as she tugged keys from her bag.

Whilst he propped his stuff against the house wall she opened the porch, stepping past two pots of pelargoniums she kept forgetting to water and an antique hat and coat stand that had come with the house when her parents had bought it thirty years ago. She unlocked the front door as well, leaving her bags and the parcel nearby. Suddenly the space felt smaller with the cyclist so near as he followed her into the hall, and she began to wonder about the wisdom of inviting him in.

'It's this way.' Daisy pointed along the passageway, his cycling shoes tapping out a rhythm on the floor behind her. The kitchen hadn't been updated in years and she loved the old-fashioned room with its freestanding oak dresser and ancient cream Aga, a worn, comfy armchair next to it. The large table was surrounded by six scruffy chairs and had been the scene of many family dinners, as well as a base for homework back in the day and the best place to be on hand to grab something delicious out of the baking oven.

She pointed to a chair as she busied herself boiling water, washing her hands and finding cotton wool and antiseptic. She added cool water to the jug she had filled with the boiled, hoping it would do as there was no time to wait; she sensed he would simply leave should any delay attempt to hold him back. Uncertainty was twisting in her stomach as she approached him, setting everything on the table and dipping cotton wool in the warm water.

Their eyes met again before hers slid to the cut on his cheek and she bent forward, concentrating on trying to clean the wound as gently as possible. She wanted to hold his face steady with her free hand but didn't dare, the gesture would seem far too intimate. He remained completely still as she continued, his stare settling somewhere in the distance.

'I don't think it will need stitches, but you might want to get it checked out properly, just to be sure.' She finished cleaning and reached for a jar of antiseptic cream nearby. 'I could put this on, if you like, as my hands are clean. Or you could wash yours and do it yourself?'

'You do it.'

His voice: politer now, reserved, suggesting he wouldn't waste words, came with the trace of an accent. Perhaps West Country; there was nothing of Yorkshire or anything northern in it. Daisy supposed he was here on holiday too or perhaps just hurtling through on his bike like so many others. Scooping out a blob of antiseptic cream, she touched his face lightly, aware of it being inches from her own, feeling the muscle in his cheek tightening as she carefully spread the cream across his wound.

She felt the brief brush of his beard as her fingers drifted lower and then straightened up, silently releasing the breath she hadn't even realised she had been holding. She reached for fresh cotton wool, gently wiping the gravel from his shoulder and applied cream once more, their eyes determinedly not meeting even as their skin continued to connect. She delved into the first aid kit and retrieved a packet of antiseptic wipes, handing them to him.

'You should probably clean the rest.'

Their eyes hitched together as he took the packet and she watched wordlessly as his gaze suddenly fell down her body, pausing somewhere below her chest.

'You've got blood on you. Sorry about that.' He indicated the lemon silk shirt she was wearing, which in all the fuss had separated from the waistband of her black pencil skirt and was dangling loose.

Daisy had left her new client less than two hours ago and already it felt like days, and the morning when she had chosen her outfit another life. She glanced down, seeing the red splash across her ribs, as well as the top button that had somehow popped undone, revealing a generous curve of cleavage and the lace-trimmed bra he couldn't possibly have missed.

'It doesn't matter. I'm sure it will come out.' Embarrassed, she turned away, quickly fastening the button and busying herself putting everything back whilst he cleaned off the last of the gravel and dirt. On a whim, she switched on the kettle and reached for two mugs. He was standing up, clutching a pile of dirty wipes and she pointed to a bin near the door. As she put tea bags in the mugs and reached for sugar, he spoke again.

'Thanks for your help. I'll get out of your way now.'

She spun around, the sugar bowl still in her hand. 'Are you sure? I don't want to delay you but perhaps you should have some sugary tea, to help with the shock?'

'I'm fine. Thanks anyway.' The stilted words sounded as though he wasn't used to having to rely on other people, and she wondered if he felt obligated to her in some way and didn't enjoy it. The silence lengthened between them as she saw him watching her tip the tea bag out of one mug and replace it on the shelf.

'Right,' she said briskly, understanding there was nothing more to be done and he was clearly impatient to leave. 'I'll see you out.'

He waited for Daisy to lead him back through the house and once he was outside again, the bike still propped against the wall, he looked at her. 'Thanks.' His voice was quieter now and she heard the sincerity in his few words. 'It was good of you to take me into your home.'

She was struggling to understand why she was so disappointed he was leaving already and that only goodbye would follow. He would not wait, she was certain, would not linger when nothing more could be said.

'You're welcome. I hope you're okay.'

He gave her a final, unreadable stare before walking slowly away, his movements careful. Daisy didn't wait but closed the door, all thoughts of sewing and the evening ahead forgotten. She returned to the kitchen and stood looking out of the window, unseeing of the view before her as she wondered whether she could have done anything else, something that would have made him stay.

But it was too late now; she had no way of knowing where he might have gone or means of contacting him had she even wanted to check on him. Remembered glimpses of his eyes and the expression in them danced before her as she trailed upstairs to change. It was only when she returned to the kitchen a few minutes later that she discovered a twenty-pound note on the table and a hurried line scribbled on the back of a box of plasters she had not put away.

'For the dry cleaning. Cheers.'

Chapter Two

Since the recent move back to her parents' house Daisy had fallen into a routine on Saturday mornings of an early walk followed by coffee in the village cafe and shop. Occasionally Nina came with her, but as a fell runner Nina found Daisy's outings too sedate and so they usually just met up whenever they could. Today, as she set off away from the village, Daisy was still yawning after the late night with Nina yesterday evening.

They'd devoured the sushi Nina had brought and had sat out in the garden long after dark, the evening warm even without the sun. Daisy had still been distracted by the encounter with the cyclist and had shared the accident with Nina, unable to help admitting that she wished she could contact him, try and find out if he really were all right.

Clever and intuitive, it hadn't taken Nina long to guess that Daisy's cyclist wasn't a middle-aged man or older, but somebody far more unsettling and attractive. Daisy couldn't explain her interest any better than confessing she was worried about him and Nina had sympathised, knowing they had no real means of identifying him.

Daisy had collected many walks over the years, but her favourite was still a footpath that climbed to a broad limestone pavement and eventually petered out through fields at a farm just beyond the village. Once a thriving business, now the farm was a quiet old place where the widowed farmer lived alone, chugging around the fields on a muddy quad bike with his faithful sheepdogs ever present.

For years Edwin Rawlinson had trained point-to-point racehorses and hadn't been able to part with the last two when he had given up his licence. Too young for retirement and not knowing any other life, a dapple-grey gelding and chestnut mare grazed the fields and pulled at bales of haylage to keep them fed in the winter months. Daisy could never pass by without stopping to talk to them. The horses knew her and would always make their way over, knowing she came armed with treats.

She had loved riding once, too, had thrived on the rush of adrenaline that came with exercising the pointers and the thrill of feeling at one with the horse underneath her. But like much else in her life during that summer after college, riding had become another thing she had given up, and life on the farm something that belonged in her former days.

Once she was through the untidy farmyard, waving as she spotted Edwin leaning against a vintage tractor, his dogs at his feet and clutching a mug of something she knew would be tea the colour of creosote, she hurried on towards the horses. She called and they came over, the mare putting back her ears and nipping crossly at the gelding. Daisy bit chunks out of an apple, chiding the mare for her grumpiness, dividing the pieces between the horses. The gelding, Flint, was quieter and Daisy rubbed his face, stroking his ears gently.

He tried to scratch his head on her shoulder and she laughed wryly as he deposited a blob of green slime on her chest. The mare, Lark, took her piece of apple and wandered away, swishing her tail as flies swooped around them, the swallows not far behind. Not for the first time Daisy wondered about slinging a saddle and bridle onto Flint and seeing what would happen if she jumped on top. But as fast as the thought arrived, she sent it away with the usual churning feeling in her stomach and resumed her walk, heading downhill away from the farm.

The village was busier when she returned, the car park already filling up with visitors and she knew she was unlikely to get a seat in the cafe now. The doorbell jangled briskly as she went inside anyway, still wanting her coffee. Her glance went to the familiar display of local arts and crafts and she pushed her sunglasses into her hair to get a better look.

The old post office had been knocked through to the cafe beside it, and when the shop had expanded into the cafe Daisy had created a series of cooks' aprons for the staff as gifts, each individually designed yet still reflecting the shop's brand. So many customers had enquired about them that she'd agreed to produce more to sell. Their shelf was almost empty, and Daisy thought about the choice of cottons she already had in her sewing room, her mind dashing ahead to how quickly she could supply a few more.

She carried on through the shop to the cafe beside it, tempting aromas of coffee and bacon greeting her as she approached the counter. Out of habit her glance fell over the scattered tables and was already returning to the queue when something caught her attention. She turned her head again, meeting the gaze of the cyclist from yesterday, sitting alone with an empty plate in front of him. She tried to restrain her naturally wide smile, hoping it had remained appropriate to their very brief acquaintance, and failed utterly.

She received only the merest nod in reply and then it was her turn to order. She rushed out a request for coffee as she wondered why the cyclist was here and if he would come over. Based on the coolness of his greeting, Daisy wasn't about to go tripping over tables and toppling into his lap in an attempt to say hello. Nevertheless, she sensed the imprint of his eyes on her whilst her cappuccino was poured and she took it with a quick thank you, returning through the shop.

She halted at the door to let somebody else in and then she was outside, waving to Charlie Stewart, the vicar, crossing the green with his little daughter on his shoulders. She saw his answering grin as she followed his progress, heard the roar of a fell rescue vehicle speeding out of the village. Distracted by the noise, Daisy didn't notice the shop doorbell again and jumped when she realised the cyclist was standing beside her.

'Hello again.'

He was facing her, his voice polite and – dare she hope – friendlier. She had to lift her head to look at him properly. The cut on his cheek had dried, reddened, and she couldn't miss the beginnings of a spectacular bruise surrounding it. His hair was wet, held back from his face by a different pair of sunglasses. Conscious of his height and air of formality, even in a T-shirt and combat shorts, she searched for a suitable response.

'Morning. How are you feeling? Did you get your injuries checked out?'

'You did that,' he reminded her. 'I'm fine, a bit sore but nothing a good recovery plan won't sort.'

'I'm really glad you're okay, it could've been so much worse.'

Silence fell over them as she sipped her coffee. It seemed almost as though he was out of practice with people and she wondered why he had followed her if he had nothing much to say. She wanted to touch his face again, to soothe the bruise that marked him, her fingers already familiar with the shape of his cheekbone. Her eyes went to her wrist, searching for a watch that wasn't there, hoping to imply that she didn't intend to delay him, much as she wanted to.

'I'd better go. Nice to see you again.' She stepped past him with a breezy smile and then he spoke quickly.

'I hope you don't mind, I called at your house earlier but there was no answer. I noticed you have a holiday cottage for rent and I wondered if it's available?'

'Oh!' Daisy had forgotten about the sign beside the gate advertising the tiny barn conversion at the bottom of her parents' garden, taken aback by his request. 'I see. I'm sorry, it's not available.'

'I was expecting you to say that, I suppose. It's the beginning of the summer holidays, I imagine most holiday properties are already occupied.'

'Oh, it's not because of the holidays,' she told him, registering the slight lift of an eyebrow as he continued to watch her. 'We're not accepting bookings until we've had a new shower installed.'

'And when will that be?'

'I'm not sure. Our plumber has broken his arm and we're waiting for him to arrange a replacement.'

'Is it usual to take so long? You must be losing a lot of business.'

Daisy shrugged, accepting the truth of his comment. 'He's the son of a family friend and we've always used him,' she explained. 'It should be done any day now, hopefully.'

'In that case I'm still interested. Would you let me have a look at the cottage?'

She had the impression of determination in his question, despite the stillness in his body, hands loose at his sides, her pulse spiking at the thought of him staying so close, even for just a few days. 'But if you're here on holiday then surely you'll be gone before the shower is replaced?'

'I'm looking for somewhere to stay for the next few weeks whilst I train for a triathlon.' His expression, never fully revealed, was already shuttering again, even as he offered an explanation for his request. 'I don't plan to be around much, I just need a base and your cottage would suit that purpose very well. What do you think?'

Taking a moment to consider his words, her glance swept across his chest and she remembered his warm skin beneath hers as she had dressed his cut yesterday. How her fingertips had lingered, wanting to explore the outline of his face and trace its unusual beauty.

'I'm still not sure we can help but I could let you see it.' She tried to replace her interest with a more business-like sense. 'I'm going home now, actually. Would you like to come back with me and see it?'

The words were gone from her before wisdom could join them and he was already nodding as he fell into step alongside her. They crossed the bridge over the river, dodging a group of walkers examining a map on the edge of the green. Daisy pointed out all that Thorndale could offer as they walked, from the excellent deli in the post office to the restaurant in The Courtyard and the new Pilates studio recently opened. He said nothing in response to her chatter and didn't offer any reply until they reached her parent's house and paused at the gate.

'Perhaps it's time we introduced ourselves.' He offered Daisy his hand and a little more friendliness in his voice. 'I'm Ben.'

His lips softened in the beginnings of a smile, bringing a hint of gentleness to his face she had not previously witnessed. She took his hand and as he shook hers firmly, the warmth in his expression disappeared as swiftly as it had come, replaced by the usual distance she was coming to expect.

'Hello, Ben. Daisy Lancaster.' She set off along the narrow path to the house to unlock the porch door. 'I'll go and get the keys for the cottage, I won't be long.'

It felt strange, not inviting him back inside after what had happened yesterday and she quickly found the keys and returned to him. She wanted to offer him another smile, unused to restraining her natural brightness, but his clear gaze invited no intimacy and they were silent as she led him around the side of the house.

She opened another gate set into the stone wall and they entered a courtyard leading to the main garden. The long, narrow plot was made wider by large herbaceous borders sweeping around the lawn, with a low hedge separating the small building in front of them from the main garden.

Ben followed her onto a stone terrace decorated with terracotta pots which brought vibrancy and cheer to the entrance of the tiny house. The cottage had originally been a single storey barn until it had been converted into a compact holiday let with another smaller room adjoining it to the left.

'This is it.' She kept her voice cheerful as she slid a key into the door. 'Welcome to Parlour Cottage.'

She stood aside so that he could enter first. Cool air met them, but the brightness of the day was undimmed, spilling through the windows. Despite the old-fashioned charm of the cottage, every appliance was modern and sophisticated, chosen to compliment the cream kitchen units and to appeal to every kind of holidaymaker, from the traditional seeking a comfortable base to those who appreciated a more contemporary touch.

Paintings and sculptures from local artists were high-lighted by simple frames and clever positioning, and Daisy realised afresh how stylish the whole effect was. The little cottage had seemed to shrink the moment Ben was inside and she took herself off to wait in the kitchen, watching him look around with a level of interest she couldn't help wishing he'd shown in her.

'It's just the one king-sized or twin beds with an en-suite.' She pointed to a door leading off the sitting room.

'That's fine, it's just me.' He was already moving towards the door to inspect the bedroom. He was back in moments and she knew that whatever decision he had made, he had done it in seconds. 'It's ideal, I'd really like to take it. Is there a solution to the problem with the shower? When do you realistically expect it to be replaced?'

'I'm sorry but I have no idea.' The thought of having Ben at the bottom of the garden for the rest of the summer, with his soulful gaze and long-limbed elegance, was a distraction from practical thoughts about showers, and she forced her mind back to the problem. 'It could be another couple of weeks and I don't see how you can manage without one. There aren't any public ones nearby you could use instead.'

Ben was silent, and Daisy wanted to kick herself for allowing him to view the cottage without any real hope of renting it. But he had barely been out of her thoughts since the accident and seeing him again this morning had wakened the unusual sense of being drawn to him. Without warning an idea fell into her head, one that had her dashing out the words before she could drag the plan into proper order in her mind first.

'I suppose you could use our downstairs shower, in the house.' She carried on, clarifying her offer. 'There's one next to the utility room, between the larder and the kitchen. We hardly ever need it so you could have it all to yourself. It would mean coming up to the house, though, which would probably be a nuisance for you.'

'No, I think that could definitely work.' Ben's hair had dried now, its untidiness making her think it had been some time since it was last cut. It was getting in his way and he pushed it back with an impatient hand, resetting his sunglasses to hold it off his face. 'If you're sure it won't inconvenience you? I don't want to be in your way, but I will be out most of the time.'

'I think it would be fine, just until the new shower is in anyway. I'll give the plumber a call on Monday to see where he's up to. The kitchen door can be locked so I could let you have a key to the outside door from the courtyard and you can let yourself in and out whenever you need to.'

'That sounds perfect.' He drew out a wallet from the pocket of his shorts. 'Shall we discuss terms? How much do you normally charge per week in summer?'

'It's seven hundred and fifty pounds a week,' she told him, wondering if her senses would ever reorganise them-selves back to the rational level where they normally resided now she'd seen him again, never mind the thought of Ben staying here. In her garden. For the summer. She dragged her mind back to money, far away in this moment, and already knew she was prepared to offer him a discount if he queried the price. 'I hope that's okay, it's pretty standard around here in the summer, even though the cottage is so small.'

'Seeing as you're being kind enough to let me use facilities in your home and that's going to disturb you somewhat, why don't we say a thousand pounds a week and I'd like it until early September so that's six weeks. What do you think?'

Daisy's mouth fell open at the offer, astonished by the amount he was prepared to spend. She shut it again quickly, not wanting him to see her gaping gormlessly. 'But that's far too much! The cottage isn't worth it, and you would definitely find something bigger and nearer the towns for that price.'

'I don't consider it too much and I'm sure it's not an unreasonable rate for a holiday property in this area.' He sounded as though he had already prepared the reply to counter her refusal. 'It's a business arrangement and it'll go some way to restoring your lost earnings. Yes or no?'

Daisy wondered if the offer of more money was the language he spoke in his own world and usually bought him success. She held out her hand and he crossed the room in two steps to take it.

'Eight hundred and seventy-five,' she said, neatly dividing the difference between her price and his. 'I'm not Dick Turpin.'

Ben almost smiled properly at that as they shook hands for the second time. Amusement flared in his eyes before they darkened suddenly with an expression of

23

wretchedness. Daisy slipped her hand free, certain he had revealed far more in that moment than he had intended. He took one last look around and followed her outside so she could lock up until his return.

Chapter Three

Daisy was in her sewing room adjoining the cottage, but she was distracted, aware of Ben's imminent arrival, and after just an hour returned to the house instead. She found a recipe book, flicking through it until she settled on chocolate brownies. She gathered ingredients, telling herself that her sudden desire to bake had nothing to do with him about to move in.

She was in the porch watering the pelargoniums when he arrived, wheeling the bike with a rucksack on his back, another on his uninjured shoulder and an acoustic guitar slung across his chest. He pushed the gate aside, leaving the bike propped against the wall and made his way to the front door. She tried to look surprised and knew she had failed when his gaze fell to the water trickling onto the tiles and missing the pots completely.

'Oh!' Daisy dropped the watering can with an embarrassed clatter and opened the door. 'You're here. I'll open the cottage and leave you in peace.'

Ben didn't seem to mind the lack of pleasantries or a proper greeting, and she wasn't expecting any more from him as he followed her through the garden. She unlocked the front door of the cottage, a jolt of misgiving returning as he dropped both rucksacks on the floor. She wasn't sure why she was hovering or searching for words of welcome, edging back towards the open door as she wondered about the wisdom of allowing him to stay for so many weeks.

'I'll leave you to settle in. I'll be in the house if you need anything.'

'Thanks.' He didn't look at her or offer any further reply.

'And I'll drop in a booking form, so you can let me have your details.'

'Fine.' Ben was rifling through one of his bags and Daisy jumped when she heard a familiar voice right behind her.

'Hey. What's going on?'

She moved aside, her eyes softening with a warmth that automatically brought tenderness to her expression as she saw a teenage boy on the threshold. The boy looked curiously at Ben before bringing his questioning gaze back to Daisy.

'Josh, this is Ben.' Daisy's attention darted between the two. Ben's face was as bland as ever, revealing nothing, whilst the boy's had firmed as he attempted to size up the stranger. 'I've decided to let him rent the cottage for a few weeks and he's just arrived. I was about to head back to the house and leave him to settle in. Welcome home, by the way.'

'What about the shower? Has it been sorted?'

'Oh, we've come to an arrangement about that.' Daisy touched the boy's arm. 'I'll tell you later. Let's go.'

'If we're going to be neighbours then perhaps we should introduce ourselves.' Ben crossed the room to stand before Josh and offer his hand. 'Pleased to meet you.'

Josh stepped forward and they shook, Ben's gaze softening to reduce the challenge he had clearly sensed in the boy. Already Daisy had noticed Josh's eyes sliding to

26

the guitar propped against the sofa and knew it wouldn't be long before he was questioning Ben, wanting to know every detail of its provenance and what music he played.

She noticed Josh was slightly taller than their visitor, certain he was drawing on every centimetre he possessed to make himself appear bigger. But apart from a similarity in height, physically they were quite different. Josh had not yet filled out across his chest and his limbs were slimmer, even though his arms and shoulders were strengthened by years of drumming.

'So, do you and my mum know each other? Is that why you're here?'

For the first time in their short acquaintance Daisy saw a flash of surprise in Ben's eyes as they raced from Josh to Daisy and back again.

'Your mum? Daisy is your mother?' His words were rushed, as though he had blurted them out without first measuring their meaning.

She was used to it, used to the searching looks and occasional judgement as people tried to guess the age difference between her and Josh. Her heart-shaped face, with its smooth, creamy skin, lively hazel eyes and full lips meant she appeared younger than her years; she had been mistaken for Josh's older sister more than once.

'So you don't know her then.' Josh responded quickly and she recognised the note of aggression in his reply as her son rested a protective arm across her shoulders.

She felt its weight lying there, implying a shield she did not need. Already over six feet tall, her usually delightful son had long since passed her in height and had to fold himself over to share the hugs they still enjoyed from time to time. Since leaving school a few weeks ago, his dark blonde hair was shorter, giving his face a maturity and strength that still took Daisy by surprise.

Her little boy, whose hand she had held through endless scrapes, moody moments and every triumph, had grown into a handsome young man. Being the drummer in a band that was attracting attention, both through their social media and increasing number of local gigs, certainly did his appeal no harm. Daisy was careful to step back, to be there if required and no more.

'No, we just met yesterday.' Ben glanced at Daisy again, curiosity sparking in the green depths of his eyes as he leant against the sofa. 'I enquired about the cottage and Daisy, er, your mum, has been kind enough to let me stay whilst I train for the Helvellyn triathlon.'

'You're an athlete?' Josh was blunt, and Daisy slipped his arm from her shoulders, wordlessly assuring both that she was fine standing by herself.

Ben almost smiled at that. 'No. I'm on sabbatical and I'll be heading back to work after the race.'

'What do you do?' Josh was curious now and she felt him shift away from her, his gaze going to the guitar again.

'Josh.' Daisy gave him a look practised over years of motherhood and one she knew he would recognise. 'We don't need to pry.'

'I work in finance; I'm based in New York.' Ben's quick reply was for both of them and she filed the information away in her mind, his answer raising more questions she wasn't sure she could ask.

'You're a banker? Your accent's British though; you're not from the US.' Josh was still curious and Daisy was happy to wait for Ben's reply before she left and took her son with her.

28

A pause before Ben replied. 'Hey look, if you want to interview me then at least let's sit down and do it properly.' There was a trace of amusement in his voice as he pointed at the kitchen table.

'Absolutely not, we're leaving now,' she said firmly. So not the explanation from Ben she had been hoping for. It was time to go and she gave Josh a quick dig in the ribs to back up her statement. 'Josh, you ought to be unpacking.'

She held the door wider and Josh nodded at Ben before backing outside. Ben was still propped against the sofa.

'Sorry,' Daisy told him, pulling the door shut as she followed her son. Josh was hovering on the terrace and fell into step beside her as they headed back to the house.

'Hey, Mum, did you see the guitar?' Josh couldn't restrain the enthusiasm in his voice.

'I did. It looked very nice.'

'Nice! It was a Gibson acoustic cutaway, a J-45. It's iconic!'

'If you say so, you know I know nothing about musical instruments.'

'What do you know about him though, Mum?' Josh sounded serious as he swiped the screen of the phone in his hand. 'Have you run it by Granny and Grandad to check if they're okay with letting someone stay for so long?'

Nothing and no, but Daisy didn't want to admit the truth to her sensible son. 'He seems nice,' she hedged, not at all sure that Ben was just yet. But she already knew she wanted to Ben to stay for reasons she didn't yet under-stand, wanted to somehow decipher the unhappiness she had sensed in him. 'Granny and Grandad don't generally ask guests to provide their life history before booking.'

Her parent's usual visitors were couples or friends who holidayed for a week or two and then disappeared back to their own lives, not a man in his middle thirties with the body of an athlete and the eyes of a poet.

'True, but then they usually book in advance with an email address and details that can be checked out. I'm not trying to worry you; I just think you need to be sure about him, that's all. And what's the arrangement with the shower?'

Josh followed her into the house, propping himself against the Aga. She realised that he must be serious indeed if he was looking at her and not his phone, and the thought made her smile. 'I've said he can use this one, next to the utility room.'

'In the house? But you're going to be here most of the summer on your own. Is that a good idea?'

Daisy still hadn't quite got used to it. Josh had finished his GCSEs and was about to start the second week of his National Citizen Service summer camp. School over, she knew a different life awaited him. She never let him see the moments of sadness she felt now he was almost grown and about to make his way in the world without her.

He would be starting college in the autumn and as it was closer to where his dad lived and meant a short bus ride instead of two longer ones, she had agreed it made sense for Josh to live with his dad during the week and come home to her at the weekends, a move she hadn't let him see she was dreading.

For all that she would miss him, she couldn't blame him, and nor would she hold him back, recognising that one of the joys of raising a loving and happy little boy was watching him mature into an accomplished young man. She felt he would always come home when he wanted to, even if it was just for her Bolognese sauce and his favourite bed.

'I'll be fine,' she assured him, beginning to wish that the last twenty-four hours hadn't unfolded in quite the way they had. Before Ben had arrived, she had known exactly how to be comfortable in this house, had known just where her life fitted in around everyone else's. Now that he was here, unfamiliar sensations were unsettling her to a degree she wouldn't have believed possible in only a few hours. 'I'll keep the kitchen door locked so there's no chance of him wandering in unannounced. Is Mia coming tonight?' Deftly she changed the subject, seeing the phone back in Josh's hand.

'Probably. Why do you ask?'

'I just wondered, that's all. Am I still allowed to do that? And how was your week away?'

She heard his laugh as he disappeared into the hall, heading to the attic. 'What you mean is, is she my girl-friend? We're talking, Mum, we're friends. The week was awesome, and you've already forgotten to lock that door.'

Daisy locked the kitchen door to satisfy Josh as she thought about Mia, a former classmate with long blonde hair and beautiful manners. She was a delightful girl whom Daisy liked, and she sighed, wondering about the complications of teenage dating and social media as she heard Josh bounding up the stairs, his suitcase dumped in the hall.

She and Josh had begun life together in this house on the top floor, and now it was Josh's domain for whatever time he would spend here over the summer, full of his clothes, the broken keyboard he was determined to mend and the ever-expanding collection of old vinyl as well as his very first drum kit that he couldn't bear to part with.

31

Daisy glanced at the old clock on the wall and, realising it was too early to start supper, reached for her laptop instead, settling to work out of habit as a practical solution to the uncertainty filtering through her mind.

Josh reappeared within half an hour, already beginning to fizz with the excitement of the gig and the evening to come. He'd spent the morning sound checking and setting up with the band before being dropped back at home to change, desperate to turn seventeen in the autumn and obtain his driving licence as soon as possible. Something else Daisy wanted him to achieve, although she wasn't wholly looking forward to the reality of him driving alone.

She followed him to the front door, waving to his friend's dad waiting in the lane. She slipped her arms around Josh, giving him a swift hug and he squeezed her back. 'Be safe tonight, have the best time and remember you're all brilliant and destined for great things. Love you. Say hi to your dad, Wendy and the girls for me.'

It was the same thing she told Josh every time he played a gig and he smiled as he let her go. 'Thanks Mum, will do. I'll be back on Friday night, okay?' He straightened up and looked at her, and she marvelled once again how that tiny little boy had so soon become a young man. 'But if you need me around, let me know and I'll try and get back.'

There was a question in his statement and Daisy shook her head. Her decision to let the cottage would not be allowed to impact his plans, of that she would make sure.

'I'm perfectly fine,' she assured him. 'But thank you, you know I appreciate your thoughtfulness and there's no reason to spoil your week away. I'm looking forward to hearing about your cooking and living in halls. Can't wait to see the posts of the band later.'

And he was gone, jumping into the car with a wave. Alone in the house once again, she couldn't settle to anything as the evening stretched before her, unwilling for once to disappear into her sewing room with Ben so close, and she knew Nina was busy tonight.

The irony didn't escape her that, as her child became more independent, many of her contemporaries had young children and were still on the school run, supervising never ending homework and cramming in after-school activities. So here she was again, not quite at one with her friends' lives and still forging her own path, somehow out of step with those around her.

Daisy looked around the kitchen for inspiration, wondering what she could be bothered to cook for supper, and her gaze alighted on the tray of cooled brownies. She realised that a few were missing already; Josh must have made an opportunistic grab as he had passed by. An idea quickly formed in her mind and she took four brownies, slid them into a container and made her way through the garden to the cottage.

She hesitated on the terrace as silence and a closed door met her, not certain Ben was still inside even though his bike was propped against the wall. She knocked and when there was no reply tapped once again. The door was slowly pulled back and apprehension fluttered in Daisy's stomach at the lack of warmth on Ben's face. She gave him a dazzling smile to counter it.

'Hi, Ben.' She carried on, aware she was rushing, her smile faltering at the sudden incredulity in his gaze. 'Sorry to bother you, I've brought you these.'

She thrust the container towards him, startled still further when he made no move to take it. 'It's only chocolate brownies. Don't worry, I'm not planning to pop in every day. Call them a "welcome to Parlour Cottage" gift if you like. Oh, I forgot to mention earlier, I left a few basics for you in the larder cupboard and there's fresh milk in the fridge.' She paused and a nervous giggle escaped. 'I promise to leave you in peace after this.'

Ben looked at the box but didn't attempt to take it. She rattled it, as though trying to prove the existence of the brownies and finally he spoke.

'That's kind of you but I'm afraid they'd be wasted on me. That type of ingredient combination doesn't form part of my current nutrition plan and I've absorbed enough fat for today so I'm going to have to pass. I appreciate the thought but I'm sure I'll find something more suitable for tonight.'

Daisy stared at him, quickly registering the quite definite dismissal of her gift. Silence tinged with tension filled the space between them as her astonished gaze challenged his steady one. She blurted out the words filling her mind, a cooler smile adding sarcasm to her meaning.

'Well, the macrobiotic shop in the village has closed for the weekend but never mind, there might still be a tin of beansprouts someone left behind if you're lucky. Oh, and the milk in the fridge? Really sorry but it's just dairy. You know, from cows?'

She glared at him as her natural kindness was doused by his indifference, already horrified by the words she had flung at him and the depth of emotion he aroused in her so effortlessly. As she whirled around to make her escape, she thought that his lips might even have been twitching but as she had never actually seen him smile properly, she couldn't be sure.

Clutching the box as though she would never relinquish it and certainly not to an ungrateful athlete, she marched furiously back to the house wondering who, ever, refused freshly baked chocolate brownies, and dreaming up all the words that rhymed with banker. She barged into the house, certain now she knew as much as she ever wanted to know about Ben, tossing the container onto the table and locking the kitchen door again to bar him an entry she doubted he would attempt to gain.

Daisy was still smarting when she eventually went up to her old bedroom at the back of the house. It had changed over the years she had been gone and although the generous proportions and delightful view of the garden remained, the pale grey walls spoke of modernity, as did the king-sized bed and comfy, if snug, lilac sofa, still strewn with the hand-stitched patchwork cushions she had made as a teenager. She went to draw the curtains to shut out the evening and her glance hurried beyond the garden to the cottage.

Light spilling from the little house was enough for her to see Ben on the terrace, perched on one of the garden chairs, head bent over his guitar. Even from this distance she recognised a relaxation in his frame she had never before seen, watching his fingers moving over the strings to draw out the music he clearly found calming. She closed the curtains before he caught her staring down at him, her mind full of questions and concerns as she changed for bed, alone here again and yet not quite.

Chapter Four

Sundays had followed a rhythm throughout Daisy's child-hood that unconsciously laced the day with familiarity. She'd have a simple breakfast followed by a service at the church in the village, followed by a sleep-inducing roast lunch cooked by her dad and one of her mum's mouth-watering puddings, often including last-minute guests.

Daisy had made lifelong friends at the church; had had her first kiss there, an unforgettable encounter with the local blacksmith's son who was her first crush and had lasted for one special Christmas holiday only. She had eventually found a new home at a larger church in town, finding friends who had supported her without judgement as she had studied and looked after Josh in those early years, when her relationship with his dad was breaking apart.

Since Charlie and Sam Stewart, the young vicar and his wife, had arrived in Thorndale, the morning service Daisy remembered had changed, although tradition was main-tained at evensong later. They still met in the building, but a band had joined the organ and the service included a simple brunch for anyone who wanted it, instead of tea and biscuits later. Daisy really liked Charlie's relaxed manner and Sam's lively, open nature. She and Sam were getting to know one another better, bonding over a community fundraising initiative they were both involved in.

But today Daisy was back at the village church and, following tradition, she left a chicken in the Aga to roast whilst she went to the service. She didn't really know how many to expect for lunch; Josh was in town at his dad's and other than Mrs Hodges, who lived between Daisy and her neighbour Connie, and was ninety-three and had her meal on a tray at home, it was likely to be just Daisy tucking into more freshly dug new potatoes than she should.

It had been another sleep-disturbed night, her second since the accident with Ben, and she was tired, unable to ignore that he was only a short stroll through the garden away. She decided it would be pointless to offer him lunch too, quite sure that such a meal would not fit with a diet probably honed by expensive New York nutritionists.

Her eyes went to the box of brownies, still on the table where she had chucked them last night, and she wished she hadn't responded to his refusal in quite the way she had. Her natural friendliness had vanished in the face of his dismissal and she still felt as though his rejection had included her along with the kindly meant gift.

The day – and seemingly the rest of the summer with Josh away for most of it – stretched before her with nothing much more than work to keep her busy. Even sewing didn't seem to beckon with its usual promise of pleasure. The booking form she needed Ben to complete was sitting on the dresser, and Daisy thought again about why he was here in Thorndale. She'd quickly googled the triathlon he'd mentioned and discovered it was taking place in Cumbria the first weekend in September.

She collected a wire basket from its usual spot on the dresser to fill with new potatoes from the garden and tugged at the latch on the kitchen door. When it wouldn't open as normal it dawned on her why it was locked, and she had to rifle through a drawer to find the spare key where she'd tossed it yesterday. She tucked the basket back over her arm and hurried into the corridor just as the door to the shower room was pulled back and Ben stepped out.

Daisy shrieked and stopped dead, the basket clattering into her hip. She had almost walked right into him, so close were they, and she hastily backed up until the solid barrier of the doorframe was pressing into her. He was wearing only a pair of crumpled grey shorts and rubbing his long, wet hair with a towel, holding a T-shirt in his other hand. He, too, halted abruptly and she saw the usual mask of indifference slide over his face, draining it of all expression.

'You startled me,' she muttered, trying not to stare at the curve of his biceps and the toned and sun-tanned chest, covered with dark hair narrowing down to a hard and muscular stomach. She noticed the angry gash on his left shoulder, reddened but apparently not infected. Sensing him watching her, she forced her eyes away, finding the basket on her arm suddenly fascinating and inched it around until it became a physical barrier between them. 'Sorry. I didn't realise you were in there.'

'I was showering,' he told her brusquely, the towel falling to his side, the tousled lengths of his hair still damp. 'We agreed, remember?'

She did, only too well, along with the realisation he was paying handsomely for the privilege. She also knew she couldn't continue reacting to him in an absurd manner every time he appeared, but the blush warming her face was already blooming as the fresh, lemon scent on his skin drifted over her in the confined space.

'Of course I do.' She paused, her feet rooted to the floor. 'How's your shoulder? It looks a bit sore.'

'It's fine. There's some pain but the skin is healing and I'm making sure I keep it mobile, I can't afford to let it stiffen up.' He hesitated. 'Daisy, look, I'm sorry about last night, and the brownies. I was offhand and must have seemed ungrateful. It was kind of you to think of me.'

'I was a bit sharp too,' she admitted, making light of the disappointment she had felt. She glimpsed a sudden softness in his expression before it was lost again. 'There isn't a macrobiotic shop in the village, as I'm sure you've realised, but the cafe serves a good range of vegan food. I expect you do have to be careful what you eat, as you're training.'

'Thanks.'

He pulled his T-shirt over his head and Daisy took that to be a clear signal the conversation was at an end and he didn't appreciate her interest. She shoved the back door open, moving away from the ridiculously distracting sight of him and the way her body had reacted with a responsiveness she had never before known. Her pulse was still thudding and she told herself firmly it was because of the surprise of almost walking right into him. She assumed Ben wasn't far behind as she walked through the garden but he made no attempt to catch up with her.

After Daisy had cleared away lunch she settled at the table with a glass of wine and her laptop, searching for a spreadsheet she needed to update. She had been keen to offer help with a fundraising project underway in the village and was now more grateful than ever to have something to occupy herself with.

Community bus transport was a vital link in areas that had no access to commercial services and Thorndale's own scheme was at risk of floundering under the requirement to update its ancient minibus. The vehicle and its fleet of volunteers and drivers were often the only method of transporting those who had no other means to travel and almost everyone in the village agreed that this service must not be lost.

The fundraising group was holding an auction of 'promises' along with a barn dance in a few weeks, and Daisy had offered to work on the promises. Her list was steadily growing as more people agreed to offer their time or skills in return for winning bids on the night.

She was still seeking a few more imaginative promises to auction off. To date she had a hot air balloon flight, a man with a van for a day and a walk-on part in a local pantomime amongst the highlights. The landlord of The Coach and Horses just beyond the village, as a direct favour to her, had offered exclusive use of the pub for an evening and the bookseller at the top of the green had managed to secure the personal appearance of a highly respected writer for a signing, no mean feat in such a rural location.

Daisy updated her list with the latest promises, her mind drifting back to Ben. Following her earlier thoughts, her fingers strayed across the keyboard to open a browser. She recalled that he had replied, somewhat vaguely to Josh's questioning, that he was a banker in New York. She knew, even as she guiltily typed his name into Google, and the results popped up – several million of them – that *Ben, Banker, New York* was going to get her absolutely nowhere. She tried Images instead with no more success and knew she would have to wait for the completed booking form, which she ought to take to him sooner rather than later.

The doorbell rang and it was Amazon again with another parcel for Josh. Heading back to the kitchen, intending to text him to let him know it had arrived, she stopped dead in surprise. Ben was standing beside the table and her pulse rocketed. She'd done it again. She'd forgotten to lock the door and alarm sent heat rushing to her cheeks.

'I found these in the garden, thought I'd return them before they got broken.' Ben's voice rattled through the space between them and Daisy saw her sunglasses sitting beside the laptop. She had been wearing them when she'd gone to dig for potatoes after bumping into Ben and had forgotten she'd left them outside.

'I did knock, a couple of times actually, but the door was open so I hoped you wouldn't mind if I came in. I can see you're busy.'

His eyes fell knowingly to the laptop and another blast of heat raced across her skin – he knew she had been searching for him.

'You googled me.' Not a question, merely a statement delivered with ice in his voice.

'Well, I thought I should try and find…'

'Why didn't you ask me if it's that important? You're supposed to be giving me a booking form to complete.'

'So this is my fault?' She crossed the room to close her laptop with an angry snap, still battling with the humiliation of having been caught searching his name. 'You've barely said anything to me that I haven't had to drag from you, and you don't invite conversation or pleasantries. So yes, I apologise if I'm prying but I believe I ought to know more about the person who I'm allowing to live in the cottage for the rest of the summer. I don't think I'm being too unreasonable, and I wasn't certain you'd tell me if I asked.'

Grabbing the booking form from the dresser, she thrust it at him, the firm width of the table between them as the booking form floated down to rest on it. His voice was low and angry as he spoke, forcing out details she knew he did not want to confide.

'Fine, if that's what you need.' He paused, as though he didn't know quite how to form the words. 'I work for a fund management company in New York and I'm on sabbatical to recover from illness. Acute Stress Disorder, if you'd like me to be specific, you can look it up later. My overriding intention is to keep my circumstances as private as possible and I will only tell you it had nothing to do with drugs, alcohol or anything of a criminal nature, so I can assure you and your family you're quite safe.

'I'd very much appreciate it if we didn't speak about this again, I won't be here long enough for it to matter. I'm sure you can find out anything else you wish to know from Google, there's enough stuff linked to my name after what happened. It's Ben Carter, by the way. Benedict, not Benjamin, just to be clear.'

Ben was still staring at her with hard and glittering eyes and he suddenly leant across the table. She jumped, backing away from him. The smile forming on his lips was ironic and then sad as he reached for the pen she had been using earlier, writing on the form and holding it out to her. 'I'm sorry I frightened you, I didn't mean to.'

He spun around and Daisy heard his footsteps hurrying across the courtyard before they were lost in the garden. She pulled out a chair and sank onto it as she wished she could take back what she had learnt, wished she had waited for his trust and confidence in her to come.

She couldn't forget what he had shared, the hurt she'd glimpsed in his expression, the circumstances she'd unknowingly drawn him back to because she'd wanted to know more, to know him. She'd allowed her concern to override her place as his host. That was something she must not repeat, even as her sympathy for his situation bloomed again.

The booking form lay face-up on the table, his email and a New York address scrawled in a blue slash across it. She reached for her glass of wine, no longer cool, and drained it anyway. She rested her head on her arms, wanting nothing more at this moment than to return to her familiar life with its usual routines and forget this had ever happened.

When she eventually became aware of her surroundings again, Daisy realised she must have fallen asleep because she was still slumped at the kitchen table and the empty wine glass had tipped over. She groaned, slowly raising her head. Glancing at the clock, she was relieved to see that it was only quarter past four.

After moving back to Thorndale, she had popped into The Coach and Horses, the pub just beyond the village that she'd always loved and frequented as a teenager. The landlord was a friend of the family and he'd persuaded Daisy to take up her old Sunday night shift. She liked catching up with old friends, making her feel part of the community again, and if she was honest, those few hours were now part of her social calendar.

She realised she'd better get on a move on if she didn't want to be late, filling a glass with water and drinking it quickly. She also swallowed a paracetamol as well to settle the pounding in her temples, praying it would not lead to a migraine.

43

Chapter Five

By the middle of the first week Daisy could only assume that Ben was going out of his way to avoid her after their exchange on Sunday. She hadn't seen him once, not even coming in or out of the house to use the shower, and she'd made sure to keep the kitchen door locked so he couldn't simply stroll in again.

The new plumber was due any day now to replace the shower and she was keeping to her routine of being in the office by eight in the mornings and staying later as Josh wasn't at home. Occasionally she'd caught glimpses of a light inside the cottage but most evenings it was in darkness, and she didn't want to think about how Ben was spending his time and where he was going.

There was no vehicle sitting on the drive near hers and she could only presume he cycled or walked everywhere. The spectre of their last conversation still lingered, and she wondered if he would simply move on at the end of the week to somewhere his story wasn't known. She hadn't googled him again or looked up his address, even though the temptation had hovered all week, her fingers ready to make the decision for her.

There was a fundraising committee meeting on Wednesday evening after an unavoidable day spent at a client's and Daisy was tired when she walked home afterwards. Her heart hadn't really been in it tonight and she took a glass of wine outside, sitting at the table in the courtyard. She was feeling strangely reduced in the house where she had always been at home, almost afraid to use her sewing room in case she ran into Ben. Perhaps avoidance was the best tactic if they were going to get through the summer without complications.

She stretched, enjoying the last of the day's warmth as she looked at her phone. She sipped her wine, looking over Josh's latest pictures from his week away on the family group chat, delighted he was having a great time and making new friends. There were other message groups she needed to respond to, including one for the Mud'n'Mire race taking place on Saturday over in Cumbria an hour or so away.

She always looked forward to it, mainly because she never took part in the actual race but enjoyed the festival atmosphere, spectacular surroundings and supporting her friends from the side-lines. Daisy wasn't the only non-runner in the group, but she was in the minority and took the teasing about not racing in good humour. She was still following the messages about the race when quick footsteps from behind made her jump to her feet in alarm.

'Sorry, I didn't mean to startle you.' Ben was standing at the edge of the courtyard, holding his hands up in apology.

'It's fine.' She returned to her seat more slowly than she had left it and reached for her phone. 'I didn't hear you, that's all.'

'Is it okay to use the shower? I'm just back from a run. Sorry, I know it's a bit late.'

She didn't need him to tell her about the run. A quick glimpse had been enough to imprint the details of his damp T-shirt onto her mind, the material clinging to the outline of his chest. A narrow sports headband held his hair back from his face, emphasising the deeply tanned skin.

'Of course.'

'I got your note about the plumber, thanks. It'll be better for you when it's done and I'm out of your way.'

'We should probably negotiate a reduction in the weekly rate once it's replaced, if you're planning to stay.' Daisy was testing him, wanting to know if he was going to disappear come the weekend. 'Seeing as the amount we agreed allowed for you having to come up to the house.' She thought for a moment. 'Actually, that sounds wrong. We should be compensating *you* for the inconvenience, not the other way around.'

'I'm definitely staying.' He seemed to be offering a plea and she was sure her smile had revealed her rush of happiness. 'I haven't changed my mind. Unless you have and you'd rather I leave?' He halted, suddenly uncertain as his voice fell. 'I wouldn't blame you, after the other day.'

'Of course I haven't.' Her reply was swift, and she tried to counter it with a rational reason. 'As you said, its good business for us to have the cottage occupied all summer.'

'Daisy, I'm sorry about Sunday, and what I said.' He faltered again, his tone serious. 'It's just I find it hard to talk about…'

'It's fine, Ben. You don't have to share anything with me.' She jumped in before he could finish, not wanting to force him into another painful admission. 'I only needed some contact details and you've given me those now. I'm sorry I didn't wait.'

He nodded, lifting a hand towards the house. 'I'll be quick, I don't want to disturb you or your family.'

'You don't need to worry about that, there's only me here.' She bit her lip, wondering if she ought to have

46

told him, ought to have spelled out her aloneness quite so clearly.

His expression altered in an instant from indifference into something more like awareness. 'No Josh?'

'No, he's away, he'll be back on Friday night.'

'Right.' Ben hesitated. 'And er, there's no one else, here, with you?' He held up his hands quickly, a towel dangling from one. 'Sorry. That's none of my business.'

'No.' Daisy's reply was steady. 'Josh's dad and I are divorced, a long time ago now.'

'I'm sorry.'

'Thank you. This is actually my parents' house; they're away and Josh and I moved in after selling ours until we find something new.' Daisy lifted her glass, casually tilting it towards Ben. 'Would you like to join me?' She wanted to withdraw the words the moment they left her, the offer sounding like a desperate invitation for company. 'Sorry, of course you won't. I was trying to be neighbourly.'

'Better not.' Ben seemed to be trying to soften the refusal with something approaching a smile. 'Thanks for asking.'

'Silly question. I don't suppose you drink alcohol as you're in training.' She took a slug of her own, trying not to see his reply as the rejection of her company it clearly was.

'Occasionally I do.' He lifted the towel again. 'I'd better go take that shower.'

He disappeared into the house and Daisy followed soon after, walking past the shower room and ignoring the thought of him inside it. In her own room a short while later she looked in the garden as she went to draw the curtains. It wasn't yet fully dark and although the light was diminishing as the hour grew later, it was enough for her to see the cottage.

The kitchen light was on, but Ben was on the terrace, a mat at his feet. Daisy stilled as she watched him practising yoga, knowing enough about it from classes with Nina to recognise him moving into a standing forward bend, folding his body from his hips, his back towards her.

Wearing the shorts he'd had on before, the T-shirt had gone, and she stared as he held the pose and then gradually straightened. He moved into the corpse position, lying down, palms upturned, legs slightly wide. Still she watched as quite different and decidedly unrestful thoughts filled her mind, bringing a quiver to her skin that was delightful and new. Slowly he got to his feet and lifted the mat to roll it up. She drew the curtains quickly, not wanting to be caught staring.

–

On Saturday morning the day began with drizzle and Daisy knew from long experience that anything could happen with the weather out on the fells in the Lake District. She stuffed both coat and sun cream into her rucksack with a waterproof picnic rug, hopeful that the promised sunshine for later would break through.

Josh had arrived home last night and disappeared into his attic after she'd cooked his favourite supper. He was supposed to be meeting friends at the Mud'n'Mire race and had promised to be up early enough to go with her. She banged on his bedroom door for the third time when he still hadn't surfaced by eight thirty, and, at the last minute, he leapt into her car with a pint of milk and a grin.

The weather was already improving when she parked in a field later and Josh disappeared at once, giving her a wave and promising to call if he needed a lift back. It was muddy underfoot as she followed and she could well imagine how filthy the runners were going to get as they slithered up and down fells, crossed a river twice and tackled twenty obstacles designed to test their endurance.

It was supposed to be fun, although plenty of people took it very seriously indeed, and she had always managed to resist Nina's cajoling to persuade her every year to enter. In the distance she saw the first few competitors striding away and found a place to spread out the picnic blanket near the finish line.

One of the reasons the event was so popular was the vibrant, festival atmosphere, as well as the location and its extraordinary views. Few were in a hurry to leave once they had completed the course and a DJ on the back of a Land Rover was whipping up the mood with loud music. A bar in a converted double decker bus was getting ready to open and she knew it would be late when the last stragglers set off for whatever passed for home this weekend.

'So, Daisy Lancaster, have you brought your trainers? It's not too late for you to enter.'

Daisy laughed, hearing Nina shouting to her above the noise of the DJ, searching through the crowd until she spotted her friend. Nina was jogging comfortably towards her and Daisy noticed lots of other people watching Nina too. They met with a hug and Daisy drew back, used to the attention the stunning young woman attracted wherever she went, recognising the competitive glint in Nina's eyes.

Nina had never been timid or quiet, and Daisy knew it wasn't only her looks that made others take notice. Tall, Nina's lean frame was honed by years of running and yoga and she looked equally arresting in sports gear or an elegant dress. Her fierce intelligence and rich brown eyes were inherited from her Kenyan mother whilst her height, natural confidence and dogged determination came from her British father.

'We both know it is. I don't care how many officials you think you can charm to get a late entry, I'm staying put. Where's Scott?'

Nina checked her watch. Her long hair was tied back, an orange headband a bright splash against her skin. 'I just saw him at the start. He's in the group ahead of mine and I'm still going to finish before him. He's my target, it's not about the time.'

Daisy and Nina had met nearly five years ago at a festival on a farm not far away from Thorndale. Nina had also met Scott, a local stonemason, at the same time and they'd been together ever since. A chartered physiotherapist, she had secured a position with a professional Yorkshire rugby league team but was gradually reducing her hours at the club after opening her own practice, and little fazed her.

Scott had entered the race last year with a group from his amateur rugby club, goaded by Nina that he wasn't up to it. A highly competitive couple, she had beaten him easily when they had started the race together and Daisy knew she had no intention of finishing second to him this time.

Daisy wished her luck as Nina set off for the start, before making her way to the furthest point of the course, staying until Nina's group had been dunked in the ice tank and had clambered out the other side. Daisy slowly headed back to the finish, where the worst of the obstacles was saved for when legs were almost dead and energy long since sapped.

She watched runners trying to scale a high wall before swinging across a large tank of dirty, cold water. Only the fittest made it without mishap and lots of spectators were waiting for friends to finish, laughing in the process as people emerged, filthy and exhausted, from a final drenching.

Competitors were streaming across the finish, posing for triumphant photographs before having their identity tags removed and collapsing over the line with a goody bag and a free drink. There was laughter as an older man tried valiantly to swing across the bars, managing the first two before falling into the water and disappearing into the filth, followed swiftly by the lifeguards in wetsuits to fish him out.

Daisy turned her attention to the course again and her heart skipped in surprise when she spotted a man dropping down from the wall and running purposefully towards the tank, the orange headband a slash against his tanned skin, holding the lengths of chestnut hair back from his face.

She stood on tiptoe, trying to get a better view and knew she had not been mistaken when she spied Ben comfortably making the leap onto the bars. She couldn't explain why her body suddenly became so tense as he swung across, making the finish easily without falling in, the crowd giving him a cheer of approval.

He barely hesitated for the photograph he clearly didn't want and was over the line, bending to catch his breath, his hands on his knees before he straightened and pulled the headband off. She saw him tug the dirty wet T-shirt up and her breath caught as he dragged it impatiently over his head, revealing once again the marvellous chest she had been picturing in her mind all week. She was standing directly in front of him, behind the metal barrier separating spectators from competitors, as he emerged and looked straight into her eyes.

Chapter Six

'Hey. Not competing?'

Daisy shook her head as Ben made his way to her through the bustle surrounding them. She hadn't been expecting him to approach, assuming he would give her a nod at the most and melt away into the crowd. He was still clutching the T-shirt in one hand, his goody bag in the other and she forced her gaze to his face, trying not to be side-tracked by the sight of his bare chest.

'No. This is a bit extreme for me, I prefer a good walk.' Surprise lent a nervous note to her voice and she tried to mask it. 'Congratulations on completing. Was that your first time here?'

Ben was using the T-shirt to wipe some of the mud from his face. A curl of desire darted across her skin as he vaulted easily over the barrier and halted beside her. She knew her mouth was open and closed it quickly, her fingers longing to smooth away the mud still smearing his skin.

'Yes, I thought it would be a decent warm up and a chance to compete on the fells but that's it now, no more races before the triathlon.' He looked down at his messy kit and pressed his lips into a wry line. 'I'll rinse this lot under the garden tap before I put it in the washing machine in the cottage, I don't want to clog it up with dirt.'

'Oh, don't worry about that.' Daisy waved her hand dismissively. 'I'm sure it'll be, oh!' The back of her knees gave way and she lurched forwards. Her balance was gone as she staggered into the barrier, aware at once of Ben's hand reaching for her arm and pulling her back.

She righted herself quickly, looking over her shoulder to see what had happened. A huge Doberman had escaped from its owner and was hurtling around excitedly, trailing its lead. The owner shot past, yelling an apology as he raced off in pursuit and somebody grabbed the lead, halting the dog before it could interfere on course.

'You okay?'

Ben's fingers were loosely wrapped around her wrist, transferring a streak of mud to her. He lifted her arm, using the wet T-shirt in his other hand to wipe away the dirt from her skin. He suddenly let her go, as though he had just realised what he had done. She didn't need another dog to knock her off balance, she knew Ben had managed it quite effortlessly with one of the simplest and yet most sensual gestures she had ever experienced.

'I'm fine.' Her heart was slamming as she looked up, expecting his gaze to be shuttered, his thoughts hidden from her. 'It surprised me, that's all.'

There was a beat, a moment as his eyes glittered on hers before dropping to the shirt in his hand. 'Right.' He cleared his throat. 'Good. So, are you here with…?'

'Friends.' Daisy hoped she sounded more relaxed than she felt, still feeling the effects of the flush on her skin where he had heated it. 'Most of them are running.'

'Not Josh?'

'He's here somewhere but he's not racing, he was always more into cycling until drumming took over.' An idea fell into her mind and she wondered how to voice it, how to frame her invitation to make it sound simple enough. 'Actually, we're staying on after the race for the band and a few drinks. Would you like to join us? You'd be very welcome, we're a friendly bunch.'

She caught a glimpse of Nina, swinging across the monkey bars, unmistakable with her tall figure and bright clothes. Nina managed the bars easily and was over the finish line with her group, arranging themselves into position for the photographer. She gave Daisy a merry wave, her eyes alighting on Ben. Daisy saw him looking across too, as Nina's group retrieved their goody bags and drinks.

'No thanks. I'm going to change, I'll leave you to it.'

He turned, vanishing swiftly into the mass of people crowding around the finish. Nina marched over to Daisy, already recovering her breath and unscrewing a bottle of water with dirty hands.

'Who was that you were talking to, D? Is he a client?'

Daisy wasn't the only one looking at Nina, her friend's confident voice carrying easily, curiosity and an implacable demand for the full story in her tone.

'Not a client as such, no. He's a guest, staying in the cottage for a bit. Will that do?' Daisy made her way past the barriers to the picnic blanket she had left earlier, reclaiming their place before it was lost to the crowd.

'It will not!' Nina caught up in a couple of strides and reached for Daisy's arm to halt her. 'What do you mean, staying for a bit? How long has he been there and why don't I know anything about it?'

Daisy bit back a smile at her friend's open curiosity. 'Only a week or so. His name is Ben and he's on sabbatical so he can have a crack at the Helvellyn event and is basing himself in the Dales to train.' She continued, hoping to distract her sharp and clever friend. 'Do you know anyone who's taking part? Any clients?'

'A couple, and I'll know Ben when you introduce us.' Daisy knew Nina was trying to fill in the details she was leaving out and she saw the second that understanding dawned in Nina's eyes. 'He's your cyclist!'

'What makes you think that?' Daisy tried to brush it off, knew she had failed as her gaze slid away from Nina guiltily.

'Your face, that's what. And the two of you looked pretty intense, kind of separate from everyone else. Well. So he did come back.' Nina gave her a cheeky grin, high-fiving someone she recognised. 'I'll call round one evening this week to say hello, we can compare training methods and injuries. Maybe even run together, he looked fit from what I saw and if he's here on his own then he might want someone to train with. And I've always got room for another client if he needs a physio.'

Daisy wondered if she ought to warn Ben, certain from the little she knew of him that he would not welcome a running buddy. Nina's determination and charm were legendary, and Daisy felt a twinge of alarm at the thought of Nina succeeding in gaining his confidence and drawing out his story where she had failed.

'Maybe. Don't call round specially, he doesn't seem to be in much.'

'So? I'm still coming.'

With a wink Nina dashed away, her attention caught by Scott and his mates tottering over the finish line, plastered in mud and gasping for breath. Nina ran across to hug him and they embraced, laughing together as he managed to transfer most of the mud onto her. Hand in hand, they headed away to shower, and Daisy settled down to enjoy what was left of the day.

Josh came over to let her know he was going back to a friend's house and they would drop him at home later, and she waved him off. The rest of Nina's group arrived, everyone sharing drinks and food as the festival atmosphere and relaxed mood increased. Children were racing around whilst dogs snoozed in the warming sun. Daisy overheard competitors comparing injuries and swapping stories of the race, the noise and laughter growing with every wave of runners that made it over the finish line. But however often she searched, she couldn't see that flash of chestnut hair anywhere.

–

After church the next day Daisy delivered some of the vegetable lasagne she'd made to Mrs Hodges and ate her lunch alone again, trying not to mind the silence in the house. Even though Josh was almost always in his attic whenever he was home and she didn't see much of him, she knew he was there, and it somehow made the house feel more alive. He'd gone for a bike ride with a friend whilst she'd been out and would no doubt come back starving so she made sure to leave him plenty to eat.

But now she had a few hours free before she needed to be at the pub and intended to spend them sewing. She changed into a denim apron dress that she loved to work in, a T-shirt underneath it, and headed outside. As her interest in designing clothes had grown over the years, her parents had vacated the room next door to the cottage when she'd sold her house, turning it into a small space where she could store her equipment and work in peace, the huge skylight allowing in the necessary light.

She noticed lots of flowers in the garden ready to pick and decided to drop some in with Connie on her way to the pub. As ever Ben's cottage was silent, the door closed as Daisy made her way along her side of the terrace, ignoring the impulse to peep through the windows. His bike was propped against the wall and she had no idea if that meant he was in the house or not.

She let herself into her room, already relaxing and anticipating the soothing diversion of sewing for a while. She loved the old-fashioned armchair losing its stuffing and the pretty walnut needlework box she'd found at a local antiques fair. She liked to sit and dream sometimes of who might have used and appreciated it before her. Having avoided coming to this room since Ben had arrived – not wanting him to think she was keeping an eye on him – she'd missed her sewing. She didn't ever go more than a few days without it and would not be able to wait until he had left and the cottage was empty once more.

Occasionally she was invited to craft fairs to demonstrate her work and she had one coming up, so would soon need to think about the projects to take with her on the day. After having made tea with the lemon verbena she liked, Daisy studied the design she'd produced for a hacking jacket she was making for Nina's birthday. Fitted, slightly shorter than usual, it was a traditional herringbone pattern and would have a bright, emerald green silk lining that would suit Nina's vibrant style.

Daisy finished her tea as she gathered what she needed and began to cut out the material for the lining, spreading the silk and working carefully so as not to make a mistake. As ever, time simply slid away and a glance at the antique wall clock later told her she ought to be heading back to the house to get ready for the pub. Reluctantly she tidied everything away, appreciating the warm afternoon sun outside as she locked up.

A row of large planters filled with clipped box hedging divided her share of the terrace from the cottage's, and she saw Ben sitting in one of the comfortable Adirondack chairs, his face, partly masked by sunglasses, tilted up to the sun. Daisy realised it was the first time she had seen him looking restful. She put one silent foot in front of the other, hoping not to disturb him and had almost reached the hedge when he spoke.

'I'm not asleep. You don't need to be quiet.'

Halting, she threw him a glance over her shoulder. 'I probably should have told you about my room, I'm usually sewing most evenings.'

'Then why haven't you been in there all week?'

She turned around, unable not to scan the half-buttoned shirt and ever-present shorts he wore. 'How do you know I haven't?'

He stood up, pulling the sunglasses off and coming to stand at the edge of the terrace. 'I'm surrounded by silence and I would've heard you.' He paused, watching her. 'Have you got a minute? I need your bank details to pay the balance of the rent. Unless you'd prefer cash?'

It was over four thousand pounds and she was already shaking her head, not wanting to have so much cash lying around until she could bank it. 'Bank details are fine,' she told him crisply. 'Shall I text them to you?'

'Sorry, no. I don't have a mobile.' Ben smiled then, the simplicity of it adding charm to his expression. 'Could you write them down for me, the old-fashioned way?' He held out an arm, indicating the cottage.

'Of course.'

She followed him to the door, and he stood back to allow her to go first. She noticed at once that he was very tidy, with nothing seeming to be out of place. His guitar was propped on the armchair and a glass sat on the draining board beside the sink but otherwise, there was no other evidence of his occupation.

'So how are you feeling after the race yesterday?' She was aware of him beside her, catching that same lemon fragrance on his skin.

'Fine. I ran a level 3k this morning and I'll swim tomorrow. It's important for good recovery to keep moving.'

'You make it sound so easy, as though there were no effort required at all.'

'Training's what I do,' he told her quietly, his gaze somewhere else once again. 'I'm much better when I keep moving.'

He reached for the pen and notepad left by the microwave for guests and she wrote down the details he needed and passed them back to him.

'Thanks.'

He pocketed the paper and Daisy was already near the door again. Struck by a sudden impulse, she decided to take advantage of his apparently relaxed mood.

'If you've no plans for tonight, would you like to call in at the pub where I work and have a drink? It's only a mile or so from here.' She saw the stiffness returning to his shoulders and hurried on, trying to clarify her invitation.

'Obviously, it doesn't have to be alcohol, they do a good range of non-alcoholic beers. I'm there on Sunday evenings and seeing as you're definitely staying, maybe it would be nice for you to meet a few of our neighbours. Most people are friendly, and they'd love to say hello.'

'No thanks,' he told her shortly, the earlier mildness she had just seen already gone and replaced by the cool indifference she was more used to. 'Not my thing.'

'Why not?' She was getting fed up with her attempts at friendliness being rebuffed time and again, disguising a sigh and trying to lace her words with patience.

'Excuse me?'

'Why not, Ben? It can't do any harm, surely, spending an hour or two in the pub. Perhaps it will help take your mind off training for a while.'

'Take my mind off training?' There was an incredulous note in his voice as he lengthened the syllables and Daisy knew she had lost him. That her invitation, issued in kindness, had gone badly wrong and horrified him in ways she did not understand. 'So go on then, how is sitting around in a bar with a bunch of strangers supposed to help me, exactly? And why would you think I need to take my mind off training?'

There was more than sarcasm in his voice now and the hint of sorrow made her press on, trying to make him realise she had not intended to upset him. He looked scathing and anxiety prickled on her skin.

'Thorndale is a small village.' She hoped she sounded calm and friendly, so he could see she wasn't trying to force anything on him. 'Most of us know and look out for one another. You're already a part of that, even if you don't realise it yet, whilst you're here. People mean well.'

He laughed, the sound utterly bereft of humour. Annoyance mingled with dismay at how he had reacted to her simple invitation, one she would never have issued had she honestly believed him to be so dismissive and unkind.

'I can only assume you've been searching online again and have decided that somehow you know what's best for me,' he snapped, the controlled fury in his voice reflected in the rigidity of his shoulders, lending his frame a severity that had her stepping backwards. 'I don't need pity from inward-looking strangers in the back of beyond who know nothing about me or what happened. And whatever the hell lives you people live here, where I'm from we don't tend to stick our noses in someone else's business without invitation, we prefer to let them get on with it until they say otherwise.'

Facing one another, every shred of his tension was mirrored in Daisy's own body as her fists balled at her side. Her face flamed as she finally gave way to her temper at his heated and scornful reply.

'"You people"? How dare you? Just because you're from a fancy city you think we're all ignorant bumpkins with nothing better to do than interfere? No doubt you can go for years without setting eyes on your neighbours but I'm glad it's different here and we usually know when something isn't right. I don't know what kind of life you do lead but it seems to be one you're clearly determined to live alone.'

She lifted a hand, waving it angrily towards the village beyond the house. 'Mike from the pub lost his wife suddenly two years ago and yet he's still here, putting one foot in front of the other every day and trying to make a life without her. We all have families, homes, jobs and responsibilities to keep us here, and just not quite enough money to run away. And whatever you think, I haven't googled you again; I know nothing more than you've already told me. I was only trying to be kind and you've proved yet again that you neither want nor need it, so I must learn to stop bothering.'

Her voice had risen with every line until she was shrieking, and she fell into an abrupt silence, appalled by her words and how far she had gone. There was a moment as they continued to lock furious stares before Ben spoke, his voice oddly quiet through the hush that had fallen over them so swiftly.

'I knew this was going to be a mistake.'

He spun around and disappeared into the bedroom, slamming the door behind him. Stunned by what had occurred between them so unexpectedly, Daisy hurried back to the house, swiping at the tears on her face. She went upstairs to change, praying that Josh had not seen or heard anything amiss, and washed her face, trying to make the hurt slip away like the water in the sink.

After quickly checking on Josh and letting him know she was heading out, Daisy left the house and marched through the village, taking a shortcut along a footpath that led to a lane and eventually the pub, her mind still reeling after the argument with Ben.

She was certain he would be gone when she returned home, his few things packed, and the cottage empty once more. When she reached the pub, she realised she'd forgotten to cut flowers from the garden and take them for Connie to enjoy, her idea obliterated in the commotion with Ben that had gone before and dragged all reason with it.

Chapter Seven

The Coach and Horses was named after its former life as an inn for travellers heading through the Dales, and Daisy had been coming here for years. She had long been a part of the pub's social life and had loved working there once she turned eighteen until other circumstances prevailed. With Josh often busy or staying with his dad, Daisy had been happy to slot her old job into her usual routine and return for a few hours each week.

It was a traditional and attractive building, painted white with black window frames. The landlord had resisted updating the decor to reflect a more modern taste so the flamboyant planters on the cobbles outside, low beams and jaunty horse brasses inside all remained. A skilful young chef continued to add to the pub's reputation for good food, along with outstanding beer brewed on site in the old stables. All this meant that the pub continued to flourish both from within its community and attracting visitors from afar.

Daisy had never felt less like being there as she said hello to people she recognised, automatically checking tables for empty glasses. It looked to be an average Sunday evening, customers propped on stools at the bar, chatting together or sitting at tables and enjoying a fine meal, and she noticed someone rifling through the stack of board games.

It was always homely in the pub and she sighed inwardly as she put her bag away and headed back to the public rooms. She couldn't forget the awful fight with Ben earlier, cringing as she remembered how they had shouted at one another. Despite his contemptuous refusal of her invitation she still wished she had not spoken to him in the way she had.

'Hey, Mike, busy day?' She smiled at the landlord as he served someone and saw him grin. She stepped behind the bar and spoke to the customer waiting for drinks and eyeing up the local beers on tap. 'What can I get you?'

Mike came over as she filled pint glasses and helped to finish the order, adding tonic to two different gins. Daisy took the payment whilst he handed out menus and they paused for a moment in the lull, experienced eyes keeping watch for the next customer or table to be cleared.

Mike Todd was a huge bear of a man, a former policeman who had retired at fifty from a career spent as a detective and had then achieved his dream of running a country pub. Cumbrian born with cropped, gunmetal-grey hair, he loved the traditional sport of Cumberland wrestling and judged at competitions whenever he could leave the pub. His son and daughter both worked in the Metropolitan Police and came up for visits when time allowed but Daisy knew he didn't see as much of them as he would like.

Since the sudden loss of his wife Linda two years ago he seemed to have shrunk physically as well as emotionally, grief trailing after him for months on end. Daisy knew how hard he tried to keep going and how much the pub and the local community had sustained him in the days and weeks afterwards. Recently he seemed to be coming back to more of the man he was before, and she was glad of the change as he gradually found a way to come to terms with his bereavement.

'Not bad, Daisy, busy as usual.' Mike waved to one of their regulars. 'I'm glad you're here, though; that new young lad from town hasn't turned up so I'll need to advertise for weekend staff again. Some sorry tale about his mate's car breaking down but he didn't sound too impressed when I asked him if he'd ever heard of buses or bikes. Anyway, I'll stay behind the bar and make sure you're not run off your feet.'

Daisy smiled, wiping down the pumps and already anticipating a large order as a group of men burst through the door, their noisy laughter causing a little dog who was lying quietly underneath a table nearby to jump to its feet. Her heart sank as she recognised a couple of them, hoping they weren't here to make a nuisance of themselves. Daisy knew Mike had recognised them too as he drew himself up to his full intimidating height, never a disadvantage in his chosen work. He spoke clearly as they clattered across to a large table in a corner beside one of the front windows.

'Now lads, keep the noise level decent please, there's people enjoying their tea.'

They were boisterously rearranging the seating and Mike looked at her. 'I'll keep an eye on them,' he told her quietly. 'They can have one round and if they're disturbing anybody then I'll get shot of them.'

'I'm sure they'll be fine.' Daisy replied. 'It's nothing we haven't dealt with before.'

'Well, if it isn't the gorgeous Daisy!' The younger of the two men who had appeared at the bar spoke, giving her the dubious benefit of a wink along with a silly grin. 'Have you missed me, darlin'?'

Daisy was reaching for glasses and she threw him an exasperated look. 'I haven't, Dex, not at all. What would you like to drink?'

She hadn't seen Steven Dexter for a couple of weeks and if she ever bothered to think of him, she presumed he had returned home to Newcastle. She had to concede he was good looking, and the time spent honing his physique generated a certain appeal, but his immaturity was apparent in ways more than just the age difference between them. His immaculate dark-blonde hair was short, and she was sure he'd chosen the tight white T-shirt to show off both his tanned skin and impressive biceps.

Dex paid for the drinks when Daisy had finished, and he winked at her again. It was a hazard of her job, certainly, fending off the mostly good-natured banter that came her way and she knew Mike would step in before anything became out of hand. She gave Dex a blank smile and he turned away to re-join his table, unperturbed.

'So who's this bloke you've got staying in your mum and dad's cottage then? Word has it he's a loner, not been seen much around the village, although Mrs Timms has informed the world at large she's had the pleasure of his acquaintance in the cafe. Said he was a bit unkempt and couldn't string a sentence together.'

Mike's curiosity was another reminder of the row with Ben earlier. Daisy took a cloth from the shelf out of habit and began wiping down the pumps again as she replied, one shoulder rising in a shrug.

'He's on sabbatical to train for the Helvellyn triathlon and hasn't said much more. He likes to keep his life private and I haven't asked.'

'What does he do?'

'Banking, I believe. Based in New York.'

Mike whistled, a low sound that had her glancing across to him. 'Sabbatical? Not sick leave? I saw him the other day in the village, running like he had half the fraud squad on his tail. You sure he's all right, Daisy? You and Josh being there on your own and all?'

She touched Mike's arm briefly, hearing the concern in his question. 'We're fine, honestly. He's fine. Thanks for asking.' She lowered her voice. 'Strictly between you and me, he's recovering from illness and I don't want that to go any further, okay? And I trust him, Mike, really I do.'

'Poor bloke,' he murmured, distractedly scratching his balding head with a large hand. 'Probably all that stress. Hope it's nothing to do with a bereavement, you can never tell. At least I've got thirty-three years with Linda to look back on and the kids to keep me going. Speaking of which, you don't fancy an extra shift on Friday night, do you? My lad and his girlfriend are coming up and they've got tickets for that new comedian who was on telly the other night. Can't remember his name but he's supposed to be very good with his one-liners, won some sort of competition.'

Daisy took the dirty glasses somebody had returned and slid them into the dishwasher. 'Should be fine. Let me check with Josh in case there's something I've already promised to do for him. I think I'm in the office all day so I could be in for six, if that's any help?'

'Sure it fits with your routine?'

'Mike! I'm not that bad. There's nothing wrong with planning and being organised, especially when you work for yourself and have a busy teenager to ferry around.'

'I suppose not. You're a good lass, Daisy, I've always said so. Thanks a million. It'll be grand to get out with them.'

More customers were arriving, and she and Mike were kept busy for the next hour or so as they served people with skilled and friendly efficiency. She wasn't sorry to notice that most of Dex's group had wandered away and the remaining three, including him, were flirting with two young women sitting on the other side of the pub, laughing over their phones.

She finished serving a couple of walkers and saw Mike chatting to an attractive middle-aged woman with short, auburn curls and a lively, intelligent face, sitting alone at a small table beside the fireplace. This wasn't the first time she had noticed the woman in The Coach, and she and Mike seemed to be finding plenty to talk about. He returned to the bar a few minutes later, looking pleased and rather surprised, giving Daisy a sheepish glance.

'Well, looks can certainly be deceptive, that's for sure.' She saw how he tried to keep his grin casual and she laughed, enjoying his pleasure. 'I was just talking to Heather over there,' he tipped his head in the direction of the fireplace. 'You know she's been in before and we've been chatting? You'll never guess why she's here?'

'Go on then, I won't, and you're dying to tell me.'

'She's a crime writer, staying nearby to research a book. When I told her what I used to do, she asked me if I'd like to meet for a coffee sometime and have a chat about my old job.'

'That sounds lovely, Mike. I hope you're going to go?'

He rubbed his chin thoughtfully, a frown creasing his brow. 'I've said yes, 'course I have. Just don't want to make a fool of myself, that's all. And she knows I can't be too specific.'

'You'll be fine, it's only coffee and a chat. No pressure.'

'Aye, you're right. Anyway she seems nice; she doesn't look the sort to be murdering people, does she? Even if it is only in print.' Then Mike grinned again. 'And I do know it takes all sorts.'

He headed off into the snug to talk about wrestling with a couple of pals, and Daisy hoped he would keep that to himself, at least for a bit, when he met Heather for their coffee. He loved the sport, but not everyone might see the appeal at first. She was still smiling as she bent to replace bottles of soft drinks in the fridge.

'So if I wanted to drink something local, what would you recommend?'

She froze, her fingers stilling on the bottle in her hand. Sliding it carefully into the fridge, she straightened up as she recognised Ben's quiet voice. Hurriedly searching for the words of apology she had already rehearsed, she turned towards him and mentally braced herself.

'Ben! I'm so sorry about what I said earlier. I didn't…'

'No, don't Daisy, please.' Ben quickly lifted a hand to halt her. 'It's me who needs to apologise. I should never have said what I did about your home and the people here. It was arrogant, misguided and very wrong of me. I'm sorry and can only ask you to accept my apology, I mean it sincerely.' He hesitated, still watching her. 'I've got pretty good at shutting out the world and maybe this will help me find a way to start letting it back in.'

'There's nothing to forgive. I shouldn't have spoken to you like that, given you must have had a very difficult time over the past months.' Her voice had lowered, not wanting to draw attention to their conversation.

Ben smiled, bringing a suggestion of affection to his face. 'My mother would've cheered if she had heard you earlier. Not that you're anything like my mother,' he added hastily. 'She would have appreciated the sentiment and said it was about time somebody took me to task.'

Daisy grinned, glad of the break in customers and so relieved he hadn't stormed out of the cottage and disappeared into the night to somewhere she would not be able to find him. 'What can I get you to drink?'

'Something local? What would you recommend?'

'The pale ales are produced in the microbrewery on site and they're extremely popular and delicious. The Nickel is lovely if you like a crisp, dry ale or have the Copper if you want a stronger hop flavour and more citrusy taste.'

'I'll try the Nickel, thanks. A pint.'

'Are you sure?' she teased, not entirely certain she was on safe ground with him just yet as she reached for a glass and tilted it under the pump. 'What about your training? Does your regime allow for pints in the pub?'

The smile was back, a little wider this time, and she knew he understood her playful comments and the spirit with which they were meant. He shrugged. 'I'll have to drink more water and run a bit further tomorrow.'

She laughed as she expertly straightened the glass to allow for a head on the ale and released the pump, placing the drink in front of him. She spotted an older man shuffling across the pub, his gait awkward as he favoured his left hip over his right. A beautiful black and white collie was at his heels, keeping close but far enough away so as not to be a hazard beneath his feet.

Daisy reached for a glass, long experience telling her that this new arrival would have first a pint of Thorndale Copper followed by a half of Nickel. He reached the bar, nodding at her and sliding his curious look over to Ben. The dog lay down at once on the stone-flagged floor.

'Now then, lass.' Tufts of grey hair stuck out from a battered tweed cap above faded but sharp blue eyes and a weathered face. Despite the warm evening, a vest, shirt and jumper were visible beneath a half open pair of dirty green overalls and thick rubber wellies. He pulled out the stool next to Ben's, tilting his head towards her guest. 'Is this yon mon what's stayin' in t'cottage, then?'

She pushed the glass towards the older man, wondering how much of the broad Yorkshire dialect Ben would understand.

'This is Ben, Edwin.' There was no point asking Edwin how he knew who Ben was. Ben had been in the village for a little over a week and that was more than enough time for word to have got around, as Mike had suggested before. 'Yes, until the end of summer. Edwin farms just outside the village, Ben.'

'Pleased to meet you.' Ben sounded polite, too formal, as he reached a hand across for Edwin to take. Edwin stared at it for a moment, and when they shook, Daisy marvelled at the size and worn strength of Edwin's huge hand, out of scale with his short body, the broad stumpy fingers closing over Ben's own narrow, graceful ones and crunching them firmly.

''Ow do. Summat to do wi' a race, is it?'

Ben laughed, a happier sound Daisy had never heard before and she loved the altered look on his face. She busied herself with another order, their voices carrying over to her anyway.

'Yes, the ultra-triathlon on Helvellyn. Have you heard of it?'

She saw Edwin take a long drink of his ale as she poured a pint for someone else, one that left his glass half empty and had him wiping his mouth with the back of his hand. He tipped his head to someone over Ben's shoulder.

'Nay, lad. Only reason to go up t'fells is to gather sheep.' His eyes slid over Ben, as though assessing him for suitability of the challenge that lay ahead. 'Ye'll be wantin' a vehicle to get ye around.'

Daisy knew what was coming as Edwin's look became crafty, and she laughed. 'Watch him, Ben. If Edwin tries to sell you an old red Land Rover that's been sat in a barn since forever, then don't say I didn't warn you.'

Edwin grinned, bringing mischief to his face. 'Gi' o'er Daisy,' he told her mildly, downing the rest of his pint. She took his glass and began filling him a half pint with Nickel. 'Let 'im mek up 'is own mind. Nowt wrong wi' it.'

'You don't, do you Ben? Need a vehicle whilst you're here?'

Ben raised his eyebrows, looking from Edwin to Daisy. 'I might. It'll be easier than cycling or running everywhere.'

Edwin accepted his second drink and downed it in one. Ben caught Daisy's eye and they shared a smile as Edwin slid the empty glass back to her. At once the dog on the floor leapt to its feet, eyes fixed on Edwin. He scowled at it but the hand reaching down to stroke its ears was gentle as he tipped his head to Ben again. 'Best come 'ave a gander, Daisy'll show ye where. Reet. Ah'm garn yam, Ah've a yow to skift.'

He turned without a word, the dog back at his heels. Ben was still smiling as he looked questioningly at her.

'He's going home, he's got a ewe to move. A female sheep,' she translated for him. She saw Mike reappear from the snug as Heather got up from her table, following her to the door and holding it open for her.

'Right. Thanks. Looks like I'm going to see a Land Rover then.'

Daisy's smile slid away as she saw Dex approaching, and she noticed the curious and unfriendly look he shot Ben. Dex pushed empty glasses onto the bar, leaving an elbow there as he addressed Daisy confidently, his back angled towards Ben.

'When are we going on that date you promised me, Daisy,' Dex said loudly, a faint slurring to his words.

Ben stepped away, taking his drink to the small table Heather had just vacated. Daisy dragged her attention back to her customer as Dex continued in the same cajoling tone. 'I'm going to be here for a week or two and I'm looking for someone to keep us company.'

'I promised you nothing of the sort.' Her tone was mild as she refilled his glass. 'You're never short of company, Dex. I don't doubt there are plenty of broken hearts scattered behind you but I'm not going to be one of them.'

'Who's the bloke?' he asked, jerking his head towards Ben, sitting quietly with his drink. 'Not seen him before. Mate of yours?'

'Just a friend.'

Dex took the drinks and turned away, tossing another look at Ben. She knew that her friendliness towards Ben had not gone unnoticed and the thought unsettled her. Gradually the evening wore on and people drifted away. Dex and his two mates were still slouched around the corner table, joined now by the two young women from earlier.

Ben returned to the bar with his empty glass and Daisy took it from him. 'Another one?'

'Better not, thanks. I do have my regime to consider, as you correctly pointed out. But you were right, the ale is very good. I'll have a glass of water please.'

She ignored the flare of delight that came with the realisation he was not yet ready to leave. She filled a new glass as Mike made his way along the bar until he was standing next to her. She made the introductions as Ben pulled out a stool and settled back at the bar. Mike's big hand reached across and took Ben's and they shook firmly.

'Nice to meet you.' Mike's words were simple and welcoming, and Ben nodded his thanks. 'You've found a good 'un in Daisy, she's got a very good heart.'

She whirled around to face the landlord. 'Mike! Don't be ridiculous.' Her face flamed as she turned away to empty the dishwasher and left the two men to chat. She busied herself tidying and preparing to close up for the evening whilst Ben sat quietly at the bar. Mike had disappeared into the office at the back and then Dex appeared again and addressed her.

'You free tomorrow night, Daisy?' he asked, his Geordie accent carrying with ease. 'For that date I mentioned. How do you fancy the open mike night in town and a few drinks?'

She stiffened, noticing that Dex had looked across to Ben as he spoke, sensing a challenge in his tone that hadn't been present before. Ben paid them no attention, his attention focused on his glass, fingers idly wrapped around it.

'Sorry, Dex,' she told him, wiping away a puddle of beer on the bar and giving him a sharp look to back up her comment. 'It's still a no. Comedy clubs aren't really my thing.'

Dex seized on her reply, mistakenly assuming he only needed to change the venue to secure her acceptance. 'A nice restaurant, then? My treat. There's a new Indian opened in town that's meant to be good.'

She shook her head firmly. 'Not going to happen.'

'Ah, come on, love. You wouldn't leave us all on us own, would you? I know how to show a good-looking lass like you a proper night out.'

Daisy opened her mouth to send him packing once and for all just as Ben let go of his glass and looked up.

'She said no,' he told Dex softly, fixing a steady look on the younger man. 'I don't think she's going to change her mind, do you?'

Dex's mouth tightened in an angry line and he banged his half-empty glass down onto the bar, sloshing more beer onto the patch she had just cleaned.

'What's it to you?' he mocked, looking down at Ben. 'Fancy her yourself, do you? You'll be lucky, I've been asking her out for weeks and all she ever says is no. Got a reputation for being a bit chilly, if you follow my meaning.'

Ben stood up and Daisy felt alarm prickling on her skin as they confronted one another. They were a similar height and build, and she saw Dex's hand ball into a fist as he tried to face down the challenge he'd provoked in Ben. The whole pub seemed to have fallen silent when a sudden voice burst in.

'Right, that's it. You can clear out and take your mates with you. You don't speak about any of my staff like that.'

Mike appeared in a rush, raising his voice and drawing himself up to his full six-foot-four height as he flung up the flap separating the bar from the pub and strode around to face Dex, who paled slightly at the size and demeanour of the man now pointing to the door.

'Sorry, Daisy, I didn't mean it,' he wheedled, trying to backtrack.

'Not interested. Get moving laddie, or I'll have to help you out.'

Mike took a step forward and Dex turned away hastily. Ben returned to his table, sitting silently and paying no attention as Dex made a fuss about having to leave. Daisy quietly continued clearing up through the commotion until Mike was beside her again, having seen the men out into the street and shut the door firmly behind them.

The two women who had been sitting with them looked a bit startled and grabbed their bags, hurrying after them. Daisy hoped they'd be okay. The last few stragglers gathered their belongings and said goodnight as they slowly made their way outside, and soon the pub was empty, bar Ben and the staff setting tables in the room next door.

'I've told him he's barred,' Mike said to Daisy with a roll of his eyes. 'I know he can be a bit gobby at times but he's not usually aggressive. Wonder what's got into him? Ah well, we'll probably never know.' His voice became more serious. 'Give it ten minutes or so before you go, let them get away. Will you be all right walking home?'

She tried to bat away his worries. 'I'll be fine, I've walked home dozens of times on my own before, it's not far.'

Ben had reappeared at the bar and he handed over his empty glass. 'I'll wait for you,' he said quietly, effortlessly catching her gaze as she swung her head around in surprise. 'I think Mike's right, you probably shouldn't walk home alone this evening.'

'Oh, for goodness' sake.' Daisy flung her impatient glare across both men as she placed Ben's glass into the dishwasher. 'I appreciate your concern, but I'm absolutely fine.'

'Makes sense, Daisy,' Mike told her, giving Ben a grateful nod. 'He is going your way after all.'

Chapter Eight

Daisy busied herself finishing the clearing up and was ready to leave within fifteen minutes. Throughout Ben had waited patiently at the bar until Mike saw them to the door to lock up behind them. Ben was checking along the lane and her eyes flew across it too, wanting to be certain Dex or his friends weren't lingering. There was no one around and she and Ben set off into the quiet evening.

'It was nice of you to stay but I am fine.' She tilted her head to look at him through the dusk, trying not to think about the comfort his presence had brought. 'Dex isn't usually rude or aggressive.'

'You think? He seemed pretty hostile to me, didn't look like he was going to take no for an answer. What's the story with him?'

She shrugged, a dismissive gesture that summed up the extent of her opinion of the younger man. 'He's a builder, he lives in Newcastle, but he's got mates here and he's working on a job locally. I met him at The Coach a few months ago and then bumped into him at a festival. We were both there with friends, he recognised me and came over. We had a chat, nothing more. He's asked me out before, but he knows I'll never go.'

'I'm not sure he sees it that way. He seemed quite persistent.'

'Oh, Dex just likes a challenge, he'd lose interest if I ever said yes. And I do have a few tricks up my sleeve.'

'Go on then, what would you do? Squirt beer in his eyes? Blind him with a dazzling smile? Set Edwin on him?'

'Very funny.' Daisy grinned, appreciating Ben's lighter tone and gentle teasing. 'No, I have a black belt in Taekwondo that not many people know about so there's always the element of surprise. I am rusty though, it's been a while.'

'Seriously? You're a dark horse.'

'Josh started going when he was about six and I decided to join in, too. It seemed more useful than sitting around watching.'

'Remind me not to upset you then, I don't want you decking me. I've got a race to train for.'

They both laughed, strolling along in silence until Ben cut through the quietness with words coming out in a rush. 'So if I wanted to see this Land Rover of Edwin's, would you mind coming with me? I think he's got the measure of both of us and you're coming out best.'

'If you think it will help?'

'Definitely. I might be an experienced negotiator, but I have a funny feeling Edwin will try to pull the wool over my eyes if I turn up alone. He obviously respects you, Daisy.'

This was the first reference Ben had made to his job and she was still mulling it over as they reached the house. Ben pushed the gate aside, following her up the path. They drew to a halt outside the porch and Daisy rummaged through her bag for keys. She found them and lifted her head, his face illuminated by the light from her home.

'I'm glad you came tonight, Ben.' She opened the door and turned to look at him. 'Thanks for waiting for me.'

'You're welcome.'

There was a long moment as they stared at one another and then he nodded, quickly heading off around the side of the house to his cottage. Daisy lingered, waiting until his footsteps had faded into nothing before she closed the door.

The next morning she dropped Josh off for his final NCS week on her way to work. She had a full day in the office and when she eventually looked at her phone, sitting outside at lunchtime, there was a message from Nina saying she would pop round this evening. She didn't need to say what for, Daisy knew she was interested in meeting Ben properly. Daisy offered to cook supper for them, pointing out that Ben wasn't certain to be in.

She also ordered more cotton so she could produce another batch of aprons for the village shop as they'd emailed her to say the last one had sold out. She knew she could put them together quickly and replied, promising to have some ready by the weekend. That meant a few evenings in her sewing room and after that she needed to concentrate on finishing Nina's jacket for her birthday.

But when she got home Nina messaged again to say that supper was off as Scott's mother had had a fall, not serious but Nina was taking her to A&E to make certain nothing was broken. Nina promised to call round if she was back in good time and Daisy replied, sending love and good wishes.

After supper she hurried down to the sewing room, wanting to make the best of whatever time she had. She studiously ignored the cottage; it was as quiet as ever and she didn't see Ben. After last night in the pub she knew something between them had shifted. They had become something a little more than neighbours separated by an insignificant physical distance. Within an hour she heard a tap on the door and opened it, surprised to see Ben outside.

'Hi. Am I disturbing you?'

She didn't seem able to restrain her happiness at the sight of him and his eyes were still cautious when they found her merry ones. 'Do you want the truth? Or shall I be polite?'

'Sorry.' He looked awkward, glancing back towards the cottage. 'I obviously am. I'll leave you in peace.'

'No, don't go,' she called after him, closing the door behind her. 'I've been staring at my laptop most of the day and now sewing, my eyes seriously need a rest. What can I do for you?'

'You sure?'

'Absolutely.'

It was a warm evening; the sun was slowly slipping behind the hills to the west and surprisingly she didn't want to resume sewing. Ben pointed to the chairs on his terrace.

'Would you like to sit down? It's, er, fine if you'd rather not.'

'Sitting in the sun would be lovely. Give me five minutes and I'll be right out.'

She went back inside and tidied everything away, leaving it ready for the next time. When she returned to the terrace Ben had rearranged the two Adirondack chairs, so they were at right angles to one another and she lowered herself into one.

'This feels so nice.' She closed her eyes and lifted her face to the sun. 'I always think the design of these chairs make you feel sleepy the minute you're in one. You can't do anything other than lie back and relax.'

He didn't reply and she opened one eye. He was watching her, not quite leaning back into his chair and achieving the relaxation she already had.

'So what did you want to speak to me about? Is it the Land Rover? Or the non-existent shower? It should definitely be done this week. If not, I'll have to…'

'Daisy?'

'What?'

'It's fine.' His eyes were still on her, softer, with the new ease that she was coming to enjoy finding there. 'The shower's fine – I'm managing no problem if you're still okay with it. It was about the car, actually. I wondered if you'd mind coming with me to see Edwin tomorrow. After work, obviously.'

'Of course. Other than sewing I don't think I have anything else planned.'

'What about Josh?'

'He's making his own way home each evening, I don't need to collect him.'

'How's he getting on? I bumped into him the other day and he said he liked living in halls and fending for himself. I was too busy competing at his age, I wish I'd taken some of the different opportunities that came my way then.'

There it was again, the tiny reference to his former life, the one before his illness. 'Oh?' She hadn't meant to make her reply sound like a question.

'This looks very cosy.'

Daisy leapt out of her chair as she heard Nina's voice and saw her friend crossing the garden with long strides. She was aware of Ben standing too as they watched Nina approach. Wearing black yoga pants paired with a light-weight jade green hoodie and trainers, her long hair tied back, Nina looked as effortlessly stunning as ever. Daisy tried not to make comparisons with her own floral shirt, the sleeves loosely rolled up, and a pair of faded old boyfriend jeans and decided it didn't matter anyway.

There was no possibility of sitting again as there were only two chairs and it didn't seem likely that Ben was going to invite them inside for a cheerful pot of tea or welcome glass of wine. She made the introductions, Nina and Ben shaking hands before launching into a conversation about running and competing, comparing experiences from the race last Saturday.

'Actually, that's partly why I'm here.' Nina had her phone in one hand, a card in the other. 'Obviously to say hello seeing as you're a friend of Daisy's, but I'm a physiotherapist and I thought you might like my contact details.' She passed the card to Ben and he accepted it. 'Just in case there's anything you need. I see a lot of runners and triathletes, so you know, give me a call.'

'Actually I probably could do with an appointment.' Ben sounded amused by her directness, although his face was inscrutable. 'I've been getting some pain in my left shoulder when I'm swimming so it's probably worth checking it out.'

'Absolutely.' Nina was scrolling through her phone in a flash. 'You really don't want that to be rotator cuff tendinitis with the race less than a month away. How about this Thursday at seven? I do a late clinic once a week and I've had a cancellation so I could fit you in no problem.'

'Sounds perfect. Thanks.'

'How's Scott's mum?' Daisy changed the subject, trying to make her voice sound normal and not twisted with jealousy at the thought of Nina spending time alone with Ben, touching him, testing the movement of his shoulder and feel of the muscles beneath. 'What happened?'

'She's fine, thanks.' Nina's look was relieved. 'She slipped and hurt her arm, I didn't think it was broken but decided to make sure as she was in quite a bit of pain. She's back at home with painkillers and swearing at the news again so I know she's okay. I'll take another look tomorrow.'

Nina glanced at her phone. 'Actually I'd better go and leave you two to it, I've got a yoga class in ten minutes. Don't forget, Daisy, you promised to come to classes again with me after the summer holidays.' She engulfed Daisy in a hug and shot a grin at Ben. 'See you Thursday. Behave yourselves.'

They were alone again as Nina dashed back through the garden, and Ben's voice came to Daisy through the fading light. 'Tomorrow then, to see the Land Rover at Edwin's? Does seven suit you?'

'Sure.' Daisy wanted to sit down again, to go back to the ease they were beginning to find before Nina had arrived, but Ben was brisk, making for his front door and she knew the moment had passed. 'See you then.'

–

All through work the next day she was impatient, looking forward to the evening ahead with Ben. She left Josh to clear up the supper she had made them and crossed the courtyard to her car, Ben joining her moments later, that same fresh, citrus scent drifting from his skin.

'Are you serious, then, about buying the Land Rover?' Daisy drove away from the village, waving at Mrs Hodges. Her elderly neighbour was slowly deadheading roses, a tabby cat snoozing on a chair, reminding Daisy she'd promised to run her to the vets next week. She had to pull over to let a fell rescue vehicle fly past, on their way to another summer emergency. 'Do you really need it, just for a month?'

'I'm thinking about it. I've kept my training local so far, but it would be useful to have a vehicle for carrying my kit and getting to the Lakes.'

'Wouldn't it be easier to hire something?'

'Maybe. I'll see what Edwin's is like first.' Ben was looking out of the window, watching the landscape changing as the houses disappeared, replaced with fields of grazing sheep and young lambs bounding over hilly ground surrounded with bracken not yet bronzed. 'Does he farm on his own?'

'Yes, what's left, anyway. There was a small beef herd at one time, and he used to produce pedigree Swaledale sheep for breeding flocks, but he let most of them go after his wife died. Edwin is hugely respected for his knowledge of the breed. He's kept a few sheep going and he still cuts haylage for winter and sells the surplus. He also breeds collies for hill work and he concentrates on that now. The puppies are promised to farmers before they're even born; they're enormously valuable and not just in price.'

Low Gill Farm was only a short drive from Thorndale and Daisy was soon swinging into the yard behind the house, parking opposite a wall separating the old building from two large stone barns. Weeds and moss were creeping along the cobbles and a few slates were missing from the roofs of the barns, a rusty trailer lying half propped against the wall.

Used to passing through on foot, she was surprised how much smaller everything looked from her car and thought it might seem very unkempt and rather sad in Ben's eyes. The first crop of this year's haylage filled one barn and when they got out of her car, four collies in their pens near the back door of the house barked loudly. Daisy ignored them as she knocked at the house, Ben standing silently beside her. She was about to knock again, the dogs still making a din, when the door was pulled back and Edwin Rawlinson leaned out past them, and roared.

'Shurrup liggin' dogs! Afore Ah wang summat!' As one the dogs fell silent and lay down, their eyes on Edwin, who turned his unsmiling look first to Daisy and then Ben.

'Is this a good time to have a look at the Land Rover, Edwin?' The old farmer didn't really do pleasantries but she was long used to him.

'Aye, it's in t'barn yonder.' Edwin was staring at Ben from beneath the old tweed cap and Daisy knew he was trying to size up this polished stranger who had appeared on his doorstep, the gloss of the city he had left still evident in his manner if not his appearance. 'Nar'n, 'ows tha been?'

She felt the sharp flick of Ben's glance on her but he answered before she could translate. 'I'm good thanks, Edwin. How are you? Thanks for letting me see the vehicle.'

Edwin tipped his head towards her whilst still watching Ben, the ghost of a smile creasing his weathered face. 'Ah can see ye not clarht–eead, ye've brought t'accountant wi' ye.'

He stepped out of the house, still in slippers beneath his overalls and leaving the door wide open. The dogs in their pen leapt to their feet excitedly but he glared at them and they lay down again, deflated. He limped awkwardly across the yard, shuffling through the odd muddy patch not yet dried into dust.

'What did he say?' Ben lowered his voice. 'I was guessing before.'

'That you must be serious as you've brought me along, presumably in some sort of professional capacity.' Ben chuckled and the sound of it brushed over Daisy's skin, leaving a trail of goosebumps in its wake. 'Just remember it's nothing to do with me if you're minus some cash and bunny hopping down the lanes after Edwin's done a number on you.'

Inside the barn they helped Edwin clear a path of sorts between tools propped precariously against the wall, half a bale of last year's haylage and a dog kennel inside a makeshift sheep pen. Daisy's eyes soon adjusted to the dim light and she saw the old red Land Rover parked at the back of the barn behind all the chaos.

'Do you have the keys?' Ben was beside her, watching Edwin clamber over to the car.

Edwin shot Ben a look as he tugged open the driver's door with a creak. 'They're in t'ignition.'

'Edwin's famous for running his vehicles on empty tanks and fumes,' Daisy murmured to Ben. 'Someone took the car once and had to abandon it up the lane because it was out of fuel. So he never bothers locking them – he knows they won't get far.'

She saw Ben stifling a smile as he followed Edwin, springing over a pair of mucking out forks lying on the dusty ground. He bent down to look inside. 'Will it start, do you think?'

''Course she will,' Edwin told him scornfully, giving Daisy a sad shake of his head, feigning surprise that the vehicle's credentials should be in doubt. 'She runs like a bairn on t'bottle. 'Ad plenty done to 'er in 'er day.'

Ben stepped back to let Edwin haul himself inside with some difficulty. Daisy was sure she wasn't the only one who was surprised as the car lumbered into life at the first turn of the key. He flashed Ben and then her a triumphant look, resting his hands on the steering wheel behind the dirty windscreen. Ben shook his head wryly.

'Ye'll be wantin' to tek 'er out then.' Edwin slowly lowered himself back to the ground, staring at the mess in front of him meaningfully, his thick dark brows furrowed. 'Just 'ave to shift this lot. Be reet when it's done.'

The barn began to fill with smoky fumes and Ben leant into the car to switch the ignition off, straightening to look at Edwin.

'I'll leave you to it,' Daisy said, backing out of the barn. Whatever deal the two men struck was between them and she crossed the yard towards the fields to see if the two horses were about.

The dogs eyed her lazily, knowing she was of no interest to them. The horses were dozing in the sunlight on the other side of the field and she hovered by the gate, unwilling to disturb them. Swallows were flitting to and fro, and she heard the call of a sheep nearby, hidden on the other side of the buildings.

A few minutes later Ben reappeared with Edwin, chatting together as they shook hands. Edwin threw an arm in her direction before he disappeared into the farmhouse, banging the door loudly behind him. Ben came over to join her, propping one foot on the gate as he tilted his head sideways.

'We've shaken on it,' he said. 'I'm coming back tomorrow, and I'll help him clear the barn and run the car down to the garage to let them service it. If it passes the MOT, then I'll pay and Edwin's going to let me use it for the next month or so in return for a bit of help around the farm. We both agreed there wasn't much point in me buying it but this way he gets it serviced and he can sell it later, if he wants to.'

Astonished, Daisy stared at Ben. 'Help him around the farm? Does he know you've no experience and you work in an office? What about your training, if you hurt yourself trying to catch a sheep or something? They're much stronger than they look and awfully hard to hold if you don't know what you're doing.'

She was concerned about him, of course she was, but she couldn't ignore the small part of her that was more worried about him leaving the village if he had no triathlon to stay for…

'I won't hurt myself, I promise.' His voice was low as he turned his back to the field and stared across the yard, his elbows and one heel resting on the bars of the gate. 'It's nice of you to mind, though.'

'Oh well, you know, of course I do, anyone would, wouldn't they, we don't want you to miss the race. That's why you're here after all and you can't possibly miss it with everything you're doing to keep fit.'

'Absolutely. It's all about the race.'

The briskness had returned, but for once she was grateful for that bit of distance. She pointed at her car. 'Good to go? I could do with an hour or two's sewing if you're ready? I've got an order to fill.'

'Sure. Sorry, I didn't mean to keep you.'

'Not at all, you haven't.'

Chapter Nine

When Daisy returned home on Thursday evening after meeting a client, she found Josh cooking supper and an email on her phone from the plumber confirming the new shower in the cottage had been successfully installed. She was already tired, having sewn long into the night on Wednesday after work to finish more aprons for the shop which she'd delivered at lunchtime.

Cynthia Timms, one of the formidable quartet who ran the cafe, had enquired after Ben and Daisy had told her little. But she did learn from the older woman that Ben liked to pop in for a coffee most days and was seemingly partial to the odd slice of flapjack. It was another little window into how he was spending his time when he wasn't training.

Daisy's energy levels felt low and the news about the shower left her feeling even more flat. She'd only bumped into Ben using theirs a couple more times since that first day, and on each occasion, they'd been slightly awkward and very polite with one another.

Now there was no reason for Ben to come up to the house and wearily she set the table for the meal Josh was busy producing, thanking him gratefully for the vegetarian pasta dish he set out. Having suffered with migraines since her early twenties, she recognised the signs and thought it likely an attack would follow over the next couple of days. Sewing would have to wait, her vision simply wasn't up to it.

Josh headed up to his attic after they'd eaten, and she was standing at the sink when she saw Edwin's old red Land Rover pulling onto the drive beside her own. She watched, blinking, her head throbbing with a bit more intent, as Ben jumped out and reached for a rucksack in the back. He glanced over, catching her watching and waved, and she decided to go and have a look.

He smiled as she crossed the courtyard. 'She's scrubbed up quite well, don't you think?'

Daisy nodded, trying pointlessly to smooth away the pain building in her head with a hand as she stared at the old vehicle. It did indeed look vastly different now that it was freed from its former home at the back of the dusty and cramped barn at Edwin's.

'I didn't notice before it had a white roof. You're braver than I thought if you've washed it.'

Ben tapped the door knowingly as he locked it. 'She's actually in very good order, or so they tell me at the garage. I've got a shiny new MOT certificate to prove it.'

'Don't let Edwin know, he'll be charging you rent. So you cleared the barn then?' The pasta was already churning in her stomach and she felt light-headed.

'Yep, although really we've just moved everything into the other one. Edwin wasn't too keen on getting rid of stuff, even a box of old nails we found that he swore he's going to straighten.' Ben halted, staring at her. 'Are you okay, Daisy?'

'I'm fine,' she muttered, aware of the alarm in his voice as he dropped the rucksack to come and stand beside her. The dizziness was gradually receding, and she took slow, deep breaths, feeling a little of her strength returning.

'Sure? You've gone a bit pale.'

'Yes, honestly, I am. It's the start of a migraine. I'll go back inside and lie down for a bit. I get them sometimes, usually if I'm overtired or spend too long sewing.'

To Daisy's surprise Ben followed her, waiting until she was inside the house and facing him at the door. 'Thanks, Ben. I'm fine now.'

He checked his watch. 'I've got to go to the appointment with Nina. Are you sure you'll be okay? Is Josh here?'

'Yes.' Daisy couldn't nod, it was suddenly too much effort. Backing away, she tried to smile reassuringly so he could leave. 'Don't miss it.'

He looked doubtful and she closed the door before he had turned away. She collected a glass of water and said goodnight to Josh before heading into her own room and curling up in bed after taking painkillers, praying that blinding pain and crashing lights would not follow. Josh promised to look in on her before he left for his final day of NCS tomorrow.

Sleep was fitful and she struggled to settle every time she woke up through the night, eventually getting up at four a.m. to make a cup of green tea and going back to bed an hour later. She checked her calendar first, thankful to see that she had no client appointments and could work from home if necessary.

It was mid-morning before she woke again, knowing she'd missed Josh and picked up her phone, squinting at it uncomfortably. Sure enough he'd texted to say she'd been asleep when he'd knocked and hadn't wanted to wake her, and to let him know if she needed him. She tapped out a brief reply to thank him and crawled back into bed, tossing her phone aside.

The real pain kicked in during the afternoon and she was sick twice on an empty stomach, wondering what had triggered such an attack when she hadn't had one so vile for almost a year. She swallowed more painkillers with a tiny amount of water, retching as the liquid reached her stomach, and tottered back to her room. She slept, on and off, all thoughts of working from home abandoned as she waited for the pain to subside.

She was in the kitchen again, still in her blue and white sheep-printed pyjamas, her hair tousled and messy, making another cup of green tea when there was a knock on the outside door. Groggily she crossed to answer it, not surprised yet horrified all at once to see Ben. She knew she looked a complete fright and even through the pain and nausea she tugged at her wild hair, squinting at him and covering her eyes from the light pouring in.

'Hi, Daisy, sorry to bother you. You're not going to believe it but— what the hell?'

She teetered backwards suddenly, feeling light-headed again as another wave of nausea flipped her stomach. Ben rushed forwards and grabbed her shoulders to steady her. She lurched, half collapsing into his arms which tightened around her, his hands warm on her back through the thin cotton of her top. Her face flushed hotter still as she felt the firmness of his chest against hers and she tensed, trying to arch away from him.

'Migraine?'

She nodded, still propped in his arms and aware of his strength supporting her. One arm went to her waist as he walked with her back into the kitchen, guiding her into the cosy armchair beside the Aga. He dropped down in front of her and she saw concern in his bottomless green eyes as she tried to control her swirling nausea.

'What do you need? Water? Pain relief? Doctor?' His voice was already soothing her with its unexpected tenderness.

'Just bed,' she mumbled, taking deep breaths and trying not to focus on the pain in her head. She tried to stand up and Ben reached for her shoulders again, holding her gently.

'You shouldn't be alone, not like this.'

'I'm fine. Just need to go upstairs.' She didn't dare move her head as another wave of nausea washed over her again and she sank back into the armchair, feeling ready to faint as his arms fell away.

'Is Josh here?'

'No. Home on Monday.'

There was a pause, a small silence between them. 'Daisy, will you let me help you up to bed?'

In all the ways she had imagined him saying that to her, it wasn't like this. Sick, faint, in pain, she only nodded, past caring what either of them thought as long as she could crawl back under her duvet and shut out the light. She stood again, expecting him to offer her a hand, and her mouth fell open in shock when his arms slid beneath her, lifting her easily, their eyes meeting for a long moment as he crossed the kitchen.

One of her arms went around his neck, her fingers grazing his hair. Terrified she would be sick over him, she fixed her gaze on her knees bent over his left arm, feeling the brush of his beard against the top of her head.

'Your shoulder,' she muttered. 'Please don't hurt yourself.'

'I'm fine.' He carried her upstairs in silence and when they reached the landing on the first floor, he paused, still holding her tightly. 'Which room, Daisy?'

She'd already given up the struggle to resist and her head was resting on his good shoulder. She lifted a hand, pointing to her bedroom at the back of the house and he crossed the landing in quick strides. He pushed the door open with his foot, carrying her across the room and laying her down gently on the bed. She hoped he hadn't noticed yesterday's work clothes still slung across the sofa, her primrose bra lying on top, or the plate from this morning's toast and cold mug of tea beside it.

'Thank you.' She pulled the duvet up to her chin. 'So sorry, how awful for you. I must look terrible.'

There was a smile hovering as he backed away. 'Would you mind if I came back later to check how you're doing?' Suddenly awkward, his glance fell on the sofa before returning to her. 'Obviously, I wouldn't if Josh were here to look after you.'

'No. Thank you.'

She wasn't really supposed to trust him. She was meant to leave the door locked to keep him away but if he'd offered to crawl into the bed beside her and hold her all through the night, she knew she wouldn't have said no. Ben was heading for the door, almost back on the landing when Daisy gasped, remembrance sending a fresh wave of pain reverberating through her head and she clutched her forehead. 'Oh, no.'

Instantly he spun around, staring worriedly at her. 'What is it? Are you worse?'

'No,' she whispered, pushing the duvet away and slowly swinging her sheep-covered legs back out of the bed. 'I've just remembered it's Friday and I promised Mike I'd be at the pub tonight so he can go out with his son.'

Ben crossed the room again, standing in front of her as she tried to get to her feet. 'Absolutely not,' he said firmly, bending down to lift her legs back onto the bed. Daisy was aware of gentle hands and warm skin and didn't resist, laying her head carefully back onto the pillow and shutting her eyes.

'I need to go.'

'You can't,' he said softly, tucking the duvet back over her. 'You're in no fit state. I'll nip down and let him know.'

'I hate letting him down, he was so looking forward to it.'

'Don't think about that now, just rest. I'm sure he'll understand. Don't get up, I'll be back later.'

She couldn't nod without setting off more pain but heard Ben leave the room, closing the door quietly. His presence and gentle strength had comforted her, and she dozed off, the painkillers doing their work. Once, throughout the long night, she thought she saw him looking in on her, trying to keep the light on the landing from falling onto her face. She mumbled some words at him through dry lips that made sense in her drowsy confusion and he seemed to be smiling as he backed away.

When she woke early on Saturday morning, she knew the worst had passed, thankful that probably only tiredness would linger for a day or two. She was starving and headed into the bathroom to brush her teeth and freshen up. A shower could wait, she decided, until she'd had breakfast.

Still in the same pyjamas, she walked through the quiet house, feeling bad about Mike and not being well enough to work in the pub last night. She pushed the kitchen door open and was met by the comforting warmth of the Aga. At once her feet halted where they stood, her lips parting in a silent gasp as her pulse rocketed. Ben lay sprawled in the armchair beside the Aga, fast asleep, his head tipped back, legs stretched out.

His expression was peaceful for once, long dark lashes sweeping over his skin and she noticed a light dusting of freckles above his beard. He'd changed into jeans and a polo shirt since she'd last seen him, and she hesitated, not wanting to disturb his sleep but desperate for some food. Bad enough for him to have seen what he had last night without waking to find her staring down at him.

She knew she ought to be alarmed that her migraine had caused her to abandon good sense and not lock up, but she wasn't, and she wouldn't tell Josh what had happened either. She'd already answered his texts to let him know she was fine now. She couldn't help it, her heart tilted as she remembered Ben's obvious concern and gentle care for her last night. She turned away, intending to go back upstairs and change before he woke up.

'Morning.'

Daisy whirled around, a blush blooming on her skin. There was an awkwardness in his greeting as he rose quickly from the chair and hovered by the Aga. She saw him taking in the same pyjamas and wild hair and she crossed her arms, certain she had never looked less appealing. He ran a hand through his long hair, pushing it from his face, the movement bringing her focus to the arms that had lifted her so easily last night.

'How are you feeling? You look much better.'

If that was the case, she must have looked like death yesterday. 'I'm okay. I'll probably be tired for a day or two, but the worst has passed.' She hesitated, searching for the right words. 'Ben, it was so kind of you to take care of me as Josh wasn't here. Thank you, I really appreciate it.'

'You're welcome.' There was a hint of embarrassment in his tone that hadn't been present before. 'Sorry, about this. I must have fallen asleep after I looked in on you.'

'It's fine, please don't apologise. Would you like a cup of tea or coffee? I was about to make some once I've changed.'

He checked his watch, the hesitation enough to let her know of his decision. 'Thanks, but I should head off. I need to go train.' He crossed the kitchen and she thought he was about to say something before he nodded once and was gone, closing the door quietly behind him.

Daisy didn't bother going to change now he'd left, and made tea instead, sitting alone at the table, the kindness of Ben's care gone with him. She knew her day held nothing much more than a gentle walk, a bit of shopping in the village. The hours stretched ahead, the weekend already feeling long. She supposed she could catch up on the work she had missed yesterday instead, the idea holding no appeal.

A long, hot bath had never felt more lovely after a light breakfast and she collected her bag and sunglasses and left the house. Edwin's red Land Rover was gone, and she knew she had a marker now, a means of letting her know when Ben was definitely not at home. She reminded herself to stop referring to it as his home, certain he never did.

She reached the village green, the monthly farmers' market in full swing, and Daisy picked up some fresh eggs and the locally grown vegetables that Mrs Hodges liked, to drop in on her way home. After a slow wander and a brief chat with Sam Stewart about the bus fundraising, she decided to go and see Mike and apologise in person for last night, hoping Ben had not forgotten to do it for her. Fifteen minutes later she headed around the back of the closed pub and found Mike already outside, chatting to one of the men who ran the microbrewery. Mike saw her and came straight over.

'Daisy,' he said cheerfully, smiling down at her from his great height. He was so big, he was blocking the sun from her sight and she was glad, her eyes still sensitive even behind her glasses. 'How are you, love? Sounds like it was a rough one, having to take to your bed like that.'

'I'm okay now, thanks, Mike. I'm really sorry about last night; I felt so awful I forgot all about working until it was nearly time to come in. Did you still manage to go out?'

''Course I did, we found a last-minute stand in for the pub, so I didn't have to miss it. Don't you worry, Daisy, you couldn't have worked with your head like that.'

'I'm so glad, Mike, I really am. I hate letting anyone down. I'll do a shift for free one night to say sorry properly when you're stuck for someone.'

'There's no need for that, lass. Like I said, we found someone to step in and from what I've heard they went down very well with the customers.'

'Who did you find?' she asked. 'Someone with experience, presumably?'

'Aye, he said he had some, anyway.' Mike was obviously enjoying drawing out the surprise. 'You know what it's like behind the bar, you need to be able to think quickly and clearly and get on with the rest of the team.'

She couldn't keep the impatience from her voice. 'But who was it?'

'It was Ben.'

'Ben?' Stupefied, Daisy stared at Mike. 'Ben who?'

Mike shook his head with another laugh. 'How many blokes called Ben do you know?' he asked patiently. 'Your Ben, the Ben that's staying in your cottage.'

'Ben? Ben Carter? *Ben worked my shift last night?*'

She was utterly astonished, so completely taken aback by the answer that she dropped her shopping, the bag sliding to her feet. She fumbled to pick it up, hoping she hadn't broken the eggs. Her mind finally began to catch up as she tried to picture Ben in the pub, behind the bar, even. Working. For her.

Mike was watching her curiously. 'Aye, he did, and made a grand job of it too. Laughing and joking with everyone and charming the ladies and a few gents until they were nearly three deep at the bar. Hey, how long do you think he's staying? I could offer him a job, you and him together could do wonders for my takings.'

'He's not my Ben,' Daisy blurted out, squinting behind her glasses. Two things struck her then; one that he had been relaxed and charming, something she had never really seen, and a sudden jealousy shot through her as she realised she had missed it. And the second, that she was always so completely unable to produce such ease and lightness in him, remembering his reserve around her, the thought enough to crush her happiness over what he had done in a moment.

'Maybe. Maybe not.'

With that infuriating comment Mike gave her a chirpy wink and Daisy headed off, her mind spinning with thoughts she tried to bring to order as she returned to the village. The farmers' market was even busier, and she had an idea then, one that had her seeking out the stalls she wanted. She paid for her purchases, promising to collect them after her walk and leaving her other shopping at the cafe.

She set out, her mind moving faster than her legs, unconsciously heading towards Edwin's farm and the horses, seeking the animals' quiet company and knowing they would bring her a degree of calm. They weren't in their usual field and she had to cross the yard to find them, another reminder of Ben when she thought of being here with him. The dogs were gone, and all was silent, so she knew Edwin must be out shepherding somewhere. Although most of his own flock had been dispersed, he still loved to help other hill farmers with the gathers that took place around them.

Edwin's horses were in the smaller field behind the barns and Daisy lingered with them, resting her head against Flint's warm and comfortable neck. The gelding seemed to sense her mood and nuzzled her gently as she apologised for not bringing him a treat. Eventually she left them and returned home, collecting her shopping on the way.

Glancing out of the kitchen window was already becoming a habit and she saw Ben's car back beside her own. She left the kitchen, her feet flying down the garden before she could make sense of her thoughts and knocked on the door of the cottage.

Chapter Ten

Ben said no. Of course he did, and through her humiliation as she hurried back to the house Daisy wondered if
she'd imagined the trace of regret in his voice. She had
rushed out her thanks – unable to disguise her surprise –
for his standing in for her at the pub and he had merely
nodded, the ease from this morning gone, replaced by
a wariness she had hoped they were moving beyond.
She'd followed it up with her invitation to supper this
evening, two fillet steaks and the rest of the ingredients
already bought, and he'd shaken his head before she'd even
finished the sentence.

They'd stared at one another for a long moment and
she'd apologised for bothering him, her disappointment
and embarrassment burning in equal part. Not wanting to
be in the house with him so close, effortlessly unsettling
her from a hundred feet away, she locked up and got into
her car, catching a glimpse of Ben gesturing to her from
the garden. She ignored him and drove away, heading for
town. She'd had the sense to grab her laptop before she
left, and she settled at a corner table in one of her favourite
coffee shops and ordered a bowl of sweet potato soup and
ginger tea.

She told herself that Ben's refusal to join her for supper
was exactly what she had needed to hear. Whatever had
occurred between them last night had passed just as swiftly

as the evening had lengthened into morning. She opened her list of promises for the barn dance in a few weeks, not ready yet to catch up with work, and added a pair of tickets to a touring musical. Josh had messaged again to check if she was okay and she let him know she was fine.

Another cup of tea and a slice of banana loaf later and Daisy was ready to head home. She'd checked the bank account a few days ago and Ben had paid the outstanding balance so there was little prospect of his leaving the cottage early. She also realised that now he finally had a functioning shower in the cottage she could ask for the house keys back and decided to write him a note with her request. There really was little reason why she should even see much of him anymore.

She drove home and although the red Land Rover was on the drive, there was no sign of him as she went inside and locked up. She made herself switch the laptop back on, sitting at the kitchen table to go through her work emails and update her calendar for next week. A knock on the outside door had her looking up warily and she frowned, wondering whether to bother answering. A second knock followed. She strode down the corridor and impatiently pulled the door open.

Ben spun around and she had a moment to notice his green shirt and jeans, unwilling to acknowledge how good he looked, his hair seemed freshly washed, falling to his shoulders. She faced him silently, holding the door to prevent any suggestion of further welcome.

'Daisy, I'm sorry about before.' There was tension around his eyes, a suggestion that his apology was at odds with his resolve. 'I didn't mean to be bad-mannered, it was kind of you to invite me to supper.'

She sighed; it seemed she was always having to balance being friendly against his desire for privacy. She had thought, hoped, that after last night, they were beyond it now. 'Right. Thanks for that.'

'If the offer's still open, then I'd like to say yes. Please.'

'Why? What's changed since this morning?' Some of her frustration crept into her voice. 'All I wanted to do was say thank you for helping Mike out. And for taking care of me, the way you did. I meant nothing else by it.'

Lifting his hands in a placating motion, Ben's eyes beseeched hers. 'I know, I'm sorry. I was surprised, that's all. I didn't do it in expectation of thanks.' He hesitated. 'Supper would be great but I understand if you'd rather not.'

Her promise to herself to avoid him, made only a few hours ago, was already disintegrating as he waited for her to tell him her decision. Never before had she felt like this, wanting to catch every glimpse of him she could for whatever time he was here. But she wasn't quite ready to make it so easy for him.

'I don't want to sit in silence with you across the table whilst you wonder why you bothered to come and how soon you can escape. Will there be conversation? Will you run away the moment your plate's empty?'

He smiled, some of the stiffness around his eyes disappearing as relief began to replace the tension. 'Yes and no. Will that do?'

Daisy's annoyance was already fading in delightful expectation of an evening with him. 'I suppose it'll have to. There's always the weather to fall back on if we get desperate.'

He grinned then, displaying something of the man he must have been in the pub last night. When she had not been there to observe it.

'I'll bring wine,' he told her. 'What time?'

'Six thirty?'

'Perfect.'

She closed the door, not bothering to lock it. She hurried through to the hall and checked her image in the mirror. Not amazing but she certainly couldn't go and change now, after clearly spelling out the evening wasn't any kind of a date. She ran a light pink lipstick across her mouth and that would have to suffice, she would do no more.

She returned to the kitchen, trying to remember the last time she had eaten dinner with a male who wasn't Josh. She took the two steaks she had bought this morning from the fridge, knowing there wasn't time enough to bring them fully to room temperature. She found mush-rooms, tomatoes and other ingredients to make a salad, putting it aside to dress later, and added cubed potatoes to salted boiling water, ready to toss in a frying pan with garlic and parsley whilst the steaks were resting.

She opened the window, seeing Ben crossing the courtyard and went to the door. In other circumstances they might have greeted one another with a kiss on the cheek, but that was impossible, given their reserve around one another, and she glanced at the bottle in his hands instead. He lifted it up to show her.

'I've opened it already to give it chance to breathe as I wasn't sure what time we'd be eating.'

'Great, thanks,' she told him, aware of him following her inside. She took the potatoes from the Aga, draining them so she could heat up a pan for the steak. 'What is it? It's definitely not one I've tried before. I think I'd recognise the label: it looks distinctive. Glasses are in there if you don't mind.'

She pointed to a cupboard and he placed the bottle on the table, then reached up to lift down two crystal glasses.

'It's a Cheval des Andes, an Argentinian blend of Malbec and Cabernet Sauvignon. I found it at the wine merchants in The Courtyard and thought it would be ideal with steak as the tannins should suit the beef perfectly. I was surprised to find something like that here.'

Daisy gave him a look and he had the grace to seem a little sheepish. 'Sorry, I wasn't trying to be dismissive. Wine's a hobby of mine.' He poured a little into each glass and passed one to her, sniffing his own. 'They are very well stocked and supplied.'

'They are, I believe; I don't buy that much from them. It's run by a couple from London who used to be barristers and decided they'd rather be here, selling to the high-end holiday market.'

She sniffed too, having no real idea of what she was supposed to find and tried a mouthful straight after. 'Oh, that's gorgeous! I know nothing about wine, as you've no doubt realised, but even I can taste fruit. Something rich, like blackberries.'

'Very good. It definitely has the intensity of the Argentinian style, blended with an elegance that's very French. I'm glad you like it.'

Impressed, Daisy busied herself with the steaks, bringing the pan up to temperature and sliding them both in. She raised her voice over the hissing from the pan. 'I'm guessing rare?'

'Please.'

The steaks were ready in a few minutes and Daisy finished the potatoes, adding parsley and garlic at the last minute. She put the steaks onto plates, dressed the salad and arranged everything on the table. Ben had sat down already, and she settled opposite him as he reached for the wine to refill their glasses.

'Please, Ben, help yourself.' She indicated the food before them.

Ben filled his plate, and she was gratified to see he hadn't taken a tiny portion of anything. There was a moment's silence and then he served her too. They began to eat and she wondered how they would ever have an ordinary conversation, how she might see beyond his reserve and decided to have a go.

'Thanks so much for everything you did yesterday. It was incredibly good of you to keep an eye on me and then stand in at the pub. So kind.'

'Daisy, please.' A smile was hovering as Ben looked at her. 'You've already thanked me, it's not necessary to say it again. And this food is wonderful, without doubt the best meal I've eaten in months.'

She laughed, trying to bat away the satisfaction she felt at his compliment. 'The wine is amazing too, it probably cost more than everything else put together.'

Ben grinned and she loved how it softened the wariness in his expression, sensing the beginnings of a relaxation in the unstiffening of his shoulders. He was devouring his food and she waved away seconds as she ate more slowly, watching as he filled his plate with everything left over. Her stomach still hadn't quite returned to normal after the migraine and she didn't want to overdo it.

'Where's Josh this evening?'

'In town, at his dad's.'

'For the weekend?'

'Yes, now he's left school he goes most weekends. The band he's in have a couple of gigs coming up and it's easier for him to get to rehearsals when he's already in town. Like most teenagers he's got a much better social diary than his mum.'

'He seems like a fine young man, you must be so proud of him.' Ben held his glass lightly in one hand, watching her with interest.

Daisy beamed, lighting her face with love. 'I really am, he's very caring and seems able to cope with whatever life throws at him. We definitely have our moments, but his teenage years have been good so far.'

'He asked me about my guitar, what kind of music I play, when we chatted the other day.' Ben was smiling now, leaning a little further back in his chair.

'He was desperate to ask you about that, he couldn't wait to tell me what make it was and how iconic it is.' She tipped her head to look at Ben, still watching her. 'What do you play?'

'Blues, some country, bit of rock. I like musicians with a story to tell.'

Daisy didn't share that she had seen him playing on the terrace, that she'd recognised the melancholy bend of his body as his fingers worked the fret and moved down the strings, even without being able to hear the notes he picked out.

'Josh did ask if I would let him hear me play some-time.' Ben tilted his glass, almost empty now, swirling the remains of the fine wine around the crystal.

'He'd love that. What did you say?'

'I said I would.'

'You don't mind?'

'Actually I don't, and I thought it would be churlish to refuse him.'

She laughed at that and saw confusion furrowing Ben's brow as she shook her head in disbelief.

'What?'

'You've had no trouble refusing almost everything I've suggested to you.'

He offered no reply, looking down at his glass and she felt an evasiveness returning to his manner, frustrated once again that he was shutting her out.

'Don't leave it too long to play for Josh. Once he has his GCSE results next week, he can breathe a sigh of relief and look forward to his holiday.' She made her voice deliberately even, giving Ben a steady glance to disguise her disappointment.

'He's going away?'

Daisy hesitated but she and Ben were beyond trying to conceal whether she was here on her own or not, especially after last night. 'Mark's family always get together in France every August. Brothers, in-laws, kids, cousins, grandparents, the lot.'

'Mark's Josh's dad?'

'Yes. They're going a bit later this year because of Josh's results.'

'Not you?'

Daisy took another mouthful of wine, savouring the taste of the rich, dark berries. 'No. I did go a couple of times after Mark and I divorced; it was a nice way to keep something the same for Josh, and they've always been close. But Mark's married again now with two little girls and even though his wife is lovely and we get on well, it's their family time, not mine.'

She felt suddenly wistful. 'I do miss it a bit, if I'm honest. What goes on there feels like real family life with all its noise and chaos and love, it's quite different to the simple little twosome Josh and I used to be.'

She stopped abruptly, startled by what she had confessed to Ben, things she usually only admitted in the privacy of her own mind. She stood up, reaching for their plates, unwilling to see his face and find disinterest or boredom there.

'Wow, sorry, no idea where that came from. So much for the company. I'd run away now if I were you, permission granted.'

'Wasn't planning to unless you want me to leave?'

There was a gentleness in Ben's voice she wasn't used to, and she turned to the dishwasher, sliding their plates in. He had stood too and cleared the rest of the table, bringing everything across to the sink.

'Of course not.' He was beside her and she tried to lighten the moment with a smile, clattering the plates into the dishwasher more haphazardly than usual. 'Why would I send you away before you've had dessert?' She gasped, a hand shooting to her mouth with a horrified laugh. 'I forgot!'

'What?'

'The dessert. I bought a treacle tart at the farmers market this morning and forgot to go back for it.' She tried to remember what was in the freezer. 'There's ice cream, I think. I'll have a look.'

'Daisy?' His hand briefly on her arm stilled her as she closed the dishwasher door. 'It's fine, I'm not really eating sweet stuff.'

'Oh?' She gave him a sly look, unable to hide the tease in her tone. 'That's not what Mrs Timms in the cafe says.'

His lips pursed together in mock outrage. 'Isn't it?'

Daisy was still smiling as he reached for the wine on the table and shared the last of it between their glasses, passing hers across.

'Thanks. Flapjacks, I believe she said, are an indulgence you allow yourself. As you refused my homemade, freshly baked brownies I had assumed you had a will of iron but I'm learning that's not quite true.'

He was shaking his head as they returned to the table with their glasses. 'What can I say? She likes me, and they are mostly made of oats, so I don't see the problem.'

They sat down again and Daisy knew they were gradually edging beyond the stilted wariness of those first days, barely two weeks ago. Silence enveloped them as they finished their wine, but it was a more comfortable one, easing them into another place.

Chapter Eleven

Unwilling to give Ben a reason to leave now that they'd finished their wine, Daisy asked as nonchalantly as possible, 'Coffee?'

'Are you sure?' Ben hesitated. 'Wouldn't you rather have some peace and quiet, after last night?'

'I'm always on my own whenever Josh isn't home. So no, unless you'd rather go?'

She presented the choice again, fully expecting him to take the opportunity to leave and escape to his own company. He shook his head and she stood up, hiding the pleasure she felt at his silent reply.

'Daisy, may I have tea instead? Coffee will keep me awake.'

'Of course, me too. Would you like chamomile?'

'Perfect, thanks.'

When their drinks were ready, she held his out to him. 'Shall we move into the sitting room? It's more comfortable than here.'

'Sure.'

Ben followed her along the hallway and Daisy was reminded of that first time, when he had just crashed off his bike. She had never imagined seeing him again and yet here they were, alone in the house after sharing supper. Her parents liked clutter and she shoved aside her father's books and medical magazines from one of the two sofas.

A piano stood in one corner, piles of sheet music heaped precariously on top, and the only splash of colour on the wooden floor was a scarlet rug in front of the fireplace. A large bookcase filled one wall, its contents stacked on top of one another on every shelf. Daisy chose one of the two green armchairs on either side of the hearth, drawing her legs beneath her, and Ben dropped into the one opposite her. A few posters were on the arm of his chair and he picked one up, scanning it quickly.

'"Family Barn Dance & Auction of Promises".' He looked up at Daisy curiously, the poster still in his hand.

'I was supposed to be dropping those off at a local farm shop and I forgot all about it with the migraine. Good thing you found them. I'd better make sure I deliver them, or my name will be mud at the next fundraising meeting.'

'You're involved?' Ben leant back in his chair, cupping his hands around his tea.

'You are looking at the official Promise List organiser.' Her lips widened into a grin, one he reciprocated. 'I volunteered to persuade people to offer time, gifts, tickets, the usual kind of stuff and a few surprises, that we can auction off on the evening.'

'I bet you're brilliant at that.'

She narrowed her eyes. 'Is that meant to be funny?'

'No! I was serious, I can imagine how encouraging you'd be, and that people would be happy to help you, that's all. What's it for?'

'We need to raise money to keep the community bus running in the village and hopefully this evening will go a long way to hitting the final total.'

'Can't people just use a regular service instead?'

'There isn't one anymore. The council route went a while ago, lost to a cost cutting exercise and the village only has the community bus now, which is run by volunteers. We need a new vehicle as it's no longer viable to keep repairing the old one, and it doesn't have proper access for passengers with mobility issues. Plus more money, volunteers and training to keep it going.'

Ben shrugged. 'But surely if there's not enough money to run it, then that's that and people will have to find another way. Nothing lasts forever.'

Daisy laughed softly, bending to put her empty teacup on the tiled hearth. 'Spoken like a true city dweller with public transport always on hand. It's not really quite that simple. Without the bus many of the villagers can't get into town to appointments, fetch shopping, socialise and stay active. Not everyone has a car and some of the elderly residents don't want to drive around here, especially in winter when the conditions are particularly challenging. It truly is a lifeline and we're doing everything we can think of to raise enough money for at least another two years' worth of funding.'

'And if you don't?'

'Then losing the bus will have a negative impact on people's lives and their wellbeing, and increase the risk of social isolation,' she replied simply. 'I'm guilty of taking my car for granted and driving off whenever I feel like it, but for some people it'll mean rarely leaving the village, having to rely even more on others for essentials and lessen their independence.'

Ben lowered his empty cup to the floor. 'I suppose it's easy not to see beyond the charm and beauty of a place like this, especially if you're just passing through.'

'Exactly. It might look pretty but we still have our difficulties, and the fight for the bus is really important. It sounds remarkably simple and possibly idealistic but there's a lot at stake, especially in the long term. If we lose it now, then it'll be much harder to start up again later on. And the volunteers love helping, knowing they're making a difference.'

She hoped he understood, as much as he could for one who was simply passing through, as he had said. A thought occurred to her then and she voiced it before she lost it again.

'When you called round last night, you were trying to tell me something, but I missed it because of the migraine. Was it important?'

Ben grinned again, relaxing into the comfortable chair, crossing one ankle over the other knee. 'You're not going to believe this but there's no hot water in the shower.'

'What?' Daisy shot forward in her seat, staring at him in dismay. 'Seriously? But it was only fitted on Thursday, I've got the invoice from the plumber.'

'If you haven't paid it then you might want to hold off for a bit. It was fine on Thursday, but it was a bit chilly yesterday. It's probably a faulty solenoid, shouldn't take much to fix it.'

'I'm so sorry.' She remembered her decision earlier to ask for the keys back and knew she wouldn't now, shower working or not. 'You've still got keys for the house, haven't you? If you're okay with it then just use ours again, you don't have to put up with cold water. I'll ring the plumber first thing Monday.'

'Are you sure?'

'Of course I am; it's only fair.'

'Thanks, Daisy. I don't mind it now and again, but I do prefer a hot shower to a cold one. Being a soft city dweller and all.'

Daisy didn't mind in the least, not about to share her pleasure at the thought of him still needing to pop in and out of the house. 'How's your shoulder?' She was remembering how easily he had lifted her last night, how she had loved being in his arms for those few minutes, even through the blur of pain. 'What did Nina say?'

'That there's a bit of inflammation and to avoid swimming for a few days, to give the muscle repetition a rest, but the skin has healed well. She's given me some exercises to do to improve the muscle stability and to make sure I'm following through correctly on my stroke.'

'She's good, isn't she?' Daisy couldn't keep the pride for her friend from her voice. 'You were lucky to get to see her so quickly, she's usually fully booked up.'

'Very good. She's got a lot of experience in top-level sport that really sets her apart. I've made an appointment to see her every week, whilst I'm here.'

He glanced around the room, a pair of tall sash windows giving a view to the lane outside, the curtains still open. 'When are your parents coming back?'

'Not for a while. They're staying with my sister and her partner in Canada. Lucy's having a baby in a few weeks and they're in no hurry to come home as they've both recently retired.'

'My sister's expecting a baby too, in October.'

'How lovely. Is it her first or are you already an uncle?'

'Her first.' Ben hesitated and Daisy knew he was wondering how much to say, how far he wanted to go. 'I haven't seen much of them recently. I need to change that when the baby's here.'

'Is she in England?'

'Yes, Dorset. That's where we grew up.'

'So you're a southerner then,' Daisy teased, enjoying how pleasure stole into his eyes, rendering his features gentler and more peaceful. 'You're doing well, surviving up here in our harsh northern climate.'

'It is summer,' he reminded her good-naturedly. 'And surprisingly warm, on rare occasions.' He shifted until he was leaning forward, resting his arms on his thighs. 'You haven't ever asked me why I'm here, Daisy.' He was searching her face, his voice lowered. 'You've trusted me with so much and I've given you nothing.'

'That's not quite true, is it?' The teasing had gone now, her quieter tone matching his. 'You helped me yesterday and you made sure I got home safely from the pub the other night.'

'That's not what I meant.' He was still watching her, and she nodded, unwilling to pretend again that she had misunderstood him.

'You made it clear, Ben, that you wouldn't discuss your reasons with me or anyone. That's why I haven't asked; I haven't felt able to.'

'I'm sorry for being so brusque.' He faltered, his expression mirroring his apology. 'I don't like telling people what happened and why I left because it brings nothing but painful memories. Then I can see it affecting their judgement of me, like my illness has made me less than I was before.'

'You don't have to share anything with me.' She reached across to touch his hand, briefly, before retreating, curling back into the big, comfy seat. 'Your being here can still be just as simple as renting the cottage to continue training for the race. Nothing more.'

'Maybe I want it to be more.' His eyes searched hers. 'I feel like I need you to know me, so you can understand why I'm here and why I've behaved the way I have. Maybe it's selfish, hoping you won't think less of me.'

'I don't. I won't think less of you, whether you share it with me or not,' she told him simply, truthfully. There were moments, at the beginning, when she had but that was long past now, especially after last night.

He sighed, despair settling heavily on his shoulders, bowing them under its weight. 'I witnessed a suicide. In New York. I… I was the last person to speak to the guy before he fell from a building.'

It was a moment before Daisy could whisper a reply. 'I'm so sorry.' She lifted a hand to her face and dropped it straight back down, her fingers fidgeting on her lap as she longed to reach for his. It wasn't at all what she had been expecting. 'I have no words, Ben, truly. I can't imagine…'

'No one can, that's why it's usually better to say nothing.' The darkness was still there, in the bite of his tone and the furrow of his brow, but she understood his anger wasn't directed at her… 'And I didn't want to burden you with my problems.'

'Oh, Ben…' There was nothing she could add, no words that could change anything of what he was feeling, and she waited to hear what would come next.

'I was at a party when a girl came rushing in, screaming that her boyfriend was on the roof and threatening to jump. I didn't think, I ran outside with absolutely no idea of what the hell I thought I could do. Just stop him, I suppose. I didn't know it at the time, but he was a banker, like me. I thought he was drunk or high, he was yelling about work and pressure and not being able to take it anymore.'

'He'd climbed over the barrier and was clinging on and I spent ten minutes with him, trying everything I could think of to persuade him to come back, praying desperately that someone who knew what to do would show up and take over.'

Ben's voice was flat, and Daisy was desperate to offer something, some form of comfort and strength and inched nearer to him, still on her chair. 'He fell about two minutes before they came. Drugs are common enough in our business and it turned out he had a serious addiction, was in debt beyond anything he could manage and couldn't see a way forward.'

'You know you did everything you could, don't you?' Whispered words, ones that had Ben looking away from her. 'If drugs were involved and he was already unwell...'

'Maybe. But the second he'd gone I knew whatever I'd done hadn't been enough to save him, that I'd let him down.'

'Ben, probably nobody could if he were so determined and his life was completely out of control.'

Ben sighed, raking a hand through long hair already messy. 'I've had months of therapy telling me that but, in the end, when it was just me and him, I failed.'

'What was his name?'

Ben looked at her, surprised. 'Aaron. I didn't even know that, had never set eyes on him before. There were weeks of investigations and I carried on, tried to keep working and socialising and pretending everything was fine. My family are here, and it was easy enough to convince them I was okay from a distance.

'It wasn't until I met Aaron's parents and they thanked me for trying to persuade him not to jump that I really knew I was struggling. They treated me like some kind of hero when I knew I was anything but. I felt I'd failed them too, and I could feel myself changing into someone

I didn't want to be. Life was good until then. I had professional success, travel, a relationship, every reward I wanted and none of it meant anything after what happened to Aaron. The job literally killed him.'

Ben paused. 'About four weeks after it happened, I was in a meeting and couldn't remember how to sign my own name or what year it was. Everything felt unreal, as though I wasn't really there. So that was the start of medication, therapy and the ASD diagnosis. It shocked me, I thought I was strong enough to just carry on. My therapist taught me I couldn't, that I needed treatment because my mind was still struggling to process what had happened. That it wasn't a matter of strength succumbing to weakness, which was how I felt at the start, like I'd let my own self down as well.'

Ben's face was utterly bleak, and Daisy felt her heart reaching for him, aching, for him and the man he had tried to help, for the family who were mourning.

'I don't mean for this to sound as though it's all about me. I won't forget that a young man lost his life, and his family and friends lost him. It's their tragedy, it's not for me to make it mine and claim it from them somehow. I'm better than I was, and I have to keep on finding a way of living with what I saw and failed to do.'

'But it wasn't your failure, Ben.'

Ben's head jerked up and he stared at Daisy.

'It didn't happen because *you* failed,' she repeated quietly. 'There must have been a series of failures that brought Aaron to that point, but it wasn't yours. At the last moment he knew someone cared enough to try and stop him and his illness took him over the edge, not your lack of knowing how to stop it. His family have that, at least, because of you. You didn't leave him, you stayed when someone else might not have been able to. Your life is a gift, Ben, one you absolutely must try to live because there's no sense in losing another one.'

Ben's head tipped forwards as he covered his face and she left her chair, crossing the few feet between them to reach him, silent tears sliding through his fingers. She lifted her hands, gently touching his shoulders until her arms were around him, slowly tugging him forwards until she felt the brush of his beard as his head rested on her shoulder, and the wetness of his tears dampened her neck.

'Your head already knows the truth,' she whispered, holding him, knowing him, trying not to love him. 'And one day your heart will catch up.'

Chapter Twelve

Daisy was up for church as usual on Sunday morning, feeling better after the migraine had departed. She was still thinking over everything Ben had shared last night and the illness he had suffered over these past months. She couldn't forget the expression of loss and hurt on his face as he'd explained what had happened, her sorrow both for him and a family she would never know filling her mind.

She was coming to understand the reserve she'd first seen in him was a means of preventing him enjoying the life he felt he didn't quite deserve after everything he'd witnessed that terrible night. They'd sat talking for a while longer as the evening moved into night, searching for a normality that hadn't quite found them yet after the intimacy of her holding him the way she had.

The afternoon stretched ahead of her until she was due at the pub, part of her routine gone and, seemingly with it, her ability to decide what to do instead. She had Nina's present to finish but it wasn't urgent, and she didn't feel like sewing today anyway, unusually for her. She let herself back into the house, thinking of something she could produce for a quick lunch as she headed for the kitchen. Mrs Hodges had gone to her son's for the day and it was just Daisy today, with Josh at his dad's.

Glancing across the courtyard she saw the red Land Rover was gone, disappointing her more than it should have done. She hadn't bothered to lock the kitchen door, there didn't seem much point after last night. She turned around, laughing in surprised delight as she spotted a chocolate brownie sitting on the table and read the note propped against it.

Didn't want you to miss dessert as well. Ben had drawn a smiling face on the note. *The door was unlocked, I hope you don't mind. Thanks, for everything. Shower felt good.*

She had the brownie for lunch. It wasn't her usual choice for a midday meal, but it was freshly baked and delicious. She thought of Ben, where he'd gone, how he was, what he was doing. Another walk to clear her head and work off the brownie seemed like the best option so she changed and headed out. She passed the churchyard and the cricket pitch, empty until the local team played again next weekend.

Ben still wasn't back when she set off for her shift at the pub and she wondered if he was avoiding her on purpose, perhaps thinking he'd said too much last night. The Coach was busy, perfectly normal for a Sunday evening in late summer, the tables on the cobbles packed as customers enjoyed the last of the day's warmth.

There had been no further sightings of Dex, although Daisy recognised a couple of his drinking buddies sitting in one corner. They were quiet and polite whenever they came to the bar, casually dropping in that Dex had gone home to Newcastle. Every table was taken and she was kept busy, pleased to see that Heather, the crime writer, was back and Mike was chatting to her whenever he got the opportunity.

When Ben walked in later, approaching the bar and easily finding her gaze, she couldn't restrain her smile and saw his own quick one in response. A new understanding was flowing between them but she still looked for a sign in his expression that he regretted what he had shared with her last night and found none.

'Hey.'

'Hi. This is a nice surprise, I wasn't expecting to see you tonight.'

He nodded at Mike, who raised a hand in welcome. 'The beer is excellent, and you were right, last week. I did enjoy being here.'

'You'll be getting a reputation as a regular if you're not careful, three visits in a week. So what can I get you? A pint of the usual?'

He grinned at that and Daisy reached for a glass, holding it under the Nickel.

'If it isn't my brilliant new barman.' Mike made his way over, his voice booming through the chatter filtering around the room. 'Just wanted to say thanks again for what you did the other night, Ben. It was good of you to step in like that.'

'My pleasure.' Ben accepted the glass Daisy slid across the bar to him. 'But no more thanks are necessary. I was happy to help out.'

'Well it really did help, and I appreciate it. I don't spend as much time as I'd like with the kids, even though they are grown up and gone. And I can always find a few hours work here and there for good staff.' Mike lowered his voice, leaning closer to Ben across the bar. 'Seeing as you're here, you don't fancy walking Daisy home again, do you?'

'I thought I might, if she doesn't mind?'

'I'm not a child,' she told the two men exasperatedly, hiding the elation she'd felt at Ben's suggestion as she handed the customer she'd been serving a card machine to pay for his drinks. 'Thanks for thinking of me but I can decide to walk home alone or not. I don't need you two making arrangements for me.'

'Makes sense,' Mike said cheerfully. 'Seeing as Ben's already here and he is going…'

'Yeah, yeah, my way. I know.'

Mike shrugged as he moved off, his attention caught by another customer and Ben said nothing, idly holding his glass. The clock on the wall caught her eye and she frowned at the time.

'You haven't seen Edwin, have you? He's not here and he always comes in on a Sunday for his pint and a half. I hope he's okay and nothing's happened.'

Ben didn't look too worried. 'Maybe he's decided not to bother and have an early night instead. He was fast asleep in the house when I went on Friday, the dogs went mad and woke him up and he didn't even shout at them.'

'It's not like him to miss the pub, though. Here and the Auction Mart cafe in town are the only places he ever socialises. I'm beginning to think someone should go and check, he could be ill or have had a fall. He won't have a mobile, he doesn't see the point as the signal's poor around the farm and if he's still in the yard he won't be able to get to the house phone.'

Ben placed his glass on the bar. 'I'll go, I can run it in ten minutes. I'll let you know as soon as I can.'

He left at once, the door closing behind him. It wasn't yet dark, which would help his search if Edwin weren't in the house or on his way to the pub. The minutes seemed to slip away much slower than usual and it was another half an hour before Mike came to find her.

'Ben's just rung,' he told her. 'Edwin's fine, still at home. Said he'd fallen asleep in front of the telly and hadn't realised the time. Ben asked him if he wanted to come for a pint, but he said he didn't, it was too late. Told him in no uncertain terms to clear off.'

Daisy breathed a sigh of relief. 'Okay, that sounds like Edwin, I'd be more worried if he'd been pleased that Ben had turned up.' She reached for a glass. 'When have you ever known him to be too tired to come for his pint, though?'

Mike's brow furrowed. 'Dunno, not since he lost Joan, I suppose.' Mike reached out, touching her arm quickly. 'But he's getting on Daisy, don't forget, and his hip is bothering him more than he lets on.'

'I know. I'll pop in tomorrow and make sure he's really okay.'

'Good idea, and if he tells you to clear off as well then you'll know he's all right.'

'I suppose so.' She moved away to serve another customer.

Before long Ben reappeared, pushing his long hair away from his face as he stopped at the bar. He looked flushed and she knew he must have run back too.

'Edwin's okay?' Daisy threw the comment across to Ben while she pulled a couple of bottles from the fridge, knocking the tops off and reaching for glasses and ice.

'I think so. He did seem tired but not confused or overly drowsy, and he looked and sounded perfectly normal. I did offer to stay for a bit, but he was having none of it and more or less threw me out.'

Reassured, she finished serving her customer. 'Thank you for going, I'll check on him in the morning.'

They were still sharing a smile when an attractive blonde man walked in, making his way straight to the bar.

'Evening Daisy,' he called, his confident voice carrying easily and turning heads. 'It must be time we caught up, I haven't seen you for ages.'

A shade smaller than Ben but broader, he had a softness around his middle that didn't speak of triathlons and a need to keep pushing himself. His hair flopped down towards his dark blue eyes, crinkled in merriment as he grinned at her with a simplicity she still found endearing.

'Henry, how are you? You're right, it has been a while. You've been away too often.'

'Yeah, first it that was conference in Paris, the one you didn't want to go to, and my parent's diamond wedding thing in London and then the kids.' He settled onto a stool at the bar, nodding at Ben. 'You know I've been in Tuscany with them? I've just got back from dropping them at their mother's. The drive up here was absolutely appalling, the M25 should be declared a national embarrassment.'

Daisy reached for a glass. 'You know you didn't need me in Paris, Henry.'

'Doesn't mean it wouldn't have been nice to take you and spend a bit of time together.'

She shot a quick glance at Ben, but he was engrossed in a local newspaper he'd found on the bar. 'The usual, Henry?'

'Please. Make it a double. Not that revolting seaweed stuff you tried to palm off on me last time.' Henry sighed. 'Bloody Monday again tomorrow. Might as well have something to eat whilst I'm here.' He tugged a menu from its holder on the bar and scanned it quickly. 'I'll have the scampi, I think. And chips. Thanks.'

Daisy finished making his drink the way he liked it, two shots of dry, handcrafted local gin with a simple tonic and slice of grapefruit, and slid the glass across to him. 'Here you go. We had to get rid of the seaweed gin, I think you killed the concept stone dead, you whinged so much when you tried it.'

'Not surprised, it was foul. That stuff belongs on a beach, not in a bottle.'

She laughed, snatching another look at Ben, who was still sitting quietly and paying them no attention. Henry looked over too, and she made the introductions.

'This is Ben Carter, Henry, he's staying in our cottage for a few weeks. Ben, this is Henry Carlyle, who runs the estate where I have my office. He's one of my clients.'

'Your best client, you mean.' Henry smirked as he reached across to shake Ben's hand. 'Good to meet you. You familiar with the village?'

'Not really, I've only been here a couple of weeks. But everyone seems friendly.'

Henry was already turning his attention back to Daisy. 'Haven't we got a meeting soon, Daisy? Sure I saw something on my calendar.'

She threw him a frustrated look as she took payment for another order. 'Tuesday, first thing. Don't disappear like you did last time. We need to go over the plans for the glamping site and it won't keep much longer if you want to make the grant deadline.'

'Right, Tuesday it is,' Henry said. 'In fact, let's make it a lunch meeting at that pub we found in the spring near Hawes, if you're free? Right, I'm off to find a table. Text me, yeah?'

He disappeared and Ben was still reading the newspaper as she worked; she was surprised he hadn't wandered off to a quiet corner table too when it became momentarily free. Mike was nattering to him in between customers and when a man bustled in from the snug next door, looking for someone to make up a darts game, Mike suggested Ben and he agreed without a murmur, folding his paper and looking wryly at Daisy.

She didn't want to miss him the moment he was no longer in sight but did, thoughts of everything they'd shared last night still fresh in her mind. The end of her shift seemed a long time coming and the anticipation of Ben waiting for her made Daisy impatient to leave. She collected her bag when she was finished, the pub empty and quiet and saw him at the front door.

'Thank you for...'

'Don't.' Ben held the door open and they called good-night to Mike as they stepped into the lane. 'Please, Daisy, don't thank me again, I was happy to wait.'

'Fine.' Opposite the pub, a young family was trying to herd a couple of children inside a holiday house and calm a crying baby at the same time. 'How was the darts match?'

'Surprising. I learnt I have poorer hand to eye coordination than I realised and that it's extremely competitive. I lost both times, so I don't suppose they'll ask me to play again.'

'Again?' She was teasing him, giving him a sideways glance. 'Are you planning to come back?'

'Are you working next Sunday?' he countered.

Daisy caught the upward tilt of his lips. 'I expect so.' She pushed away unwelcome thoughts of walking home alone when he would no longer be staying in the cottage and had returned to the city, where his real life was waiting for him.

'Then I suppose I'll be there too. No, don't say it.'

They both laughed and when the silence came, as it usually did between them, it was a more comfortable, more knowing pause in their conversation than any that had gone before.

'Henry seems nice,' Ben remarked, nodding at a man strolling with a dog on the other side of the green as they reached the edge of the village.

'He is, he's been a good friend to me over the years. He gave me lots of help and advice when I was starting my business.'

'You've known him a long time?'

'I had a summer job in the shop on the estate after I left school. We're the same age and we hung out together for a while.'

There was more to tell than that, but she wasn't about to share the details of the lovely summer she'd had with Henry when they were sixteen, until studying, travel and a first job took him away. Over the years he'd married, fathered a boy and a girl and then followed it up with a divorce. But he'd never forgotten his friendship with Daisy, and he'd been happy to appoint her as his accountant once she'd qualified. She'd always appreciated that first professional opportunity and the ability to carry the recommendation of the estate into other businesses.

She was also aware that, single again, his interest in her beyond their professional relationship had re-awakened, even though she had no intention of letting things change. The business she had developed and grown over the years was far too important to risk for something that she knew would never last.

'He likes you.' Ben's statement was matter of fact.

'I like him too, he's great fun and good company but it won't ever be more than that.' She wasn't very interested in Henry just now. 'So did Edwin really seem okay to you?'

'I think so, there wasn't anything obvious like slurring his speech or not knowing where he was, and he hadn't fallen. But he ought to see a GP if he'll go. If anyone can make him it's probably you, Daisy.' Ben was looking sideways at her. 'He told me the other day about you growing up and spending hours in the yard with him, helping him with the horses.'

'Oh!' She hadn't expected that. 'That was years ago, when he was still training point-to-pointers and had a small herd of native ponies.'

'He said you were one of the best riders he knew, that understanding the horses was an instinct not everyone had but you were brilliant with them and they really responded to you. That you probably could've ridden professionally if you'd had the chance.'

Daisy shrugged, the familiar squeeze of anxiety at the reminder suddenly clutching at her stomach. 'That's nice of him. I did love being there, but you know how it is, studying takes over everything when you get to a certain point. I knew I didn't want to work on a yard, the hours are so long, and the winters are brutal, especially here. I wanted a job I could rely on.'

'That's not why you gave up, though, is it?'

She increased her pace as the house came into view, wanting to end the conversation, dismayed at the real-isation Edwin had been discussing her with Ben, had presumably told him things she didn't share with anyone.

'Daisy?'

'Did Edwin tell you why? Have the pair of you been gossiping about me, raking over my past?' She hated the worry in her voice trying to steal her breath, ignoring the memories of those days. They belonged in a different life, to a different Daisy. One who hadn't been a mother then, with responsibilities and a tiny baby to nurture and love and raise into a good man.

'Of course not. He didn't tell me anything, he just clammed up after he told me how brilliant you were, wouldn't say another word. There's a reason why you don't ride anymore but it's nothing to do with studying, Daisy. I saw it in your face just now when I spoke about Edwin and the yard. It bothers you.' Ben hesitated. 'I'm happy to listen if you want to share it. You did that for me.'

'You don't owe me, Ben, for last night. You don't have to pretend you're interested, just to even us up in some way.'

'I am interested.' His fingers were gentle on her arm before falling away. 'If I can help...'

'Riding was something I did then and now I don't,' Daisy jumped in, swallowing back the tears hovering at his kindness, the desire to confess how riding had been part of her soul, how utterly alive and free it had made her feel. She didn't expect him to understand: living in the city, he'd probably never sat on a horse in his life.

'It makes me the same as loads of other teenage girls who rode and then stopped to do other things.' She opened the gate, waited for Ben to disappear towards the cottage. But he was still watching her and she unlocked the porch and hurried inside, the irony of running from him, as he had done from her, not lost on her. She offered him a goodnight and he still hadn't moved by the time she closed the front door.

Chapter Thirteen

Daisy was still feeling unsettled when she left work at lunchtime the next day to call in on Edwin. He seemed fine, busily training one of the younger dogs, and he shooed her away, telling her he would be quite happy to drop dead at home with his boots on and there was nothing she could do about it. She'd been cross with him for a minute and then they'd both laughed, and she'd left him whistling to the dog in the small field behind his house, a few sheep skittering this way and that.

She was upset about running away from Ben last night after he'd tried to encourage her to tell him why she had really given up riding. She didn't like the way everything felt between them now when they were beginning to trust one another, didn't yet know quite what to do about it.

Josh was coming home today and she was so looking forward to seeing him. Daisy knew they couldn't stay at her parents' forever after selling her own home, and she and Josh had a house to view tomorrow and she texted to remind him. She cooked carbonara with linguine when he crashed in later and he demolished a huge bowl, starving after his few days away.

Ben's Land Rover wasn't in the drive and Daisy had had a message earlier to say the plumber was coming, due any minute. She found the spare key and followed the plumber down to the cottage after he collected tools from his van. He apologised for the shower not working and she left him in the bathroom. She waited in the kitchen as he worked, her attention caught by small details of Ben's life in the tiny house.

The Gibson guitar that Josh had so admired lay across the sofa, a book was folded in half on the armchair and the yoga mat was rolled up behind the front door, its presence reminding her of Ben practising on the terrace. The plumber reappeared before too long, having replaced the faulty solenoid valve. Daisy scribbled a note for Ben, confirming the repair and apologising for entering the cottage when he was not at home.

The house she had arranged to view the following day wasn't what she was looking for, and Josh didn't have much to say about it. She knew as well as he did that in a couple of years he'd be heading off to university or maybe on a gap year, and until then he'd mostly be living with his dad and spending every spare minute with the band.

-

The next day she locked up her office, drove home and changed out of her pencil skirt and teal blouse, swapping them for old jeans and a sweater and pulling on her leather Chelsea boots. She grabbed her phone and coat and set off through the village on foot. She was soon approaching a riding school about mile away, a jumble of old brick stables converted from farm buildings and extended by another couple of dozen wooden ones.

The yard was beautifully tidy and well-kept as ever. Daisy had been coming on and off since she was about seven, when she and her sister Lucy had begged for riding lessons until their parents had eventually given in. For

Lucy, the attraction had lasted until the first winter when ice had frozen the water in the buckets and thermal layers were required to step outdoors.

Daisy had loved it all and kept going, eventually spending every Saturday mucking out and helping to get the horses ready in return for more lessons. She hadn't paid much attention to the Riding for the Disabled Association group back then; they were just more people who frequented the yard during the week when she was there in the holidays.

But since those days she had come to understand that they were a very dedicated group of volunteers who gave up their time to enable others to ride who otherwise wouldn't without some form of assistance. An assorted mix of people, who had about eighty years' experience between them, now turned up twice a week. Once Josh was settled in high school, Daisy had joined them on Wednesday afternoons, when he went straight to his dad's for tea. She had missed being here these past couple of weeks, her busyness at work keeping her from taking her usual time off.

She adored the smell of the yard, and however she felt about riding, she still loved being around the horses. The yard never changed, the haylage adding a sweeter note to the fresh air than that of the immaculate muck heap, piled high and usually the resting place of at least one of the yard dogs, and with a few chickens scratching at the bottom.

Daisy opened the gate and crossed to the room where all the tack was stored, the headcollars and bridles hanging beneath saddles with the horses' names stuck above. All the necessary paperwork to run such an enterprise was fastened to a board below a shelf of riding hats in boxes, with the odd spare coat and pairs of suitable boots.

She slipped inside to check from the list which ponies needed to be tacked up first and said hello to the woman she had known for years. Gwen Radcliffe was busy filling in paperwork, and a friendly grin lit her face.

'Oh Daisy, I'm glad you're here. We're running late, do you think you could tack up all three in double quick time please? Blossom, Dora and Samson? It's just the usual three riders for the first lesson but we won't need Samson for the last one as we've had a cancellation.'

'That's fine.' Daisy was already reaching for the first saddle and bridle, only half listening to Gwen chattering as she pulled down what she needed, piling everything over her left arm.

'Can you believe it, we go all these months and months without any new volunteers and then two come along in the past fortnight.'

'Mmm.'

'Two! Two sets of paperwork, two DBS checks and two green cards to complete before we let them loose with the riders. But isn't it marvellous, I might be able to retire after all?'

Daisy had heard this conversation many times before. She knew Gwen never would retire, not whilst she still had two working – if dodgy – hips, two feet to stand on and a voice to roar encouragement. The RDA group was a big part of Gwen's life and she loved throwing her energy into making their little branch the absolute best it could be; Daisy knew it would soon falter without her.

'Wonderful,' Daisy said. Gwen beamed back and Daisy quickly crossed the yard and let herself into the first stable. Blossom was an adorable little brown and white Welsh pony, sturdy and strong enough for the lighter riders and, like all their horses, utterly dependable and quite capable of understanding the sensitivity required to carry their differently abled riders.

Daisy quickly tacked her up, connecting the reins to Blossom's headcollar so the riders wouldn't tug directly onto the horses' mouths, and shut the door. Dora, a solid black cob, was bigger and she dozed, one back leg bent, whilst Daisy got her ready. She went in to Samson last – the largest of the three and another cob, black and white this time; he loved to have his neck scratched and Daisy indulged him until she heard the riders arriving in the yard.

She led Samson out and handed him over to his leader for the afternoon while another volunteer fetched Blossom. Daisy was working with Dora for the first lesson and she chattered nonsense to her as she led her to the indoor school. Dora was known to be grumpy occasionally with some of the yard staff but she never put a foot wrong with her RDA riders and Daisy loved her for it.

Dora's first rider was a young man called Aidan, who had been coming to the centre for about two years and was almost blind. Daisy knew that Aidan rode with a volunteer leading him and an extra person on his right side to keep him secure. His confidence had grown over the time that Daisy had known him, as had his adoration for Dora, repeatedly reaching down to stroke her neck once he was on board. He knew Dora's heart rate was slower than a human's and her big, clumpy feet pattered out a steady rhythm that he seemed to find soothing.

Daisy understood Aidan better now and sometimes she would chat to him, while at others she would be quiet, when she sensed he wanted silence. His riding had improved, too, and he was capable of trotting and stepping over a row of poles on the ground, which he loved, always keen to go faster. Gwen came bustling into the arena to take the lesson and made her way over to Daisy first, raising her voice as she approached so Aidan would know she was there.

'Hello Aidan, you're looking good up there. I've got another leader to help you and Daisy today, it's one of our new volunteers, actually. All the paperwork's in order so I'm happy to let him have a go, if you don't mind showing him the ropes, as it were, Daisy. We've covered all the training, but this will be his first proper lesson.'

'Of course not.' Daisy looked over to the wide, open doors of the school as Dora stood rock still beside her, always happy to have another doze. Daisy's mouth opened in astonishment as she saw Ben making his way across and their eyes met for a long moment. She hadn't seen him since they'd walked home together on Sunday evening and he gave her a nod, her own reply a stilted smile.

'Daisy, Ben; Ben, Daisy.' Gwen was oblivious to Daisy's unease as she spoke between the two of them. 'Ben's got plenty of experience with horses, Daisy, so you'll be fine.'

Daisy was trying her best to focus on Aidan and Gwen, even as her conversation with Ben from Sunday rushed through her mind. She forced her attention back to what Gwen was saying to Aidan.

'Aidan, you've got Ben today on your right side, he's assisting Daisy and is there if you need him, okay? And no trying to canter today,' she said in a playfully stern voice. 'It's not that I wouldn't let you, but the poor old leaders can't keep up and Dora's forgotten she ever had a third gear.'

Daisy's mind was buzzing with questions she was desperate to ask as Ben positioned himself on the other side of the pony and introduced himself to the younger man. She asked Aidan to get Dora to move off and he squeezed his legs against the mare's side. Aidan was chatty today, wanting to know Daisy's news. She tried to talk as usual, aware of Ben listening. She was full of praise for Aidan's riding, encouraging him to sit a little straighter, to try and keep his weight balanced in the centre, explaining how his own movement affected Dora's.

Then Aidan wanted to know more about the new person at his side and Ben explained a little about his job and taking time off for the triathlon. She and Ben barely exchanged a word, other than for her to tell him what to do and what was happening next. Even though the half hour lesson was soon over, it was an uncomfortable one for Daisy. Her next rider didn't need a second leader and once Dora was untacked and settled in her stable again, Daisy carried the tack across the yard to the storeroom. Ben met her as Gwen was switching on the kettle.

'Well done you two, thanks for that.' Gwen reached for mugs and an ancient tub of tea bags. 'That's us finished until next Tuesday. Right, who's for a drink? Daisy, you'll stay, won't you? Ben? You usually have one, don't you? I've bought some green tea specially.'

More questions and confusion chased through Daisy's mind as she tried to imagine why Ben was here. Gwen's comments implied that he was a regular but Daisy couldn't see how that could be. She wasn't quick enough to stop Gwen from making her a drink and passing over a well-used mug. She saw Ben accept one too and Gwen looked up, seemingly surprised by the silence as she handed out a packet of chocolate biscuits. Daisy refused and yet again Ben surprised her as he took two biscuits.

At a questioning look from Gwen, Daisy explained, 'Actually Gwen, Ben and I know each other. He's staying in the cottage at home.'

'Ah, it's yours, is it? He mentioned he was staying in the village; I'd forgotten you're at your mum and dad's. That didn't matter for the DBS, we had to check your home address in London, didn't we, Ben, and your address in New York. But it was all fine and very quick.' Gwen smiled at Daisy, cradling her mug and blowing gently across the top. 'So you know all about him, then? All about his years with horses and being brought up on a farm.'

Daisy's eyes flew to the man standing silently opposite her, holding his mug of green tea, the biscuits gone. She saw an apology in his gaze, knew she was gaping and closed her mouth hurriedly, horrified by her reaction and the little he'd shared with her about his life.

Years with horses? Brought up on a farm? She tried to swallow her tea without burning herself. Gwen was still talking, her back to them as she pulled out a diary and read through it, oblivious to the tension between Daisy and Ben.

'Well, I can't tell you how much we appreciate having someone of your experience helping us, Ben, we really do. Mucking out and tacking up for lessons, you've no idea the difference it makes. Most of the staff and volunteers have been here for years and we're not getting any younger, present company excepted, Daisy.'

Daisy had heard enough. She gulped down a bit more of her tea and grabbed her jacket. 'Thanks for the drink, Gwen. Don't forget I won't be here next week; I'm on holiday. See you in a couple of weeks.'

She hurried out of the tack room, across the yard and set off back towards the village at a furious pace. She was almost home again when she realised Ben must have followed soon after. He caught her up and they didn't exchange a word until they were outside the house and she was searching her pockets for keys.

'Daisy, stop, please. Can we talk for a moment?'

'Why? What about?' Her laugh was hollow. 'You don't have to explain yourself to me. It's really none of my business how you spend your time here.'

She shook her head, hurt replacing puzzlement as her voice fell. 'It's just… It feels as though everything you've ever told me is because I've *made* you, and yet you turn up at the stables and they know so much more than I do.'

Daisy knew she was being unreasonable, that she was allowing herself to step further than she ought, as though she had a right to know anything of him at all.

'I had to give them my personal details, they can't let me volunteer otherwise.' She heard the patience in his tone, the attempt at practicality. 'You know that.'

'Of course I do.' She hadn't meant to snap. 'I'm not a complete idiot. And yet you let me blather on about not hurting yourself at Edwin's as I thought you'd no experience of farms!'

'I'm sorry, I didn't mean to mislead you. But I need to do something whilst I'm here, something that makes a difference, however small. The training isn't enough on its own to focus on.'

'But don't you see, it's… Oh forget it, we're going around in circles!'

She found the keys and jammed them in the door, almost falling inside as it opened. To her surprise Ben was still hovering as she turned, watching her, his hands pushed into his pockets.

'I can't stay here, Daisy. Once the race is over, I have to go back to New York. And the less I give you, the easier it will be for me to go.'

He took half a step forward and Daisy felt her body responding, her skin quivering with anticipation. His gaze fell to her mouth and her lips parted as he raised one hand, reaching for her face. But shock suddenly registered in his eyes, as though he had just realised what they were about to do. He muttered a savage goodbye and spun away, leaving her standing in the porch and staring after him.

–

The next morning Daisy was still on edge and not all of it was due to waiting for Josh to collect his results. They were at school in good time and she was happy to see his dad Mark and step-mum Wendy there to support him too. Josh had worked hard, and she was sure he had done well, but still the nagging feeling wouldn't quite disappear until he knew what he'd achieved. She'd planned to take the day off, or at least not go into the office until Josh was off with his friends, hopefully all celebrating.

Suddenly there was a great rush of students emerging from the school and Daisy felt a blast of nerves racing through her stomach. Josh was heading towards them, clutching his envelope and beaming, and the air rushed out of her lungs in relief.

'I got ten,' he told them triumphantly. 'French was a bit of a car crash but I still passed, and I got all the grades I wanted for college. I even passed English Lit as well.'

Daisy was crying, and Mark was too, throwing their arms around him and enveloping Josh in a tight hug as they laughed through the tears, both trying to congratulate him at the same time. Wendy hung back for a moment and then Josh hugged her too, and Daisy was glad. Wendy had long been a part of his life and Daisy appreciated her love and care for him.

They'd already arranged to take Josh out for brunch and soon headed to the busy cafe in town that Josh had chosen. He was messaging constantly, and Daisy's phone was buzzing with non-stop alerts from the family in Canada. It was only as they were about to leave that Josh suddenly produced a birthday card, giving her a hug and singing Happy Birthday, turning heads in the small cafe as Mark and Wendy joined in. Daisy thought he had forgotten – he'd been so busy with his time away and then working up to his results.

Mark and Wendy gave her a card too, with a lovely bottle of champagne and she thanked them, insisting she was perfectly happy to go back to work and didn't need to be taken out for a proper drink. Josh was in a hurry to go and meet up with his friends to continue their own celebration, and they all shared another hug as he disappeared off down the high street, school officially over. Mark arranged to collect him tomorrow morning for the long drive down to Brittany and Daisy left them to head for her office.

Chapter Fourteen

Daisy replied to her birthday messages from the office and worked all afternoon. Henry was out, his assistant on holiday, and everywhere was quiet when she eventually locked up. It was still warm and the sun bright, promising a glorious sunset later on. Tiredness was hovering and there was a slight pain behind her eyes, although it didn't feel like the start of a migraine, and she prayed it wouldn't be – she didn't want another weekend like the last one.

Ben's Land Rover wasn't in the drive when she got home and a look across to the house made her laugh in amazement. Instead of the usual stillness she had expected, she saw Josh, along with the rest of his band, setting up instruments and running through a sound check on the courtyard. The tiredness forgotten, she hurried to meet him.

'Happy birthday!' Josh spotted her and called his greeting through a mike, making her laugh again as his voice boomed down the garden. He dropped the mike and came over to fold her into a hug. 'You're getting a private gig from the band, Mum, and we needed you out of the house so we could set up. You don't mind?'

She drew back to look at him, heart completely full of love for her almost fully grown boy. 'Mind! How could I mind? Of course I don't, it's wonderful of you all and I'm so excited.'

'We thought we'd Instagram it later, but you don't have to be in it if you don't want to.'

Daisy sniffed, blinking back happy tears. 'Are you kidding? And miss my chance to be revealed as the mother of the fabulous young drummer in the coolest new band around?'

'No one ever believes you're really my mum, you know. You look too young.' Josh squeezed her shoulder as they strolled over to the others. 'Dad and Wendy are coming with the girls, they're bringing the food and we've set up a table outside for drinks. Nina and Scott are coming too, and Henry said he would if he was back in time.'

'You've thought of everything. Anyone else?'

'Mia, obviously, she'll be here any minute with Ollie and Zach.'

'I missed them this morning, did everything go well for them?'

'Yeah, Mia did brilliantly. Ollie was fine but Zach missed a couple. And Ben's coming, as he's already staying here.'

'Right.' Daisy swallowed. It made perfect sense, at least in Josh's eyes, and he had no idea how things were between her and Ben. 'He probably won't turn up, you know how private he is.'

'He said he would, I've asked him to play with us on a couple of tracks. I heard him in the garden the other night and he sounded great.'

'Play with the band?' Daisy knew she sounded shocked. 'And do you think he will?' ·

'Don't see why not, he gave me a couple of suggestions for the set and everyone's good with them.'

Still unconvinced that Ben would make an appearance, she went to say hello to the rest of the band, thanking the three other boys and Elodie, who was their lead singer. They all wished Daisy a happy birthday before beginning to tune up, and she could tell they were already fizzing with the prospect of a performance, however low key. Josh had got a playlist going over the speakers and she caught his eye, sharing a grin, as she heard some of her favourite Eighties tracks adding to the lively atmosphere.

Feeling overdressed in her usual work uniform, she disappeared into the house to change, choosing a flattering green and floral dress, with gathered short sleeves and a ruffled skirt falling above her knees. Pale pink heels picked out a shade in the material and she quickly applied mascara and lip-gloss and ran her hands through her hair. She spritzed on perfume and made her way back outside.

The garden table was laden with drinks and glasses, and the band was already helping themselves. The speakers were booming out a track by The Style Council and Daisy was beginning to feel relaxed and ready to party. Scott and Nina arrived, hugging her and leaving a gift-wrapped package in the house. She thanked them, busy pouring drinks as Mark and Wendy followed, carrying huge bowls of pasta and salad. Daisy hurried over to help and they spread everything on the kitchen table so everyone could help themselves when they were ready.

Through the window she saw Josh's twin sisters run straight to him and she watched her lovely boy with his other family, her heart clenching with a funny mixture of happiness for him and sadness for her, the evidence of the life he lived without her. He was swinging them under his arms as they shrieked with excitement. Putting the girls back down, Josh bent to say something to them before heading to the improvised stage, and Daisy returned outside.

'So this performance is for my mum, Daisy, who doesn't look old enough to be thirty-five or my mum.' Josh was grinning and she laughed with everyone else, aware of their eyes on her. 'Happy birthday, Mum. Enjoy the set.'

Josh began to tap out an intro and the others joined in, making the seemingly effortless transition into performance and Daisy realised at once how much they had improved since she had last heard them playing live. They began with *Summer of '69*, the keyboard player singing lead vocals with Elodie backing him. It was one of Daisy's favourites and she caught Josh's eye and mouthed a thank you.

The band played a couple more tracks from the Eighties, which she knew were for her, and then two of their own songs. Three of the four boys, including Josh, were songwriters and their first was a beautifully lyrical love song, with Elodie sounding exquisite on lead. Daisy's eyes met Mark's and they smiled together in a way that spoke of all they'd shared with Josh over the years. The band finished the first half of the set with a cover of *Don't Stop Believin'* and suddenly everyone was dancing and singing along, Scott most enthusiastically of all, with Nina laughing good-naturedly next to him.

Daisy's attention was caught by movement on the drive and she felt herself tense as Ben's car pulled up. He jumped out, holding a sports bag, his gaze roving over the noisy party until it found hers and settled there. Everyone else had wandered off to top up drinks or find food in the kitchen and she looked away as Nina appeared and handed her a plate.

'Here, eat this.' Nina raised a hand when she spotted Ben and he waved back, heading down the garden away from them. 'You look gorgeous, by the way, that dress really suits you.'

Daisy dragged her focus back to Nina, trying to suppress the tumult of emotions that Ben's presence had brought. 'Thank you. Haven't you got a clinic soon?'

'Did it yesterday instead. Josh got in touch a few days ago to ask if we'd come tonight. He was pretty confident about his results and he wanted to do this for you as well.'

'That's so lovely of him.' Josh was currently standing with Mia, surrounded by the rest of the band, drinks in one hand and plates of food in the other. Seeing him like that was another reminder of how quickly he had grown up and Daisy felt the familiar dread as she thought of him moving to Mark's in a couple of weeks.

'You okay, D? You've gone all quiet.'

'I'm fine, just thinking about Josh, that's all.'

'Right. So not Ben then?' Nina eyes were sharp as Daisy's flew back to hers. 'I saw you two looking at each other just now.'

'No!'

'He came to the clinic for another assessment on his shoulder last night.'

'How's he doing?'

'Really well, the inflammation seems to be settling down and he should be able to start swimming again soon. He's in great shape, Daisy. He's naturally athletic, although his body is probably best suited to swimming as he has a narrow waist and broad shoulders, but he'll smash the triathlon, no problem.'

'Right, yes, makes sense.'

'He's tapering now, winding down the long runs into shorter bursts and he'll take more time off training too. He needs to watch he stays healthy and doesn't pick up a virus, but good nutrition, his yoga and plenty of sleep will help.'

'Oh?' Daisy's voice was tight as she pictured Ben with Nina, trying to subdue the awful jealousy rising inside her again at the thought of Nina's hands exploring the shape of his marvellous body.

'He's booked in for a massage next week to try and keep muscle tension to a minimum and help prevent injuries. His quads are…'

'Don't Nina, please,' Daisy begged, unable to listen to any more descriptions of how good a shape Ben was in. She knew it for herself, from the yoga she saw him practising on the terrace to the easy way he had lifted her that night and how his simple T-shirts seemed to mould themselves to the outline of his chest. 'I really don't need to hear it.'

'Oh Daisy.' Nina's hand was on Daisy's arm. 'I did wonder, ever since I saw you that night with him in the garden. Are you saying you're falling for him? Are you seeing each other?'

'Of course not. It's just, I'm drawn to him, I can't explain it any better than that.'

'Okay. So you know I love you but it's time to be tough.' Nina's hand moved to grasp Daisy's fingers. 'He's gorgeous, enigmatic and very charming, when he bothers to let it show, Daisy, what's not to like? But he's a traveller and there's probably a girl pining for him in every city he's been to. So date him, sleep with him, whatever you both want but know he's not staying and *don't* let yourself fall for him, okay? He's already got a therapist and he doesn't need another one, you can't let him lean on you and then just disappear.'

Daisy laughed without humour, understanding that Nina was speaking perfect sense born out of care. 'I don't even know if he's single.'

Nina looked surprised. 'He is. He told me his last relationship ended before he left New York. We were chatting, and it came up.'

Something else Ben hadn't shared with her. Daisy knew Nina was right, she would be a fool to let herself fall for a man like him.

'It's not as if he'd ever find me attractive, is it? He's used to New York women and I hardly compare with that level of glamour. Galloping towards middle-age, a mum, boring life, back in a village where everyone knows everyone else, totally averse to risk.'

She tailed off as Nina's expression changed, her dark brown eyes flashing as she shook Daisy's hand angrily.

'Don't ever say that. You have no idea how wonderful and loving you are, and how everyone else sees you. And if you really believe you're not beautiful then you need to look in a mirror more often. There's a good reason why you get more than your share of attention in the pub, and you know Henry would probably marry you tomorrow.'

'That's because he thinks he'd get a free accountant and sex thrown in, as well as someone to sort his life out.'

Nina's grin told Daisy she agreed with her. 'Stop trying to persuade yourself you're just a mum and an accountant when you're so much more, and Ben knows it, believe me.'

'What do you mean?' Daisy's voice dropped to an urgent whisper, spotting Scott heading towards them. She grabbed Nina's arm urgently, trying to delay her friend for a few seconds more.

Nina's gaze was gentler now. 'Because it's in everything he doesn't say, Daisy. And every look I've ever seen him give you.'

Scott joined them, bringing drinks, and he and Nina wandered off. Still astonished by Nina's final remarks, Daisy crossed the courtyard with her untouched plate, meeting Wendy halfway, who was helping her two little daughters to carry a cake carefully. Josh spotted them and then everyone was singing happy birthday to Daisy and she bent to hug the two little ones.

'The girls were so excited to bake for you, although they've been experimenting with a new recipe,' Wendy told her. 'Not sure peanut butter is the best flavour for a sponge cake but we're about to find out.'

Daisy laughed, thanking them as she took her plate indoors to find a knife for the cake. She returned moments later and the nerves in her stomach rocketed into complete awareness of Ben when she saw that he had turned up. He was leaning against the wall at the far end of the courtyard and talking with Mark. Josh was there too, she guessed he must have introduced them, and they were all examining the guitar Ben was holding.

Ben was wearing his signature combat shorts and plain grey T-shirt, his hair still wet and smoothed back. Daisy walked towards the table where the girls had left cake. Someone had produced napkins and Daisy cut the cake, busying herself sliding pieces onto the napkins for the others.

'Happy birthday.'

Ben had joined her at the table and she saw that Mark was following Wendy with a pile of empty plates.

Ben startled her, bending to skim her cheek with his lips, his beard brushing briefly against her skin before he straightened up, the guitar slung across his back.

'Thank you.' The simple words belied the sudden warmth in her body, her pulse beating a little quicker, his eyes still holding hers. They stood at the edge of the courtyard, separate from everyone else and Daisy searched for words of explanation and apology for Sunday night, but Ben was quicker.

'Daisy, I'm sorry about the yard. Not telling you.'

'It's fine, I shouldn't have expected it. I'm sorry I was angry with you.'

'I don't blame you. I think we both know how to keep things to ourselves.' He paused. 'So if I promise to tell you anything you ask me from now on, can we still be friends?'

'What's changed, since yesterday?' Her voice was low. For all that she wanted to agree, she needed to understand why first. 'I'm not sure we've ever been friends, not really.'

The twist of his lips then was wry. 'I like it here and I thought maybe I should try and stop fighting it. I appreciate the understanding and support you've shown me, and I'd like us to be friends, if you would?'

'I would like that, Ben.' She couldn't disguise the growing joy she felt and touched his hand gently, the quick gesture confirming her acceptance. 'Are you serious, then? You'll tell me anything? That could be dangerous.' She was teasing him again, any remaining tension falling away in her reply, the cake forgotten. 'Stocks and shares? Best place to stay in New York? Worst?'

Ben took a step closer, reminding her of the last time they had spoken before he'd spun away into his usual solitude. 'Long as it's legal.'

She laughed, filling a wine glass from a bottle already open. 'I'll keep that in mind. Would you like a drink? Beer?'

'No thanks.' Ben reached for a bottle of water and unscrewed it. 'No more alcohol now until after the race.'

'Of course.' She wondered if that also meant no more Sunday nights in the pub. 'You don't have to do this,' she told him. 'Play, I mean, if you don't want to. Josh won't mind, and no one will notice if you'd rather disappear.'

'I think it's too late for that, everyone's watching. And I told Josh I would.'

Ben crossed to the band and she joined Nina and Scott as Josh introduced everyone. The band gathered around Ben, presumably confirming which of the songs in their set he would play. They took their places, Ben standing somewhere to the right of the lead guitarist, and the music began, the bass guitarist taking the lead this time on vocals with Elodie and Josh backing him.

They performed a classic hit from an American singer songwriter, the lyrics speaking of broken dreams and changing lives and Daisy struggled to take her eyes off Ben. He looked comfortable, lighter than she was used to seeing him as he played and utterly relaxed, his fingers reaching effortlessly for the notes. His hair was drying, falling over his face as he looked down, the evening sun lighting the choppy chestnut lengths. She understood he and Josh had found a bond in their love of music and ability to lose themselves in the moment, and she was loving the performance.

They all clapped when the song had ended and Daisy wished it hadn't, longing to watch the band play again. Elodie stepped to the front again, leading them to perfection through two more of their own songs that Ben sat out, before he joined them again to play a famous ballad that had Daisy wiping her eyes. They finished with a cover of 'Hey Jude', her favourite Beatles song. Everyone was singing along, and suddenly the lyrics seemed incredibly poignant. She couldn't look away from Ben, captivated by the relaxed man who seemed to be singing the words to her and her alone.

Huge cheers rang out as the music ended and she saw Mark snapping more pictures on his phone, no doubt for the band's Instagram Stories later, as well as the family group chat. Josh left his place behind the drums, coming over to shake Ben's hand and the set was over. Mark and Wendy were trying to gather up the girls, who were still skipping around in the garden, and Mia's dad had arrived to take her, Ollie and Zach home. The party was drawing to a close and Daisy wasn't surprised Ben had already disappeared. Nina and Scott were collecting empty glasses and Daisy was glad they seemed in no hurry to leave.

'Mum?' Josh had come to find her, and she recognised the elation that followed the adrenaline of a performance. He was exhilarated, still clutching his drumsticks. 'Dad's suggested I go back with him tonight; it'll save them having to pick me up first thing.'

'Absolutely, makes perfect sense.' She didn't want Josh to notice her holding in the tears that were a strange mix of happy and sad. 'Have you packed?'

He was already jogging off to help the band load the van. 'Shorts and T-shirts, that's all I need.'

'It's not, you know you should take…'

He was gone already, so she gave up and went inside instead, stuffing rubbish into bags. Mark was helping to get everything into the van as well whilst Wendy wrangled the two tired and grumpy girls into her car and then Josh was back, standing in front of her with his case. She stepped forwards to hug him, holding him tightly and he squeezed her back.

'It's not even a couple of weeks, Mum,' he told her with a grin, letting go, and she knew he was indulging her. 'I've got to be back for college enrolment.'

'Love you,' she called as he left the house. 'Have a great time. Thanks for everything tonight: it was perfect. The band was perfect.'

'Love you too.'

And he was gone, her little boy who had left childhood behind, heading to France before moving on to college. She felt the tears sliding down her face now he was not here to witness them, sighing as she looked at the chaos in the kitchen. She couldn't seem to stop crying now she'd started so of course it made perfect sense that Ben chose that particular moment to walk in.

'Right, I'm back. What can I do?'

She dropped her head, pressing her hands to her face to swipe at her skin, trying to summon a smile.

'Hey, what's the matter?' He crossed the kitchen to stand in front of her. 'Is it Josh? I saw him leaving with his dad.'

She nodded helplessly, Ben's words drawing another rush of tears. 'It's so silly, he goes away every year with Mark. It's just, this time it feels different. It's like he's left home, with school and Mia and then college and everything. I'll be fine in a minute.'

'I think mums are allowed to cry when their boys leave home, even when they haven't. Mine usually cries when I come back. Not sure what that says about us.'

She heard the smile in Ben's voice and she sniffled even as she recognised how ridiculous she was being. 'It's not that I don't want him to grow up or keep on needing me. It's wonderful seeing him becoming more independent, making his own choices and being happy with Mia. There are just moments when I miss our little twosome, and it's true what everybody says, the time flies by when you're not even noticing until suddenly, they're away.'

'Please don't cry, Daisy,' Ben murmured and then he was holding her, wrapping her into a hug and drawing her against him with a tenderness that almost undid her all over again. 'No one should cry on their birthday.'

She tensed for a second and then her arms crept around him, barely breathing as her head lay against his shoulder. His hands were gentle and warm on her back through her dress.

'Daisy, are you coming outside for a drink? Oh, sorry.' Nina had appeared behind Ben and Daisy moved away.

'Absolutely, just let me find clean glasses.'

She busied herself to avoid looking at Ben, waiting for him to make an excuse and disappear. He hovered silently before taking the bottle of wine she was trying to balance and following her outside. Scott was dragging a few chairs together and Daisy was absurdly pleased as Ben pulled out a seat to join them.

The last of the sun had left the courtyard in dusk and the air was cooler now, making Daisy shiver in her summer dress. Nina was pouring her a glass of wine and Scott already had a bottle of beer. Josh's playlist was still quite loud, and Daisy reached for her phone and turned it down so they could talk more easily. It was already buzzing with notifications from Instagram and she couldn't wait to see the comments about the band later.

'Are you not having one?' Daisy accepted her glass from Nina, looking at her friend.

'No, I had one earlier as it's your birthday, but that'll have to do: I've got a 10k in three weeks.' She'd found two bottles of water and handed one to Ben, giving him a wry smile.

Scott rolled his eyes, a frustrated gesture Daisy knew he didn't mean. Their relationship had surprised Daisy at first; they'd had such different upbringings and she hadn't been sure Nina would want to stay in the countryside Scott loved. But she had and gradually Daisy had come to realise how well they complemented one another, their relationship supporting each other through the highs and lows of starting and running their own businesses.

'Are you okay, Daisy?' Nina was still looking at her and Daisy wished she'd washed her face with cold water. 'Is it Josh?'

'I'm fine, really. I'll get used to it.'

'How's the house hunting going? You find anything yet?'

Daisy looked at Scott, smiling. 'No, I've looked at a couple recently and there's one coming up in a few days. They didn't seem right – you know how it is. And I'm on holiday next week so I'll have plenty of time to search.'

'Holiday? On your own?'

Daisy bristled at Nina's tone. 'Yes, on my own. Why are you so surprised?'

'Because you always work when Josh goes away.' Nina's hand reached for Daisy's, squeezing it quickly. 'I wasn't expecting it, that's all, you taking time off when he's not here. You know you like your weekly routine. So what plans have you made? What are you going to do?'

'Plans?' Daisy laughed nervously, taking a gulp of wine before answering. 'That's the whole point, surely, to not make plans?'

'Come on, D, you always have a plan. Even if it's to do nothing, you like to schedule it.'

'Well I haven't, other than the christening on Sunday for Sam's brother's baby.' Daisy said stubbornly. 'There's loads of things I can do, and I might go away for a few days.'

'Good. Make sure you do. I want a list at the end of the week.'

Throughout Ben had said nothing but Daisy sensed him listening, no doubt realising how opposite from him she really was, with her fondness for familiarity and willingness to cling to routine. They chatted of easier things for a while and then Nina and Scott said goodnight, leaving Daisy and Ben alone in the courtyard.

There was a moment when she was about to ask him to stay, to have another drink, but she changed her mind and stood up, making her excuses about the state of the kitchen and giving him the opportunity to leave. Again he surprised her, following her indoors and coming to stand next to her at the dishwasher, his arm brushing hers.

'Shove over. I'll unload, you put them away as you know where everything goes.'

Chapter Fifteen

For a wild moment on Sunday morning Daisy wondered what Ben might say if she invited him to the christening for Sam's brother's new baby son. The invitation had included a guest and Sam had even suggested to Daisy, when they'd met at the last fundraising committee meeting, that she might bring Ben if she wanted to. Sam explained that she had met Ben a couple of times in the cafe, and Daisy had rolled her eyes at the knowing grin Sam gave her when she suggested inviting him.

Daisy had thanked her and said she would mention it to him if the opportunity arose. After the evening with the band, she wondered now if the opportunity had perhaps arrived. She knew she could've invited Henry but much as she liked him, she thought he might interpret it with a meaning Daisy wasn't implying.

She hadn't exactly meant to leave it so late to invite Ben and the decision was made for her when she walked into the kitchen for breakfast. The red Land Rover was gone and Daisy sighed. He probably didn't even have a suit here anyway, although she knew Sam and Charlie wouldn't be bothered about such a thing.

Daisy crossed the green in good time, chatting to Connie and Mrs Timms, who had joined her. It was a lovely day, warm, with a suggestion of autumn colours already showing in the leaves around the village. After the service she had an informal appointment with Jon and Annie Beresford from the Thorndale estate and Daisy was looking forward to meeting them properly.

She'd seen them both around the village since she'd been back and noticed Jon hurtling by on a call-out with the fell rescue occasionally. Sam had told her that the Beresfords' own accountant was retiring and Daisy had been happy for Sam to suggest that Daisy might be interested in taking over.

The church was open when she arrived with Connie and Mrs Timms, and they weren't the only guests already in the cool interior as the two older ladies went to join someone they recognised. Daisy spotted Sam at the front chatting to a woman who was holding the new baby in her arms. Sam's blonde hair was softened by shades of caramel and honey, quite different to the shades of pink and plum she'd had before, and Daisy saw her excuse herself and head towards her.

'You look wonderful, Daisy. I love your dress, you're going to tell me you made it yourself, aren't you?' Sam scooped up her little daughter Esther, snuggling her onto a hip.

Daisy smiled at them both, the little girl watching her shyly. She smoothed her hands over the cornflower blue wrap dress that she knew clung in all the right places. 'I did. So long ago that I wasn't sure it would still fit me.'

'Oh, it absolutely does – I'm so envious of your curves! Thank you so much for Esther's dress, we adore it. She's worn it three times, under strict supervision, which means that Charlie isn't allowed to let her have chocolate when she's wearing it.'

'My pleasure. You know I can always make you another when she's a bit bigger.'

'Yes please, I'd love one for summer parties next year. You know I'll never say no to one of your creations; I've got two aprons now and I've been meaning to ask you about making some for Christmas presents. And you are absolutely not leaving until I've heard every last thing about that gorgeous man staying in the cottage.'

'Well, that won't take long,' Daisy quipped. 'I bet Mrs Timms has told you everything there is to know.'

'Hmm.' Sam gave Daisy a sideways look. 'She's told me everything she knows, which we both know isn't the same thing at all. He couldn't make it this morning?'

Daisy didn't exactly want to confess she hadn't plucked up the courage to ask Ben. 'He's busy with his training, Sam; I didn't want to put him on the spot. Thank you for thinking of him, though.'

'Never mind. Seeing as you're here early, come and meet Annie. I know you'll be chatting with her and Jon later anyway.'

Daisy touched Sam's arm as they walked to the front of the church. 'Thanks for the suggesting me to the Beresfords, Sam. I really appreciate it. If it works out and they take me on then I'd be absolutely full up.'

'I was happy to help. You know I think you're brilliant, and Annie's really keen to support other women in business. You'll love them. And if you move further away, that won't matter, will it? Practically everything's online now anyway. We're live streaming the christening so my aunt in New Zealand can watch it before she goes to bed.'

Sam introduced Daisy to Annie Beresford, who was slightly taller than Daisy with gorgeous auburn curls pulled back in a loose ponytail at the nape of her neck. A small, neat bump was visible through her dress and when the formalities were over, Daisy congratulated her on the pregnancy.

'Thank you, Daisy, that's so kind.' Annie's smile was wide, one hand resting on the little bump. 'I'm very glad to be past the morning sickness stage. I wasn't actually sick that often but I felt it all the time. I'm looking forward to hearing all about your business later. I think Jon's hoping to meet with you after your holiday, Sam mentioned you're taking a week off?'

'I am, yes. My son Josh is away with his dad so I'd thought I'd have a few days on my own. A meeting sounds great, I'd really like to know more about your business, and I appreciate Sam passing on my details.'

Charlie emerged from a door and he hurried over to Daisy, his welcome just as warm as Sam's. They all laughed as Esther squealed and he took her from Sam, making the toddler squirm as he tickled her. The church was filling up now and Daisy excused herself to find a seat.

The christening service was lovely and relaxed. Everyone wandered outside when it was over and Annie brought Jon across to meet Daisy. She liked him at once, it was impossible not to. He was tall with laughing blue eyes and she saw how he and Annie touched one another often, his hand straying to her bump and emphasising the loving intimacy they shared.

Daisy had forgotten that Sam had told her Jon had grown up in America and it was obvious at once from the accent he still retained. They made plans to meet in the second week of September and Daisy couldn't dismiss the realisation, as she dropped the details into the calendar on her phone, that the date of Ben's leaving was coming ever closer.

Half the village seemed to have turned out for the service and the hall was packed at the party afterwards. Daisy left around four and drove to a pub high on the Dales and Cumbria border to have supper on her own. She nearly sent a photo to Nina to prove she could be spontaneous and then decided not to; Nina would not be impressed by such a little thing. Daisy resisted the urge to head for The Coach when she got home to see if Ben was there with Edwin, after having taken the night off.

On Monday, after a walk and later-than-usual break-fast, Daisy was trying not to reach for her laptop until she remembered she hadn't updated her email with an out of office message. She switched it on, automatically checking her emails anyway, pleased to see there was nothing she ought to deal with now. She made a cup of tea and was back at the kitchen table when there was a tap on the door and Ben stuck his head round.

'Morning.'

'Hello.' Surprised, she pointed to her cup. 'Would you like some tea, I've just made it.'

He shook his head, his eyes narrowing as they fell on the laptop. 'What are you doing?'

'What do you mean, what am I doing? What does it look like?' She couldn't keep the defensiveness from her voice but his was exasperated as he replied, coming to stand at the table and stare down at her.

'It looks like work and you're meant to be on holiday.'

'So?' She started to laugh, reaching for her cup and cradling it in her hands.

'So it's ten a.m. on Monday and you've already packed in your holiday.'

'No I haven't. I was actually updating the out of office.'

'Good. Then grab a coat, we're going out.'

'What?' Nervousness suddenly replaced amusement. 'Ben, you can't just stroll in and say we're going out, as though I can disappear whenever I like.'

He was already at the door and spun around to face her. 'Why can't you disappear? Josh isn't here, your parents are away, your clients aren't expecting to hear from you this week and it's not a Sunday, so Mike doesn't need you at the pub. Edwin was fine when I saw him yesterday, Mrs Hodges is still upright, as far as I know, and Henry will have to manage without you for a bit.

'Your list of promises sounds great and the auction is apparently still going ahead, even if you do take the week off. I know you've made more aprons for the shop because I bought one this morning, which nearly sent Mrs Timms into a meltdown, by the way, because I wouldn't say who it's for. As you've already told me about the gift you're making for Nina's birthday and it's not until next month, I reckon her present can wait for a few days.'

Daisy stared at him in astonishment, unsure for a moment whether to be offended or to laugh at the longest speech he'd ever made in her presence. His lips began to twitch, and she laughed, ready to ditch everything to go on a silly adventure with him. She closed the laptop and found a jacket in the utility room, heart racing when Ben appraised her suddenly, glancing at her T-shirt and jeans.

'Bring those,' he said, pointing to her worn Chelsea boots. 'They'll be better.'

'That's a relief.' She was still smiling as she pulled the boots on. 'For a horrible moment I thought you were going to make me go on a run.'

They crossed the courtyard, reaching the cars and Ben pointed to his. 'Let's go in Edwina. Do you think you can do without air conditioning and heated seats for once?'

'You can't call it that! What if Edwin finds out?'

She got inside and Ben jumped in next to her. 'I don't think he'll really mind, do you? And I don't usually give cars names, but this seemed appropriate somehow.'

He backed onto the lane and she loved how this new lightness suited him, rendering his face less severe and more approachable. The car was noisier than hers, the inside much more functional and basic. Daisy hadn't seen such an old-fashioned dashboard for years, with its switches and dials and an ancient radio cassette player fastened to the passenger side. She pointed to it. 'Got any good music for that?'

'Do the Nolan Sisters count? I found a tape under the seat.'

'Probably came with the car. I can't imagine Edwin listening to that, can you?'

'Not unless he's got a secret love of Seventies pop.'

They were both still chuckling as he drove through out of the village, dodging a fell rescue vehicle hurrying in the opposite direction, and she recognised Jon Beresford at the wheel. He was gone before she had time to raise a hand in greeting.

'So where are we going? Am I allowed to ask?'

'I'm taking you to collect your birthday present.'

Stunned, Daisy's gaze flew to Ben's face. 'You haven't really got me a present? Have you? Because there's no need and I wouldn't expect you…'

'Daisy?'

'What?'

'Shush. It's done and we're going, now that I've managed to get you away from the laptop.'

'So who's the apron for?'

He grinned again as he looked at her. 'My sister. She'll love it once she's given birth to her bump.'

Ben drove north along a busy main road for about thirty minutes. He seemed to know exactly where he was going when he eventually turned off, passing through a hamlet and following a track, its muddy ruts separated by a grassy middle. A smart wooden sign was attached to a stone wall as they approached a set of farm buildings and alarm prickled on Daisy's skin the moment she read it.

'What are we doing here?' The swirling in her stomach was back and a wave of nausea had her swallowing quickly as she stared at him anxiously. 'Ben?'

'I thought it might be nice to go riding together.'

His quiet, calm words did nothing to dispel the hot, angry tears already hovering, and she was acutely aware of his stillness as he parked the car behind the buildings. He shifted to look at her but she stared straight ahead as she fought to control the fear pounding through her veins.

'It won't. You can ride if you like, I don't mind watching.'

'What is it you're afraid of, Daisy?'

'You have no idea!' She grabbed the door and jumped out, gulping in fresh air as her heart raced to a new rhythm. 'Is this supposed to be my present? I don't want it.' She snatched her bag from her seat and began marching back the way they had just come.

'Then at least tell me why you don't want to do it.' Ben caught up with her, gentle fingers reaching for her arm and drawing her to a halt.

'Ha!' she exclaimed, the sound entirely without humour, spinning around to face him. 'How dare you say that to me? You turned up from nowhere on my doorstep with your silence and your sadness, and yes, I know I should've left you in peace, treated you like any other paying guest. But I only meant to be kind, for you to understand that you weren't alone if you didn't want to be, and every time you pushed me away.

'I tried not to make you reveal what you didn't want to and then you bring me here, out of the blue, knowing I haven't ridden for years and have the absolute gall to question me because I don't want to. You're unbelievable.' She shook her arm free. 'I'm going home.'

'That's fine. I would never force you to do something you weren't comfortable with.' Daisy froze at his next words, skittering to a halt as she heard him continue.

'Everything I've learned in therapy these past months has helped to bring me back, Daisy, taught me ways to try and cope, and I needed it. I think I know that I shouldn't spend the rest of my years punishing myself for not being able to save Aaron because I'd be wasting another life when one has already been lost. That maybe it wasn't my fault.

'But I've become good at not letting anyone see how I really feel, outside of that room. And then I met you, endlessly kind and supportive, helping me to hope that my life could be different and it won't always define everything that comes after, if I try not to let it. That maybe there is still more for me. Something that makes a difference.'

Ben paused, his voice gentler as it drifted over her. 'You have no idea how expressive you are, and I saw what working with the RDA riders meant to you and how much you love being around the horses. I know you're not frightened of them, they're part of you. If you really don't want to share why you're afraid to ride, then of course I'll understand. But please don't let what happened in the past define all of your future. It's what you said to me and now I understand its truth. And we can leave right now if that's what you want.'

Slowly, she turned around to stare at him. His hair was blowing across his face and he turned his palms up, asking her to decide.

'What did Edwin tell you?' Her voice was a whisper, but she knew he had heard her.

'Just that he still hopes you'll come back to it because he doesn't think the love you had for riding ever left you. I know it's not because you're not brave. People who aren't brave don't bring up a great son after a divorce or make a success of their own business when they probably had to give up plans for university. People who aren't brave don't put themselves out there the way you do or teach others to ride in their place.' Ben was watching her steadily. 'It's Josh, isn't it? You don't ride because of him.'

Daisy tried to gulp down the fear rising in her throat. 'It was a fall,' she whispered. 'I came off one of Edwin's pointers; one of those silly things, I wasn't even cantering. He didn't know about the baby and he'd never have let me near them if I'd told him. I was about thirteen weeks and I'd planned to give up riding when I got to four months. I wasn't hurt in the fall but I started to bleed soon after and ended up in hospital for a couple of days until they managed to stabilise me and we knew Josh was going to be okay.'

She blinked, swiping at the tear slipping from the corner of one eye. 'I almost lost him, Ben, and it was all my fault. I felt so guilty afterwards because I'd assumed I could carry on as normal for as long as possible and resented my life changing. I had a plan for my career after university and whilst I was in hospital, I finally realised it was gone.'

'So you've spent all these years trying to prove to yourself that you're worthy of Josh by giving up something you love, because you had an accident?'

Daisy stared at Ben with huge, anxious eyes. 'But I could've prevented it, not taken the risk. Given up as soon as I knew I was expecting him. It terrified me afterwards, the thought of losing him. You can imagine he wasn't planned as I was only eighteen when he was born but until I nearly lost him, I had no idea how much I already loved him. Riding didn't seem worth it by comparison and I kept putting off trying again until I let the thought of it frighten me.'

Ben moved first, catching her in his arms and holding her, as she had held him.

'I wouldn't have done this if I truly thought you didn't want to ride again. I think Edwin's right, it's part of you and somewhere deep down you want to try but aren't sure how. I never meant to frighten you, just show you a way, if you want it.'

He pulled back and the understanding in his amazing green eyes almost made her cry again. 'You're the most wonderful mum, Daisy, I'd know that just from having met you, even if I'd never set eyes on Josh. You didn't lose him, he's fine and you've kept him safe all these years. Pretty much everything in life is a risk and if he knew all this, do you think he'd want you to give up something you love so much?'

She shook her head slowly. 'I know exactly what he'd say.'

'Funnily enough, I think I do, too. Because he's brave, just like you.' Ben's arms fell away, just far enough to grasp one of her hands. 'If I promise to keep you safe and I will, Daisy, will you ride with me?'

'You're rubbish at giving presents,' she muttered, letting him lead her back towards the yard. 'What's wrong with flowers from the garage?'

Chapter Sixteen

It was a smaller yard than the RDA one closer to home but the smell of the stables, the snuffling noises the horses made as they leaned over their doors or tugged at haynets was no different and Daisy swallowed worriedly. Ben's hand was still gripping hers and she shook it lightly.

'I won't run away,' she told him, trying to prise her fingers free. 'Not again.'

'Sure?'

There was teasing in his tone and she nodded, nervousness tinged with excitement beginning to fizz through her. They entered the office and filled out the required paperwork, the cheerful young woman obviously expecting them. Daisy listened carefully as she explained everything they needed to know. Then they were outside again, the woman happy to let them carry on once she'd explained where to find their two horses.

'There's no rush,' Ben said quietly. 'I've booked for two hours and paid for extra insurance so we can tack up ourselves. I thought you'd prefer it.'

'And they let you?' Daisy was trying not to be distracted by every friendly head peering over stable doors.

'I explained that I had a bit of experience and they were happy enough.'

'You've been here before.'

It wasn't a question and he gave her a reassuring look. 'I came on Saturday to make sure I was happy with her before I brought you.'

'Her?'

'Nell. She's over here, let's go and see if you like her.'

Daisy smiled the moment she saw the little black pony staring curiously over her stable door. 'Oh, she's sweet!' She reached out, stroking Nell's neck and already murmuring nonsense to her. 'She's a Fell pony. And so small.'

Ben removed a headcollar hanging beside the door and passed it to Daisy. 'I know she's probably not what you were used to, but I think she'll be a good pony to start on. Why don't you put this on and I'll bring the tack?'

Daisy was happy to have a few moments alone with the pony. She had done this hundreds of times before, but this was the first time she was planning to ride herself and she hoped Nell wasn't picking up on her nerves, deliberately slowing her breathing. Nell seemed oblivious thankfully and then Ben was back, watching as Daisy tacked up.

'Give me five minutes,' he said, already walking away. 'Meet me in the outdoor school, behind the office. I'm joining you.'

Daisy nodded, making sure her hat was properly secured before she led Nell onto the yard. Two horses were grazing in a paddock next to a barn whilst others stared over their doors, dozing and ignoring Daisy, which suited her fine. A couple of people crossing the yard said hello and she smiled back. She found the outdoor school, staring at Ben when he appeared moments later leading a beautiful dapple-grey mare, much bigger than Nell and more alert, her head flicking from side to side as she took in her surroundings.

'Oh, she's stunning.' Daisy watched as Ben tightened the girth and lowered the stirrups. He was so obviously at home with the horse, giving off a quiet confidence Daisy recognised: she had had it herself, once.

'She is.' He patted the mare's neck, looping the reins over his arm. 'This is Harley. Happy to get on? There's a mounting block over there, do you want to try that?'

Daisy was already leading Nell towards it. 'Probably best.'

Nell stood patiently whilst Daisy lengthened her stirrups and tightened the girth. Excitement, nerves, fear – she couldn't quite tell which – hovered as she climbed the two wooden steps and gathered the reins into her left hand. She tucked her foot into the stirrup, Nell still standing quietly, and sprung across the saddle, coming to rest easily on the little mare.

She wasn't a great deal higher now that she'd left the ground, but Nell hadn't budged, and Daisy was thankful. The swirling anxiety began to recede as she looked down through the long black ears, feeling the small, solid bulk of the pony beneath her. She shook her head in wonder, having not moved an inch, her muscles remembering of old as she settled in the saddle.

'Okay?'

'Bit better than okay, actually.'

She watched as Ben swung up onto the grey mare with an easy grace speaking of years of familiarity and practice. She saw the lead rope in his right hand for the first time and he lifted it.

'Would you like this? I promise I'm not trying to patronise you or treat you like a complete novice but if you'd be happier...'

He tailed off and Daisy was already shaking her head, squeezing Nell's sides gently to encourage her to move forwards. Slowly the little pony put one foot in front of the other and Daisy was on her way. 'Don't think so. Let's see how I get on.'

Nell plodded onto the track worn around the school through years of use, snorting gently and stretching her neck to try and grab a chunk of long grass poking through the post and rail fencing.

'No, you don't!' Daisy sent the mare forward and Nell responded, trundling steadily. Ben had quickly followed, slowing the bigger horse into a shortened stride to walk at her side, keeping Nell between him and the fence, and Daisy looked across to him.

She knew at once this was no part-time rider, someone who trekked across the countryside when the mood took him or went around in circles as he tried to learn to rise to the trot. She saw that here was a man perfectly at home with his horse, holding the reins in one hand, his body moving with a relaxed ease and grace as the mare shuffled impatiently beneath him. He sat straight, tall in the saddle and yet seemed a part of it, as though he and the horse really were one.

'You can ride,' Daisy blurted out, her heels touching Nell's side as they crossed the shorter end of the school, using her bodyweight as well as her left leg and a gentle pressure on the reins to turn Nell. 'I mean, really ride. You're obviously incredibly good.'

A sheepish grin brought a pleasure to Ben's face she was coming to love seeing on him. 'I started when I was about five.' Harley was getting impatient at the slow pace and he stroked her neck with a hand, soothing her.

'And? You promised, remember!'

He laughed. 'I rode all the time on our farm as a kid and being quite competitive, ended up doing three-day eventing until I went to university.'

'What?'

Daisy's voice rose in a small shriek and Harley's ears flickered in surprise, listening for Ben to tell her how to behave. Daisy already knew the mare trusted him, knew he would keep her safe and again he leaned forward to quickly reassure her. Nell ignored them, still walking.

'Eventing? Go on then, tell me you won Badminton or Burghley or something.'

'Of course I didn't.' He was still smiling. 'But I did win a silver medal with the British junior team at a European championship, about a hundred years ago.'

Daisy shook her head, wondering at this man at her side, taking such pains to encourage her to ride again and shuffling around at practically zero miles an hour when he could have ridden any horse in the yard and galloped away into the sunset. He could have sat and watched someone else give her a lesson but had wanted to do it himself, to gain her trust and push her beyond what she would have done for herself.

'You are full of surprises,' she muttered, giving him an embarrassed glance. 'I'm holding you up. It must be like riding with a toddler.'

'Small steps,' he told her quietly. 'Do you want to try a trot?'

Daisy nodded, appreciating his understanding. 'I'll be fine on my own,' she told him. 'You go and do your thing and we'll do ours. It's like you're driving a Porsche next to a Morris Minor. Nell will look after me.'

Ben turned his horse with a movement of his body Daisy couldn't distinguish and he practised a few simple dressage moves whilst Daisy shortened her reins and prepared to trot forwards. A quick flare of nerves and they were gone the moment she squeezed her legs against Nell and the little black pony began to quicken. Her stride was so much shorter than anything Daisy had been used to but instinct and years of experience had her rising in the correct rhythm immediately and she laughed, sending Ben a triumphant, happy look.

'I'm riding,' she called, encouraging Nell to lengthen her stride a little without going any faster, her body knowing exactly what was required as the little pony responded, softening the deep muscles in her broad neck. 'I'm really doing it!'

Daisy changed direction, crossing the diagonal length of the school so that her right leg was next to the fence this time and slowed to a walk before trotting again, practising the transition between the two paces.

'Want to try a canter?' Ben asked idly, alongside her again, the grey mare in a collected, shorter trot so they could ride side by side, Nell's little legs working hard.

Daisy blew out a breath and nodded. Ben moved away effortlessly, using his legs to send Harley sideways without changing the pace or balance. Daisy sat down, feeling herself bumping in the sitting trot as she adjusted from the rising one, and in the next corner, where Nell would already be leaning inward, asked her to move up to canter.

Nell seemed uncertain, her little legs gathering pace until they were trotting faster, and Daisy laughed, slowing her again and repeating the question in the next corner. This time Nell cantered, and Daisy tried to sit still, knowing she was hopelessly out of practice as she bounced on top, wishing she still had Ben's relaxed and fluid movements to balance her.

It was an inelegant canter but her first, and she knew her face was glowing, not just from triumph, as she drew Nell back to a walk and halted beside Ben, waiting in the centre of the school. His horse wasn't impressed by the lack of activity and was fidgeting impatiently, Ben using his body and legs to keep her still.

'That was amazing,' Daisy said quietly. She had no trouble encouraging Nell to stand, the little mare had plodded to a halt and was ready to doze as Daisy lengthened the reins, allowing her to stretch her neck. 'I don't know what to say, how to thank you.' She hesitated. 'I would never have done it on my own.'

'Then don't thank me.' His eyes were gleaming, reflecting her joy. 'Just promise me you'll think about doing it again. You rode really well; you're obviously good, Daisy. And brave.'

'Hardly.' She laughed, utterly relaxed now and idly stroking Nell's warm neck. 'You practically frogmarched me in here and made me do it. But I'm so glad you did.'

They settled the horses back in their stables and left the yard, Daisy still glowing. It wasn't just the effort or satisfaction of riding but rather the unexpected delight of sharing the experience with Ben as they headed back down the track in the car.

'How would you like to eat award winning fish and chips in stunning surroundings?' She looked at his hands, relaxed and comfortable on the wheel, and the way his hair had flattened under the hat he had worn earlier. She ran a hand through hers, tousling it into something she hoped was a little more attractive. 'Don't worry if you need to get back, I'm sure fish and chips are hardly high on the list of best meals for triathletes.'

'Daisy.' There was patience in his tone, and she waited for the refusal.

'What?'

'Stop trying to give me a reason not to say yes.'

She burst out laughing. 'I've never needed to, you've always managed to find your own reasons quite easily.'

They'd reached the end of the track where it met the road and he looked at her. 'Which way?'

'For what?'

'Fish and chips, obviously. You had me at "eat". I do need to keep refuelling after all, and if it's just this once and we don't tell Nina, then let's go.'

'I'll have to tell Nina.' There was mischief in Daisy's voice now and they were both smiling. 'I need to show her a list to prove I haven't sat in the office or at home all week, and this is definitely going on it. It's left, by the way.'

She directed him and it wasn't long before they pulled over in a small village. They had to queue for the fish and chips and then they were back in the car, climbing up along a narrow lane, the houses behind them. Ben drove to the top of a moor and they left the car to wander to the edge of a wide, flat tarn, surrounded by grassy banks and trees parting on one side to reveal a huge Georgian house, set back from the water.

They found a group of flat stones to perch on, the water rippling in front, sunlight breaking through the clouds above to glint on it. They weren't alone, groups of walkers were making their way along the paths surrounding the tarn.

'Okay, you were right. Definitely stunning.' Ben was already tucking in, breaking the fish with his fingers. 'Both the view and the food. I can't honestly remember when I last ate fish and chips. Probably not since I was eventing, and they came from a van at a competition.' He found the bottles of water they'd brought and passed one to Daisy and she thanked him. 'It would be amazing to swim here.'

'You're not meant to, it's part of a nature reserve with some rare species that are protected. Swimming is discouraged.'

'Makes sense, I suppose. It must be managed by an authority.' He tipped his head, looking at the view, the water bordered by trees and land reaching up to the limestone crags surrounding it. The warm sun was leaning over them, the sparkling water rippling in the shallows nearby and she couldn't remember when she had last felt so at peace.

The thought frightened her, and she tried, knowing it was hopeless all the same, not to enjoy it too much. This time with him, this ease together, was temporary and she couldn't hope for anything different. The triathlon was less than three weeks away and then she knew he would leave. But still she loved how he was leaning back, his legs and lean frame stretched out in complete surrender to the moment.

'My sister and I used to love swimming outdoors when we were little.' Daisy's voice was wistful. 'Leaping in and out of freezing water and screaming our heads off. I haven't done it for years.'

'Tomorrow then. Let's swim together tomorrow.' Ben's voice was casual, and he was watching to see her reply.

'What?' The wistfulness had gone, replaced in a moment by alarm as she sensed another challenge in the few words he had spoken. 'You're not supposed to swim yet.'

'Nice try.' His comment came with a knowing grin and he chucked his empty water bottle at her, letting it bounce harmlessly off her arm. 'My shoulder's fine, Nina said so, and you don't get off that easily. You need something else for your list or you'll be back on your laptop working. We should go early, eat light before and I'll sort something for after.'

Chapter Seventeen

They'd arranged to meet at five and Daisy was awake before her four thirty alarm. She had packed a bag last night and tried the wetsuit she'd not used for ages, thankful that it still fitted. She swallowed a cup of tea with a few mouthfuls of cereal and locked the house as Ben was loading his car. It was a gloriously warm morning already, the sun rising over the house and lighting the dew-covered garden, clouds non-existent in the cornflower blue sky.

'Morning.' He took her bag and dropped it in the back next to his. 'All set?'

'Think so.' She hadn't known what to expect yesterday but this was different. Today was not a surprise for her birthday, the thought of appearing in front of him in her swimsuit alarming, and she bit her lip.

'Daisy?' His voice was reassuring as they drove through the silent village. 'Stop worrying. I won't let anything happen to you.'

How could she tell him she knew that already? His words soothed her but still she couldn't quite banish the anxiety building in her stomach. She dismissed the thought, it wasn't like he was even going to notice her.

'Am I allowed to ask where we're going this time?' She had to raise her voice over the noisy old engine, gradually building speed as they drove along the narrow lanes.

'Of course, it's not a secret as it's not for your birthday. We're heading over to the Lakes, to a tarn I found not long after I borrowed Edwina and I've swum there a couple of times. Mostly I swim in Ullswater as that's where the triathlon swim will be, but this is quieter.'

'Don't think I will have seen it. Lucy and I used to muck about in rivers and Windermere on days out but not so much in tarns.'

'Hopefully, you'll enjoy it all the more then as you're not familiar with the location.'

She knew he was pleased he'd found somewhere she didn't know, and they chatted as he drove. It was rare she got to be a passenger and she made the most of it, looking around and appreciating the startling beauty of the landscape she had lived with all her life. Fell walkers were out already as they drove into Cumbria, their early start able to beat the busyness that would come later and giving them the best of the day's views.

Ben eventually turned off down a narrow lane and over an ancient packhorse bridge. Still climbing, they passed an old bothy, tucked off the road and sheltered between trees. The road petered out into a tiny hamlet, only a handful of cottages propped together opposite a couple of farms and he pulled over. Daisy got out, excitement replacing nervousness and distracted by the view.

The tarn, glistening different shades of blue, looked as still as glass and surprisingly inviting, and she was so looking forward to swimming in its waters. Something else she used to do but had forgotten how, happy to sit on the shore and watch Josh crashing about in shallow rivers with friends over the years. Ben was unloading the car and she went to help.

They passed the silent houses and crossed a footbridge, walking along the side of the tarn until they reached a small, stony beach, virtually hidden from the hamlet by a narrow belt of pale birch trees. He dropped his bag, swiftly pulling his T-shirt over his head, and she pretended not to notice. His ever-present shorts followed, and she was still standing there as he tugged a wetsuit from his bag and straightened up, facing her, wearing only swimming shorts.

'You okay?'

'Absolutely.' She bent down to pull her own wetsuit out. His body was glorious, and she couldn't drive the image of the lean and muscled frame from her mind. She knew she was fretting about the stomach that had never quite returned to the flatness before she'd had Josh, or the curves she'd never minded or really noticed but were emphasised now by the fitted pink and green swimsuit, her cleavage suddenly appearing as if by magic as she took off her top.

Ben was busy stuffing his clothes into his bag, paying her no attention whatsoever and Daisy quickly stepped out of her walking trousers. What did her undressing before him matter when he wasn't ever going to notice her? The wetsuit went on fairly easily and then she was beside him at the edge of the water, shivering with nerves that weren't entirely stilled by his smile. She pulled goggles over her eyes and saw him do the same.

'If you know everything I'm about to say then tell me to shut up.' Ben was looking at her, idle waves gently lapping over their feet, her toes already feeling chilly. 'Walk in slowly, it's not very deep here but it drops away to a couple of metres about twenty feet out. Before we get that far and can't stand up, let your shoulders go under, not too quick or slow and lie back, okay? This will let water into your suit, and you'll acclimatise sooner. The water temperature could change, and you'll be swimming slower than in a pool but try to relax and keep a steady rhythm, keep your kicking minimal to save energy and oxygen. Good to go in?'

She gave him a thumbs up, trusting his confidence, his knowledge of how to keep them safe. The water was swirling around her knees, suddenly changing from blue to black and looking more challenging and less inviting than it had from the shore. She wanted to gasp at the chill but didn't dare, didn't want to gulp a sudden breath that would shock her body – and then they were in, still standing but able to tilt their shoulders underneath, as Ben had said. He was watching her as the water trickled down her back and she kept her arms and legs gently moving.

It was so different from leaping off wooden jetties with Lucy in their swimsuits on sunny days, holding hands and screaming every time they hit the water before bobbing back up to do it all over again. It was cold but Daisy was beginning not to mind as she glimpsed the soaring fells around them, sunlit into a brilliance that looked so different from this new perspective. She tipped over to her front and let her face get wet as she doggie-paddled, keeping moving, getting used to the cold, her mind telling her body with her slow, steady movements that this was actually okay.

'Ready to swim?' Ben was near enough to grab his arm if she needed to and she nodded excitedly. 'We'll stay close to the shore and you go on my left, okay? If you need to stop for any reason, then raise your hand and head in to where you can stand. We'll go as far as that oak up ahead and stop for a breather but keep moving.'

She was too busy concentrating on achieving a decent crawl as they set off to worry about how slow she was and how far from his usual pace he must be swimming with her alongside him. She saw the quick dart of fish, felt the brush of plants, her body responding to the challenge she had set it as she sliced through the water, the waves rolling around them. She stopped after a few minutes, startled from her stroke and doggie paddling when she felt Ben's hand gentle on her shoulder and saw his exuberant grin.

'We've gone way past the oak,' he said, turning to point behind them. Her eyes followed and she laughed. They'd come double the distance of the tiny beach to the oak already and she was thrilled, loving the experience and most especially because she was sharing it with him.

'I didn't want to stop you, you were swimming so well, but I thought we should have a quick breather. It can tire you out pretty quickly if you're not used to it.'

She flipped onto her back, more confident now, letting the water trickle over her as her breathing gradually slowed. She felt stronger, more alert and aware of everything around her, as though she was fully immersed in the beauty of landscape within reach.

'Let's go,' she called to Ben. Daisy swam forward, her body remembering the rhythm. She didn't really want to stop when he halted them again a bit later.

'Probably a good point to turn back,' he said, so comfortable in the water beside her. 'It's more tiring than you think, and it would be better to find that out nearer to the beach than in very deep water.'

She knew he was right, glimpsing the bright green of a cattle meadow on the opposite shore and a narrow path winding up the stony fell at the far end of the tarn. They turned around, steadily making their way back to their starting point. She didn't want to end their swim yet but knew it wouldn't be wise to exert her body beyond what was sensible this first time. They were almost at the point where they could stand and she knew she was glowing, her skin pink and eyes glittering with exhilaration. She saw him grin, and knew he understood.

'That was wonderful.' She was still bobbing about in the water, letting her arms and legs move gently. 'Absolutely amazing, and on such a stunning day too. Thank you for suggesting it.'

He stood, reaching for the zip on his wet suit and tugging it down. 'You're welcome. Now you've got another one for Nina's list.'

Daisy pulled a face. 'This won't do,' she said unthinkingly. She flipped over onto her front, reaching for the shallows to stand up. 'She'd take ghyll scrambling or wild camping, but this is a bit too normal for her. I'd probably have to be skinny dipping to make it count.'

A beat of silence followed, broken by Ben's comment. 'Come on then. Let's make it count.'

Her eyes widened as she saw him pull the wetsuit down over his arms and lower it to his waist, his chest out of the water.

'What are you doing?' Her response was a strangled cry as he managed to tug the wetsuit off and toss it to the shore.

'Making it count.' His sudden grin was wide, and she dropped her eyes from the challenge she read in his. 'Come on, Daisy, you too. One for the list.'

'What? Don't be ridiculous, Ben.' She saw him stepping backwards, lowering his shoulders beneath the water and then the swimming shorts were off too, flung towards the stones near their belongings. 'Absolutely not! It's freezing and I'm not doing it.'

Daisy moved, making for the shore and the safety it provided. But then he was behind her, reaching for her hand and drawing her gently to a halt.

'Why not?' His fingers were loose on hers and she couldn't fix her eyes on anything other than the landscape above his shoulder, couldn't let herself think of how he looked beneath the water. 'Being in here without the suits feels incredible and we're acclimatised if we do it now and don't stay in long. I'm not going to leap on you if that's what you think.'

Of course he wasn't. 'Someone will see,' she said desperately, casting an arm over the extraordinary view, empty of people. 'There's the houses we passed and there's bound to be early morning walkers. One of my clients might spot me and then what would they think if they saw me flailing about.'

'Daisy, stop making excuses.' Ben swept his long, wet hair back from his face in a way that lit her nerve endings even further. 'There isn't anyone here to see you. I'm going to turn around and swim. I promise I'm not going to look, that's not what this is about.'

She watched him slicing through the water, a flash of pale bottom obvious beneath the tanned legs and back. Could she really do it? She had to decide, she would get too cold if she lingered any longer. Angry with herself for dithering, she wondered when she'd begun choosing safety over fun and stopped pushing herself to try new things.

Overcome with a blast of recklessness, she dropped her shoulders into the water and tried to get the wetsuit off, eventually managing it with an ungainly wrestle. She slipped the straps of her swimsuit down and then the top, a flare of anxiety making her doubt before she pulled the rest of it off too and threw it to the shore. She slid her face into the water and began to swim, hoping the tarn was dark enough to conceal her from his sight.

At once the sensation of the water was entirely different. The ripples felt like a caress over her body and she felt lighter, colder too but so exhilarated she laughed out loud, hardly able to believe she was doing it and knowing she would never share this with Nina, list or not. It was too intimate; it belonged only to her and Ben. She saw him swimming towards her, hovering a few feet away. She read the triumph blazing in his eyes, knowing it was reflected in hers.

'Well?'

She laughed again, doing a sort of self-conscious doggy paddle, her arms bobbing in front of her. She wanted to confess she felt more alive than she had done in years.

'It's amazing.' Somewhere high above them birds were calling, the sun warming the air, and right now Daisy wasn't sure she would have cared if half the village had strolled past and shouted good morning.

'Let's get back,' he said, his voice brisk through the noise of waves lapping around them. 'I don't want you getting cold. You go first and when you're ready, give me a shout and I'll get out.'

He turned away, his back to her, keeping his promise. She reached the shore in moments and threw a glance over her shoulder and another anxious one towards the hamlet in case anyone should see her. But there was no one about and she dashed across the stones and grabbed the towel she had left ready, wrapping it firmly around her. She didn't want Ben to have to linger and she called him, waving for good measure and saw him raise an arm.

She backed away, busying herself with getting dry, allowing him the degree of privacy he had given her. She sensed him nearby wrapping a towel around his waist and using another to dry himself and wished she had thought to bring two as well. He was quicker, letting the towel fall once he had underwear back on and pulling his T shirt and a hoodie over his head. She was starting to shiver, drying herself with one hand whilst trying to keep the towel in place.

'You're getting cold.' Ben came and stood behind her. 'May I?'

He indicated the towel in his hand, and she said yes, wanting only to be able to dress as soon as possible. He began to rub her shoulders efficiently, sweeping down her arms with a circling motion that left her skin pink and warm. He moved to her bare back, the towel clutched high in front of her, and did the same. She would have stood there all day, wholly unused to the delightful sensation of being dried by someone else. Slowly she turned and his glance fell instead to the damp towel in his hand.

'You'll be fine now.' He moved, bending to retrieve something from his bag.

Daisy's skin was still glowing from his touch. A part of her had wanted to let the towel slip a little, to see if his eyes would follow. Now she was glad she hadn't, and Ben returned to the car as she quickly fastened her bra and pulled a T shirt and jumper over the top.

She finished dressing and he was back by the time she had packed her things. He hung their wetsuits inside out over a nearby branch to dry in the warm shade near their beach, safely out of the sunlight that could harm them.

'You hungry?' Ben was dangling the cool box she had seen earlier in the car. 'I thought it might be nice to eat here: we've earned it. Please don't tell me you have to get back? Is the out of office still on?'

'Yes, you'll be happy to know I've fixed the date to next Tuesday, after the bank holiday. And I'm starving.'

'Good.'

He dragged a few rocks together to make a table of sorts near the bank so they could sit on the grass. He opened the box and handed her a tub of something that looked like porridge, along with a spoon. Daisy took the lid off and her mouth watered the moment she saw the oats laden with fruit and smothered in yoghurt. Ben leant over to squeeze honey on top.

'Thank you, this looks amazing.'

'It's just overnight oats, it's really good for eating after a swim.'

'Are you back swimming every day now?'

He shook his head, dribbling honey over his own pot and diving in, taking a hungry spoonful. Daisy was slower, enjoying watching him.

'Not quite, every other day because of my shoulder and I'll drop it to shorter swims soon. The idea is to reduce the training load to lessen fatigue but still maintain peak performance, so I'm shortening the runs first then the cycling and the swimming last.'

'It all sounds very technical.'

'It is, I suppose; I've been trying to take it seriously.'

'Do you always train in the morning?'

'Mostly. Sleep comes and goes. I'm usually awake by first light. Yoga at night helps.'

She nodded, understanding, even as her face flamed at the memory of him on the terrace. 'How are you, after everything?' She spoke quietly, not certain he would offer more.

His head had tipped forward, the long, drying hair hiding his face and then he looked at her. She saw the honesty, the openness there, so different from those first days.

'Better than before.' Ben hesitated. 'Better than I expected to be right now.'

'Do you miss New York, and your job?' Daisy wondered if she'd gone too far, questioned him beyond where he would let her see.

'No, not at all. I keep thinking I should be. A year ago I wouldn't have known how to make a life without work or the city but somehow I'm starting to.' He lifted a hand, pointing at the extraordinary beauty spread before them. 'This helps. And training, helping Edwin and the RDA. And there's always therapy if I need it again.'

'Do you have to go back, to New York?' She almost whispered the words, hoping to hear something other than the answer she expected. She had finished her food and Ben saw, reaching across to take the empty tub and drop it beside his own.

'I've given my word. The company I work for has been very understanding but they want me back. And I need to know if I can rebuild something of the life I had, if I can live in the city and do my job again. If I can make it count for more than it did before.' He smiled. 'But my career doesn't compare to what you've achieved, Daisy. Raising a son, starting your own business from nothing, making a life in a place where people really look out for one another.'

Daisy's laugh was astonished. She'd never thought of it like that, had never considered what her life looked like from the outside to a stranger who'd appeared from nowhere and challenged her to do things she never imagined doing again. She was happy and grateful; she knew herself to be blessed, but in her eyes that steadiness and routine didn't measure up to investment banking and the risks he must have taken daily.

Ben reached for a large flask and poured a steaming cup, handed it to her. 'Sorry, it's coffee. I know you prefer tea in the mornings, but I did lace it with a shot of brandy to warm us up. I found some in the cottage.'

'How do you know I prefer tea?'

'You told me when you had the migraine. You told me a couple of interesting things in fact.'

'Like what?' Daisy almost spat out her mouthful of coffee, good as it was, and he laughed.

'Nothing too shocking, don't worry. There was the tea, obviously, and the bit about your bra size.'

'Whaaat?' Her voice rose to a shriek as a scarlet blush raced over her cheeks and she lifted a hand to try, unsuc-cessfully, to hide it. 'I didn't! I wouldn't have.'

'Oh you did, Daisy, you did.' Ben was still laughing, and his eyes were teasing her. 'Whilst you were apologising for not wearing one.'

'Stop,' she muttered. 'Please stop.' She raised her head sharply. 'Is that it? Or is there anything worse?'

'No, I think that's it. You were funny and very sweet.'

'Remind me not to have another migraine when there's a hero on hand to lug me upstairs,' she said dryly, trying to regain control of her own body and tame the wild thoughts chasing around in her head, remembering being in his arms as he'd carried her to her bed and how she hadn't wanted him to go. But it did also remind her of how she imagined he saw her, and it helped, disappointing as it was.

'I was glad to help you and there was absolutely no lugging involved.' He leant back on the grassy back, his elbows supporting him. 'How's your list of promises going, for the auction?'

She wrapped her arms around her knees, the sun high and warming them as a few clouds bounced across the sky. 'Really good thanks, I think we probably have just about enough now. The barn dance should be great, most of the tickets are sold.'

'Good job I've got mine then,' Ben said idly, his smile lazy.

'You're coming to the barn dance?' Daisy couldn't keep the surprise from her voice.

'Absolutely. Did you know that my morning coffee from the cafe usually comes with a shot of free gossip from Mrs Timms? She was most insistent that I buy a ticket because apparently she heard from someone, who'd heard it in the pub, who presumably got it from Mike, probably via Edwin, that I spent most of the summer on a ranch and therefore that gives me some sort of advantage when it comes to the actual evening. Absolutely no idea why, maybe it's the boots. Or the Stetson.'

'A ranch?'

'That's what you heard, in all that? The ranch?'

'You know I did. Come on, tell.'

He shrugged, and Daisy's smile fell away as she saw the seriousness return.

'Once I left work, I knew I couldn't stay in the city, for a couple of reasons. There were all the reminders of what had happened to Aaron, and I felt like the city was too big, too loud for me then, like I'd lost the ability to be at home there. I was also in a relationship, which ended not long after Aaron died. We were living in Juliana's apartment so clearly, I had to be the one to leave.

'I was already having treatment for my diagnosis and looking for something else beyond the medication, hoping I'd be able to stop taking it eventually. I found a ranch in Montana which specialises in therapy through their wilderness programmes and it seemed like the perfect choice, given my background. They offer rehab for horses as well as people and after a month they let me start working with the horses alongside treating me.'

'The ranch sounds amazing.' Daisy's voice was soft, and she saw Ben smile. 'Perfect for you, even though it was because of difficult circumstances. I'm sorry about your relationship.' And she meant it; she hated the thought of anything wounding him.

'Thanks. It was probably for the best. I haven't got much to offer anyone right now.'

She didn't want to reveal just how glad she was there wasn't somebody at home in New York waiting for his return. 'How did you end up here, so far from the ranch?'

'My parents had been out to see me, and they wanted me to come home for a visit. After a couple of months on the ranch I could feel myself starting to recover, getting comfortable there and knew I couldn't stay indefinitely so I came back to England. There was an ultra-triathlon taking place near home and it gave me the idea. I'd done a few triathlons before and felt I was fit enough to enter the next one I if took the extra training seriously. Helvellyn was the next one. I'm trying to learn to slow down, but it doesn't come easily.'

'You miss the ranch though.'

It wasn't a question and Daisy saw him nod. A walking group were passing, calling a cheerful good morning and she knew their peace, their early morning solitude was at an end. She was glad the walkers hadn't appeared half an hour before as she shared a grin with Ben.

'Ready to go?'

'Absolutely.' She was still smiling as they stood to gather their things. 'I've had an idea. Do you like bread?'

Chapter Eighteen

'So what is this place?'

It was Wednesday and Daisy had driven them to a cluster of converted farm buildings not far from town and found a space to park.

'You'll see.'

She led Ben across the courtyard, ignoring the busy cafe and tempting farm shop, to a small barn, its double doors open to reveal a bakery wedged inside. The counter offered an array of gorgeous looking loaves, some on wooden trays, others propped into wire baskets.

They were met by an attractive middle-aged woman who gave Daisy a hug and Daisy introduced Ben. The woman led them into a larger room, its length bisected by two long tables facing one another. She disappeared to bring coffee and they pulled out two stools next to each other. Ben was looking around and Daisy was enjoying his interest.

'Okay, I think I get it. We're here to make bread?'

'Got it in one.' She dropped her phone in her bag. 'Not just any bread, though. This is artisan sourdough bread with true Northern heart. You might live in New York, but I am prepared to guarantee you've never tried anything as good as this.'

'Is that right?' He was amused and she felt herself responding to the easy relaxation his teasing tone was suggesting.

'Absolutely. And you have to take it slow. No other way.'

His eyes narrowed then, the mossy green darkening and she was caught, trapped in his gaze as a quiver darted across her skin.

'How did you get us in here? Aren't these things usually fully booked?'

'Kathy's a mate, she used to work for a client of mine. I called her and she squeezed us in.'

The door opened and four other people, chatting excitedly, strolled in and came over to introduce themselves. They all shook hands and Daisy saw again Ben's ease with others, how they responded to him. Everyone watched carefully as the baker led them through the basics and soon they were all having a go, learning about the sourdough starter and techniques for preparing the dough. She kept darting glances at Ben. He grinned back, looking relaxed as he worked his dough.

'Stop worrying, I'm fine.' He lowered his head to mutter close to her ear. 'This is brilliant, and I would never have thought of it.'

'So you don't mind that it's not a hundred miles an hour?'

'Not in the least. I'm finding it very therapeutic, even if my feet aren't actually moving.'

When the course finished an hour or so later, Daisy and Ben walked to her car, stashing the loaves they had been given in the back.

He glanced at his watch as they got in. 'I need to go train. Would you mind dropping me back at the cottage so I can get changed?'

'Of course not. I hope I haven't made you lose any time.'

'Daisy?' Ben's hand reached for hers, squeezing for a second and then letting her go just as suddenly. 'It was perfect, thank you. I can't afford to get behind, that's all. I'm too close now.'

'Absolutely. I need to check on some things for the auction anyway.'

'I have a suggestion about the auction if you'd like to hear it.'

'Definitely, all ideas welcome.' Daisy joined the main road, idling behind a queue of slower drivers before she put her foot down to pass them.

'Could you use another promise or are you full up?'

'I'm sure we could use another. Do you have one in mind?'

'How about a wine tasting evening, or do you have something similar already?'

'No, we don't. The merchant from The Courtyard has offered a case but we don't have an actual tasting.' They were past the slower traffic now and she looked at Ben, pleased. 'Are you thinking of doing one?'

'If you thought it would be interesting enough and people would go for it.'

'Ben, I'm sure they would. Thank you, that's so kind.' Daisy couldn't restrain her happiness at his offer, even as practicalities bustled into her mind. 'But how would you manage it? The auction is on Saturday, only a week before the triathlon. Won't you be going back soon after the race?'

She was dreading the answer. The cottage was paid for until the weekend after the race and he had said nothing to suggest he was considering extending his time here. Already his leaving was looming, and she was finding it harder now to plan for the coming days, days when he would no longer be in Thorndale.

'I'd have to do the tasting before the triathlon.' Ben was twisting a bottle of water in his hands. 'The race is on Sunday, how about we offer it for the Friday before? I know it's not much time for people to decide but I can't see another way.'

'I'm sure that could work. Do you have a format in mind?' Daisy wondered if he had ignored her question about his leaving on purpose.

'It should be easy enough. Say a maximum of six people, then two reds, two whites and a champagne. I'll choose a theme and source the wine from the merchants in the village. What do you think?'

They were drawing into Thorndale now, the usual clusters of visitors strolling across the green and popping in and out of the few shops or making for The Courtyard. 'It sounds wonderful,' Daisy told him truthfully. 'I'm sure it will go down brilliantly.'

She pulled up on the drive and Ben jumped out, bending to look at her. 'I want to help you make it a success if I can. I know the community bus is important. Mrs Timms is always telling me, so it must be right.'

He'd slammed the door and disappeared before she could reply, thrilled he was coming to understand why they were trying so hard to raise the money and what the bus meant to everyone who relied on it.

On Thursday Daisy was glad of the opportunity for a day's uninterrupted peace to sew, woefully behind on more aprons for the shop and cafe. They sold faster than she was producing them now, but she couldn't regret the time spent away from her sewing with Ben instead. She wanted to spend every moment she could with him whilst he was here, pushing aside thoughts of him leaving.

She was still sewing late into the afternoon, stitching the bib and skirt together on an apron when there was a tap on the door. She was already smiling as she stood up and put her work down – she knew it would be Ben; the family were all away and no one else disturbed her in here.

'Hey. Am I interrupting you?' Ben's head appeared around the door, followed by the rest of him. He was still in running kit, the fitted vest wet with sweat, his damp hair held back by sunglasses and mud splattered up his legs.

She shook her head. 'Not exactly. I was still sewing but my eyes are clamouring for me to stop.'

He came over to look at the material laid on the table. 'I won't touch anything, don't worry. Would it be wrong to ask if I can buy this one too, before it goes to the shop? Do you think Mrs Timms will run me out of town if she finds out? Sorry, I'm not trying to give you more work when you're on holiday.'

'It can be our little secret.' Daisy was laughing as she tidied up, laying the almost finished apron out neatly. 'I won't tell if you don't, I'll just need to make another. Who's this one for?'

'My mother, she'd love that design, and she was really interested when I told her about you.'

'You told her about me?' Daisy's voice was high-pitched with surprise.

He raised his eyebrows, his tone more indifferent. 'She wanted to know a bit about where I'm staying so

I explained about the cottage and you living here with Josh, that's all.'

'Right.'

Ben stepped away and she followed him outside and locked the door. He lifted a hand and she noticed the DVD he was holding for the first time.

'I found this in the cottage along with a load of other old movies. I'm guessing it has something to do with you?'

'Oh, *The Man from Snowy River,* that's one of my absolute favourites. I'm a big fan of Eighties music and films, and my parents used to offload the DVDs in the cottage. Most of them came with me when I left home, but I haven't seen that for years. I thought it was lost.'

'Do you fancy watching it with me tonight? I've never seen it and it does have horses and a ranch, even if it is set in Australia. You'd be helping me to slow down again.'

Was this a date? Or not? How would she know the difference? She thought of Nina's remarks about Ben leaning on her, but it was pointless, Daisy wasn't going to refuse him. 'That sounds great.'

'The cottage, seven o'clock? I could make some supper if you like but I need to shower first.'

'Lovely. The supper I mean, not your shower, obviously!' She was remembering their skinny dip yesterday and had to clear her throat. 'What can I bring?'

'Nothing,' he called, already bounding over the planters dividing the terrace with a quick leap. She winced, her thoughts going to the triathlon in less than two weeks. 'See you later.'

Never before had Daisy been invited to the cottage for a social occasion. She was pleased with her appearance when she was ready, having aimed for laidback but flattering in a pair of skinny jeans, ballet flats and a floral V neck shirt.

Not wanting to arrive without a gift of sorts, she picked some flowers from the garden on the way through. She caught sight of Ben through the window, his back to her as she reached the terrace and knocked on the door. He answered it moments later, wearing Levi's – not shorts, for once – with a faded cream T-shirt and boots.

'For the table, I thought they'd be pretty.' Daisy held up the flowers, waving an arm towards the kitchen as she followed him inside. 'There should be vases under the sink.'

'Thanks.' He sounded amused. 'Would you mind?'

'Of course not.' She found a vase and busied herself arranging the flowers. Standing the vase on the table laid for two, she couldn't help but think how intimate the setting seemed and hastily tried to banish the thought from her head. He'd invited her as a friend, nothing more.

'Daisy? What would you like to drink? I've got a great rosé if you'd like that, or sparkling elderflower?'

'What are you having?'

Ben's smile was wry. 'Just water. The race is getting close.'

'The rosé, please, if you don't mind opening it for one.'

'Not in the least. I chose it for you.' He took a bottle from the fridge, popped the cork and poured a glass.

'Oh.' She was pleased, thanking him as he passed her drink across. 'Why?' She sniffed the wine, none the wiser.

'Because I thought you might like it, that's why. It's English, with a great taste of summer fruits balanced with enough acidity to keep the freshness.'

Daisy tried the wine, savouring the taste as it swirled around the glass. 'I can confirm it's delicious, thank you, and I'm definitely getting fruit. Just no idea which ones. So, no more pints in the pub for you then?'

Ben shook his head ruefully. 'No pints, just the pub.' He poured tap water for himself and added ice.

'Oh?' She hadn't meant it to sound quite so much like a question. 'You'll still go to The Coach then?'

'Absolutely.' His eyes rested on hers. 'It'll be my last chance to sit down with Edwin over a drink. The race is the following Sunday.'

'Of course.' Another reminder she didn't want, and she changed the subject. 'Have you seen him this week? I know there's a trial coming up he's planning to run the dogs in.'

'Yeah, he mentioned that when I was there the other day. He seemed okay, still tired maybe. He wants me to go back and help him clear the stables out. By clear out, I've learned that's code for shifting a load of stuff somewhere else on the farm, not get rid of it.'

Daisy laughed. 'You're obviously getting to know him.' She was enjoying watching Ben preparing the meal as he moved around. 'It smells lovely, I hope you haven't gone to too much trouble.'

He lifted a tray from the oven, placing it on the hob. 'Nothing too amazing, only a Mexican salmon salad. It's a bit of a cheat because it looks colourful but is easy to make. And there's no dessert; I'm sorry, The Courtyard and the post office cafe were already closed when I remembered.'

'Don't worry. I think that makes us evens now, as far as desserts go. Thank you for inviting me, it's very kind of you.' She saw Ben grin as she watched him deftly whisking oil with lime juice and zest, then used it to dress the salad, adding warmed chunks of tortilla and tossing blackened salmon on top. 'Maybe I could put tonight on my list for

Nina, say it was a date. She's always telling me it's time I was dating again.'

Daisy wanted to gasp the words back the moment they left her lips, but they hovered – awkwardly – somewhere between her and Ben. He said nothing, lifting the tray to the table and setting it down. He crossed to the fridge and took out the bottle of wine, while her mind reached for other words that wouldn't come to laugh away her comment.

'Sure, if you think she'll go for it.' He backed away after filling Daisy's glass, replacing the bottle and pouring more water for himself. 'Shall we sit down?'

She moved first, her remark still suspended in the now heavy silence between them. The meal was delicious, and she thanked him again. Conversation seemed a little more difficult and Daisy felt as though she had become a guest in somebody else's world, sitting in the tiny holiday house with Ben opposite her. She wanted to find a way back to the ease they had been enjoying before tonight.

'So what drew you to this movie?' Her old DVD was sitting beside the television. 'You know it's a period film, based on a poem by the man who wrote "Waltzing Matilda"?'

'No, I didn't get past the horses or the ranch. I just liked the look of it.'

'Then I hope you enjoy it; it's a wonderful film. Even Josh enjoyed it when I managed to persuade him to watch it, but that was years ago.'

Ben offered her seconds, sharing everything that was left between their two plates. 'How's he getting on, have you heard from him?'

'Barely. He does put the odd photo on the family group chat if we're lucky. But I know he's fine and Mark would let me know if there was anything wrong.'

'You and Mark seem to get on well. You've obviously done a great job with Josh.' Ben sounded casual, but she heard the question in his tone.

'Thanks. Mark has always been a brilliant dad: he's from a big family and he took it for granted he'd have kids, even though it was obviously incredibly early for both of us. We were over a long time ago, and had we not had Josh I doubt we'd have lasted as long as we did.'

'How did you two meet?'

'At the pub.' Daisy saw Ben grin. 'Mark's family had moved up here from London and he was so different to the young farmers group that I usually hung out with. We were soon together, and I found out I was pregnant not long before we sat our A levels.'

'That must have been hard.'

'It was quite the surprise. We were both planning to go to university, and in the end neither of us went. Our parents helped and Mark was adamant he was going to support us and got a job with a building firm where he eventually became a partner.'

'And there's no one else? You're, er, still single?'

'I was with someone for a couple of years but we're not together anymore.'

'I'm sorry.'

'Thanks. Adam was a chef and it wasn't always easy to get time together, with work and kids and stuff. Then he was offered a great job in Cornwall and we couldn't find a reason for him not to go.'

They'd finished eating and Daisy cleared the table whilst Ben loaded the dishwasher. He topped up their drinks as she slid the DVD into the machine.

'Sofa okay? Or would you prefer the chair?' He tipped his head, waiting for her to decide.

She chose the sofa, pleased when he came to settle beside her. She tried to match this seemingly relaxed man to the one who had carried such tension and despair with him those first days and failed. New York and his real life, his career, seemed far away in this moment.

Dusk was slowly falling, the light in the room fading around them. Her enjoyment of the film was undiminished by the number of times she had seen it before; the story of a boy becoming a man and falling in love with a woman who was as strong and capable as him.

'So?' Daisy drew the word out as the credits filled the screen. 'The million-dollar question?'

They both turned at the same time and her breath caught at the raw yearning on Ben's face before he altered it quickly, replacing it with blankness and a quick smile.

'Loved it, it was a great story and I really liked Jim. The riding scenes were amazing.' Ben jumped up, heading back to the kitchen. 'Coffee? Or tea?'

Daisy didn't want to linger, to stay beyond her welcome and witness further withdrawal. She realised she didn't know quite how to end an evening such as this. So much like a date, and yet not quite. He'd seemed happy enough earlier to let her pretend to Nina that it could've been a date and she wasn't going to be foolish enough to read more into that than he'd intended. He was simply helping her to show Nina how she had spent her week, nothing more.

'Thanks, Ben, but I think I'll head back.'

With that reply, she knew she should leave yet still she didn't want to. But she forced herself to walk to the door, opening it and letting the cool night air in. Ben followed and she knew she had the means then, in his acceptance of her leaving, to walk away. This evening together should have changed their being together into something more, and yet it had not. Instead the moments of awkwardness and everything they'd left unsaid seemed to strengthen the fact that they were nothing more than friends.

'Thanks for supper; it was gorgeous. And for suggesting the movie, I loved seeing it again. Night.' She reached out, touched his hand.

'Daisy?' Ben's fingers caught hers, held them gently.

'Yes?'

'Are you going to let Nina think this was a date, put it on the list?' His voice was low through the night around them.

Surprised, Daisy stared at him. 'Don't think so,' she said lightly. 'You know what Nina's like. She'll be wanting to know when we're going to see one another again and how we'd manage, when you're back in New York.' She paused, wondering why it seemed to matter to him, conscious of her fingers in his. 'It was just a throwaway comment.'

'Right, yes.' The awkwardness was back as their hands separated. 'I guess it was.'

Chapter Nineteen

Daisy went for a brisk walk in the morning and called in at the farm to check on Edwin. He was reasonably happy to see her, although he did ask if she and Ben were ganging up on him as he didn't seem to be able to go more than a day or two without one of them turning up to pester him.

They wandered over to the horses, calling them across. She wondered if Edwin knew about her ride with Ben but didn't want to tell him yet. She felt it was perhaps a beginning rather than a one-off but wanted to get the idea of doing it again straight in her mind before Edwin started hunting for saddles and fetching the horses in for grooming.

Ben's car was on the drive when Daisy returned so she headed down to the cottage to find him. He was stretching on the terrace, bike propped against the wall, hair flattened where his helmet had sat. It reminded her of that very first day and already the end was in sight. But not today. Today she had a plan and the dull, cool weather wasn't going to spoil it.

'Morning.' Her voice was clear, bright, belying none of the disappointment of how last night had ended. 'How was the ride?'

He turned, giving her a smile. 'Shorter.' He picked up his helmet and there was a beat of silence, a moment when neither of them knew quite what to say.

'I've got a suggestion if you'd like to hear it. Seeing as we're friends and I've still got a day off.'

He was grinning now, their ease with one another already re-emerging. 'Definitely.'

'I've been thinking, you can't leave without spending at least one day being a typical tourist. I know it's August and therefore probably madness given the number of visitors around, but hey, I'm back at work soon and you need a guide who knows the best places to see.'

'What time are we leaving?' Ben's enthusiasm was contagious and Daisy felt her pulse jump a notch.

She glanced at her watch. 'The minute you're ready. The roads will already be busy.'

'Give me fifteen.' He disappeared into the cottage and she returned to the house to collect her bag and lock up. When he joined her on the drive soon after, he looked questioningly at her. 'Yours? Or Edwina?'

'Mine,' she told him. 'If you're going to be a tourist at least you can look at the view whilst I drive.'

First she took Ben to a creamery, famous for its range of tempting, artisan cheese, and he bought a hamper to send down to his parents in Dorset. They carried on to a medieval castle and watched a falconry display and battle re-enactment, marvelling at the swooping hawks and admiring the owls with their solemn faces. They moved on to a small village, where a tiny museum housed in a former workhouse had them both laughing when Ben said the some of the items on display reminded him of Edwin's place.

She knew Ben had an early evening appointment with Nina and they just had time to squeeze in coffee and cake at a tearoom Daisy informed him was one of the most famous in the country, not just Yorkshire, having to queue for their turn. He bought another hamper, for his sister this time, after asking Daisy to help him choose.

They couldn't do any more, the hours together running away just like the days and weeks since he had arrived. She had packed as much as possible into their trip, certain he had enjoyed it as much as she had when they eventually parted back at her house.

–

Henry had generously offered a large barn for the auction and barn dance, and Daisy spent most of Saturday helping to set up. Tables and chairs were brought in and a double row of straw bales was lined up on three sides of the wooden dance floor, leaving the space in front of the low stage free for dancing. Henry kept popping in and out to waylay her and eventually asked her if she would like to be his date for the evening. Not entirely surprised, she told him no as gently as possible.

She was a bundle of nerves, praying the auction would be a success and people would actually bid for the promises she had managed to obtain – so much of the future of the bus service depending on this evening. They were running out of time to raise the last twelve thousand pounds and more would still be required, no matter how well tonight went.

Ben's car – or Edwina as Daisy now thought of it, never without smiling – wasn't on the drive beside hers when she got home from the barn. She caught up with a few chores, her usual routine having been abandoned after her time out with Ben these past days. When she went to change for the evening she still hadn't decided what she was going to wear, and she found a dress she had made and not worn for ages.

A pale pink appliqued material with a fitted bodice and a short, ruffled skirt, it felt like the perfect dress for the occasion and she put it on. She found the obligatory denim jacket and a pair of ankle boots, adding loose waves to her hair. She spritzed on the Jo Malone perfume she loved and was ready, grabbing her laptop and purse.

A Ceilidh band was playing when she arrived back at the barn, adding to the energy and excitement, fiddles and accordion flying on the low stage. People kept on arriving, setting children loose to play and claiming tables before every seat was taken. Daisy began to relax, feeling sure now that the evening would be a success.

Nina and Scott had arrived, and she went to join them. They weren't alone: a group of runners from Nina's club were with them and Daisy gradually tuned out of the conversation when it inevitably turned to racing. Nina soon swapped places to sit beside her, wanting to know how she had been spending her week off. Daisy laughed as she took Nina through some of what she had done.

'You actually got on a horse? But you've never done that, in all the years I've known you. And then Ben comes along, and you just hop on.'

'It wasn't quite that simple.' Daisy didn't want to share her conversations with Ben, the way he had encouraged her to see beyond what she thought she could do. 'I know you're worried about me and I appreciate it, but I trust him, I really do.'

'Good, because he's been standing at the bar for the last five minutes and I don't think he's taken his eyes off you yet.'

Daisy checked and there he was. Their eyes met for a beat before he gave her a brief smile, falling into conversation with Charlie Stewart and someone Daisy recognised from the pub. Ben looked wonderful, so at home in his surroundings in faded jeans, a check shirt open over a white T shirt and low-heeled cowboy boots. But it was the hat making her smile the most, a weather-beaten, brown leather Stetson, its rim tipped up, his sun-lightened chestnut hair falling beyond his collar.

Asking everyone at her table for their drinks order, she crossed the barn, dodging children skittering on the dance floor and people returning with plates of food. Ben was still in conversation when she halted beside him at the bar and after a minute or so he turned to her. Charlie said a cheerful hello and disappeared into the throng, drinks in hand, to join Sam, who'd bagged a table near the stage with Annie and Jon Beresford and others.

'Hi,' Ben greeted Daisy warmly, the Stetson making it hard to see his expression clearly. He nodded to the barman. 'I'll get these.'

'No it's fine, I'm ordering for our table.'

'I'll still get them.' He was handing over cash before she could even get her purse out and she thanked him.

'I love the hat. You look like a proper cowboy.'

'I am a proper cowboy. I've got the boots to prove it, still covered in Montana dirt.' He stuck out a foot and she laughed as she looked down; the boots worn and dusty, telling more of his story.

'Are those actually the ones you rode in?'

'Yep, every day. There's probably still horsehair stuck to them.'

Her drinks were ready, and they both moved at the same time, reaching for the tray. Ben got there first and Daisy was quietly elated that he'd decided to join her as she led the way back to her table. He was quickly drawn into the group as Nina introduced him, the conversation turning to the ultra-triathlon next weekend and what his training schedule looked like. Despite Nina's comment earlier, he barely looked at Daisy and she swallowed her disappointment, pasting on a smile when she saw Henry making his way over.

'Might be a good time to get started, Daisy, if you're ready? Most people have got food now, we don't want them wandering off before the auction.' Henry leaned in to speak over the noise.

'Absolutely.' She looked at Ben briefly. One hand was wrapped around a glass of water, his hat tipped low so she couldn't see his face clearly. He was still ignoring her, so she turned back to Henry as she stood up and reached for the laptop she had stashed away earlier.

Henry's arm went to her shoulders in a friendly hug as they walked away to the stage. The barn was packed now, and Daisy was over the moon to see so many people. It looked as though the evening truly would go brilliantly and they just might be able to save the community bus.

But first there was the auction to hold. She had worked hard to bring the list of promises together, now it was down to Henry and everyone here to do the rest. The band were taking a break and a podium had been positioned on the stage for Henry, with a microphone, gavel and iPad left in place for him. Daisy had a small desk off to his right and she opened her laptop, checking once again that they had everything they needed.

'Ready for the off?' Henry had picked up the gavel, cheerful and relaxed, and she had every confidence in him. Naturally at home in a crowd, he loved a gathering and she was so pleased he'd offered to do the auctioning. She nodded, her list of promises about to be put to the test.

He welcomed everyone, telling a couple of jokes and reminding them why they were all there. He was charming and funny, thanking everyone for their hard work and making Daisy blush as he drummed up a round of applause for the eclectic and brilliant list she had produced.

The first promise was soon sold, and Henry moved on to the next one – a walk-on part in the upcoming Christmas pantomime in town. This went for more than she had anticipated, everyone laughing at Henry's comment about the number of frustrated local actors apparently desperate to play an Ugly Sister.

One by one the promises were sold and the total grew, and Daisy already knew the evening was a success. They'd been right to hold it in August when their community was swelled by holidaymakers, having made sure to include a few promises to suit those who were not local. She was curious to see what Ben's offer of a wine tasting would generate; his was one of the three surprise lots that hadn't been advertised in advance.

Finally it was time, and Henry introduced Ben to the crowd, encouraging him to step forward and raise a hand. He did, a reluctant grin on his face, and Daisy wondered if it would look too obvious if she tried to bid. But she didn't get a chance, hands were shooting up all around the room. Henry was enjoying himself, drawing out the tension, playing guests off against one another as the bids steadily grew.

To Daisy's surprise, Nina joined in and soon it was between her and one other person. Typically determined, Nina's hand went up time after time, her table egging her on until finally Ben's promise was hers. A round of applause broke out and Nina darted over to Ben, drawing all eyes as usual, and hugged him. Daisy took a minute to check over the final figure they'd raised. She texted it to Henry, who called for silence as he picked up his phone.

The applause turned to deafening cheers as he announced the money raised was almost six thousand pounds, leaving the community bus fund short by around another six. They didn't yet have enough to declare it saved but there was still time. Daisy laughed and Henry hugged her tightly, planting a kiss on her cheek.

The auction over, a few families with younger children left while people shuffled round, changing seats to go and talk to others. The band was back on the stage as a group of line dancers began a demonstration, and then there would be an opportunity for everyone else to take part.

The queue at the bar was huge so Daisy returned to Nina's table instead, reaching for a glass of wine from the bottles the table had bought between them. She watched the line dancers, enjoying their coordination and timing as they moved across the floor to the music. They were all in jeans, checked shirts and Stetsons like Ben's and her attention wandered as her gaze flitted over to him.

The demonstration was over, the leader was calling for participants and Daisy jumped to her feet. She was fed up with sitting around, tired of Ben refusing to notice her and she marched over to the bar and grabbed his hand, apologising to Scott, who grinned at them.

'Daisy?' Ben tugged her hand, delaying them. 'Congratulations on this evening, everyone clearly loved the promises.'

'Oh well, that's not down to me, it's for everyone who offered, including you.'

'It wouldn't have happened without you, though, would it? I was starting to realise just how much the bus means and tonight proves it.'

'Thank you for saying so. Come on,' she told Ben as she towed him away. 'My holiday's not over yet and this is definitely something for the list.'

'Yeah?'

Daisy threw him a glance over her shoulder and saw him smile. 'Yeah. I've never line danced before. You're probably the only person in this barn who's lived on a real ranch and I hope you know what you're doing. Put your hat back on, it suits you.'

He did as she asked and they lined up with more people, all waiting to be taught how to follow the steps.

'Okay everyone!' The leader was calling through the mike, a couple of his team already up front to demonstrate. 'We're gonna learn the Cowboy Hustle! Weight on your left foot, fan twice to the right.'

Everyone copied, tapping their right toes sideways and back without moving their heels. Daisy learned to take her heels forward and toes back twice, then just once and it all got a bit complicated when they had to step forward and kick and step back, and the grapevine came in with a quarter turn.

Everyone was laughing and she was loving every minute. Slowly the group seemed to manage to put the steps together, then the music started, which helped, and they were dancing. Ben was good, much better than Daisy and she tried to copy him.

'You've done this before.' She had to shout as they moved sideways in another grapevine. He shrugged, smiling in agreement. 'The way you move your hips! You're really good.'

They made it to the end and stayed for 'Cotton Eye Joe', which was faster and more complicated. Nina and Scott joined them, and Nina was typically brilliant and even Scott was quick on his feet for such a big man. When it was over the four of them strolled over to the bar and Nina leaned in to speak to Daisy.

'So, Friday night.' Nina was smirking as she scooped her long hair over one shoulder. 'The wine tasting. You will come, won't you?'

'Of course, thank you. Who else are you inviting, I think you can have up to six?'

'Just the four of us. I thought it would be fun.'

'What, you, me, Scott and Ben?' Daisy was already exhilarated at the prospect of another evening with Ben when there were so few left now. 'Are you seriously going to drink wine on the night? Haven't you got a race soon? I thought Scott can't stand the stuff?'

Nina rearranged her lovely face into a more patient expression as Daisy waited for the explanation. 'I can have a taste. Anyway that's not the point.'

'Oh? But you bought a wine tasting session, surely that is…'

'For a very bright woman, you can be awfully dim sometimes. I bought it for you, Daisy, and it's mine and Scott's contribution to the bus.'

'Me?' Daisy was astonished and completely touched at the same time. 'Why?'

'Because I love you and you're amazing, but mostly because you and Ben need to decide what's happening and get on with it.' Nina narrowed her eyes. 'Unless you already have?'

'Of course we haven't.' Daisy's voice was sad, and she could see Scott and Ben collecting drinks, about to re-join them. 'I just don't think he feels the same, Nina. I'm not going to throw myself at him and wait for the "it's not you, it's me". We've practically had the conversation. And there's probably some special rule about not having sex so close to a race.'

Nina snorted. 'See? Awfully dim sometimes.'

Chapter Twenty

The Coach was packed when Daisy arrived early on Sunday evening, perfectly normal for the last bank holiday weekend of the summer. She didn't have an opportunity to speak with Ben in the queue at the bar when he arrived later, walking in with Edwin when most of the early diners and young families had been replaced by those likely to stay until closing time.

Someone made room for Edwin to perch on a stool, the collie at his heels, and Ben joined him once the queue had been dealt with. Daisy smiled at the two men, her glance coming to rest on Edwin. He looked much as normal, but it was difficult to tell properly beneath the cap and weathered face.

'The usual, Edwin?' She already had a glass tilted under the Copper pump.

'Aye, lass.' Edwin tipped his head to Ben. 'This 'un'll only 'ave watter.' He shook his head disbelievingly. 'No point comin' in t'pub if 'e can't 'ave a drink.' Edwin smirked, giving Daisy a knowing look. 'Don't know why 'e bothers.'

She flushed as she passed Edwin his pint and filled a glass with tap water and ice for Ben. He thanked her, sliding the money over to pay for Edwin's drink. Mike was further along talking with Heather, the crime writer, and Daisy wondered if they'd had coffee together yet. From the look on Mike's face and the smile Heather was giving him, Daisy guessed that they had, there was an ease to their closeness that hadn't been evident before.

'You know Ben's training for the race, Edwin.' Daisy was busy with another order, glancing at Edwin as she poured two glasses of red wine. 'He can't let up now, not when it's so close.'

'Aye, mebby, an' Ah've told 'im about that, too.' Edwin's disgusted gaze was back on Ben. 'Waste o' time, when 'e could be doin' summat 'e really wants.'

'Oh?'

'Nowt to do wi' us. Better ask 'im.' The stubbornness was back in Edwin's tone and Daisy knew she wouldn't get anything else out of him. He took a long drink, wiping his mouth with the back of his hand and giving Ben another grumpy stare.

'Are you still running the dogs tomorrow?' She wondered if Edwin wanted to bother. The trials, held on a farm near Hawes, was always well attended, attracting a crowd of late summer holidaymakers as well as the usual farmers and locals.

'Aye.'

'And is Ben going with you?'

'Sez so, if 'e can fit us in between chasin' 'is tail.'

Ben laughed and Daisy knew Edwin must have really taken to him, the old farmer only bothered to be rude to those he liked. Edwin had almost finished his drink and she filled a half pint glass with Nickel as he nodded at someone emerging from the snug. As the hour grew later, the pub finally began to quieten and Edwin drained his second glass and got down, with a little difficulty, from his stool.

Ben was watching and he stood up too. 'I'll drop you back if you like. See what you think of the Land Rover now she's running.'

She was sure he had made the offer of a lift purposefully casual, knowing Edwin wouldn't take kindly to the idea he couldn't manage the walk he'd been doing for dozens of years. Edwin scowled but made no further protest and Daisy felt a spark of alarm as he raised a hand to Mike and hobbled away, it wasn't like him to resist so easily.

'I won't be too long.' Ben leaned over to speak quietly. 'I'll just see him in and make sure he's okay. I'll be back by closing time if you're walking?' He hesitated. 'Doesn't seem real, does it? My last Sunday in the pub.'

Next Sunday was the race and the Sunday after that Ben would be in New York, far from Thorndale and even further from her. There would be no extension, no possibility of whatever this was continuing or evolving and that meant he had less than two weeks left in the cottage. It all felt horribly real to Daisy, and the smile she summoned was sad. 'I'll wait for you.'

As she served the last few customers, she was thinking about the evening when she and Ben had watched the old movie, her suggestion that they tell Nina it had been a date, Ben's casual agreement. Perhaps it wasn't too late for tonight to end differently to those that had gone before, for them to finally be more than they already were, whatever the future held for them.

By the time Mike started to lock up, Ben still wasn't back and Daisy was growing increasingly worried as she went outside for a sign of him or the red Land Rover. She pulled her phone out to check it and saw that she had three missed calls from Edwin's number.

Fear began to replace alarm when she rang him back but no one picked up in the house. She hurried back home as it was nearer and ran straight to her car, flying down the lanes to the farm. The red Land Rover was in the yard with a note propped on the windscreen.

Edwin fainted and I've gone with him in the ambulance. He's okay but needs checking out. I'll call again when I can. B

She was in her car and speeding towards the town in moments. Parking was easy enough at this hour and she dashed into the A&E department, eerily quiet with a few gloomy looking people waiting their turn. Ben was there and he stood up as she reached him, catching her hands in his.

'How is he? What happened?'

'He's okay, Daisy, they're running some tests. He fainted in the yard after he got out of the car. He came round again in a minute or so, but I wasn't taking any chances and called an ambulance. He was furious, he spent most of the journey complaining about them taking his wellies off and who was going to replace them if they got lost.'

'That sounds like him. I'd be more worried if he'd gone quietly.' Daisy bit her lip. 'It's my fault, I should be keeping a closer eye on him. It's become a habit to take him at his word when he tells me he's fine.'

'Of course it's not your fault, you're not a relative and you can't make him do anything he doesn't want to do. He told me in no uncertain terms that he wants to go on the farm with his boots on and if I weren't so interfering then he probably could've done.' Ben smiled and

223

she responded, despite her worry. 'He can't go on forever, Daisy. He'll be eighty next spring.'

'I know.' She couldn't keep the sadness from her reply. 'It's just he's such a part of Thorndale, its history and heritage, and I can't imagine the farm without him, that's all. He won't want any fuss, whatever happens.'

'Might be a bit late for that. They're doing a scan to make sure it wasn't a stroke and running some bloods.'

'Good.' Reassured, Daisy felt a bit better. 'Why don't you go back, Ben, you need your sleep with the race so close. I'll stay with him, I don't have plans for tomorrow I can't change.'

Ben was already shaking his head. 'Of course I'm staying, I'm not leaving you on your own.'

Before long a nurse came to find them to say the scan was clear and Daisy felt a rush of relief. They had found Edwin a bed and were keeping him in overnight whilst they waited for the results of his blood tests. Anaemia was suspected, and the nurse told Daisy and Ben that they could go and sit with Edwin if they wanted.

They followed the nurse to the ward off A&E and Daisy had to bite back a gasp when she finally saw Edwin. He looked so reduced from his normal self, surrounded by white sheets and shrunken by the large bed, his huge hands clutched together. He tried to scowl when he saw them and failed, his pale blue eyes strangely softened in something she thought was relief.

'Who's gaan to look after t'sheep?' he said at once, his worry about his animals increased by his unfamiliar surroundings. 'An' us dogs, that's what Ah want to know. They drag ye in 'ere to mek ye better but they've no idea about t'livestock.'

'I will.' Ben was standing at the end of the bed. 'I'll go to the farm once you're settled here and check on everything. I'll head back at first light, I know what's what and they'll be fine.'

Edwin said nothing, which Daisy knew was high praise indeed. They eventually left him when he began to doze, his eyes closing as he drifted into sleep.

Back in the cool darkness of the car park, Ben spoke as he got into Daisy's Land Rover. 'I might kip at the farm tonight, if I can find somewhere not buried in piles of stuff.'

'You sure? Don't do anything to injure yourself, not now. I haven't been upstairs in the house for years, I doubt there's a comfy bed in the spare room.'

'I'll be fine, the car's already there. I was thinking, maybe some help around the house and the farm would be good. I haven't seen much of the house, but I think he lives on pies and tins.'

'Yes, and you know he'd say they haven't killed him yet so we should stop fussing. You're right though, help would make sense, but knowing Edwin he'd hate having people popping in and out all day when he wants to be in the yard or away on the fells for a gather.'

'I can just imagine the swearing.'

They both smiled at that and Daisy drove them back to the farm to drop Ben off, saddened by Edwin's sudden visit to hospital and hoping that he would be okay. She was back at the farm at first light too, despite her tiredness.

She helped Ben feed and clean out the dogs and he went to see to the sheep whilst she made sure the two horses were fine and had fresh water. They didn't need anything else just yet, the late summer grass still enough to sustain them.

Lark, the mare, ignored her but Flint came over for his usual treats and neck scratch. Daisy was happy all was good, pleased to see that news had got around and a couple of other local farmers had turned up too, doing their bit for Edwin and offering help with the livestock should more be needed.

She called the hospital for news, Ben beside her as they stood in the yard, the sun glinting above the hill behind them. Edwin was definitely anaemic, and they were going to have to investigate the reasons why as well as have a word about his diet, but otherwise his test results were good. He was apparently surprisingly robust for someone of his age and they thought it likely he could come home the following day.

'He doesn't have any children or relatives near here, does he? Someone who might be able to help him?' Ben looked troubled and Daisy understood his concern.

'No, it's so sad. He and Joan had a son, but he died years ago in a car accident and Edwin was an only child; he lost his mother when he was young. Joan had a brother, but I don't think Edwin's been in touch with him for years, he was in Germany last I heard. Edwin's always been very independent, he'll find it hard to accept he might need help.'

'Okay.' Ben's nod was sympathetic. 'So I'm guessing your out of office expires tomorrow?'

'It does. I had a very, let's say, interesting week. Mostly thanks to you and everything you encouraged me to do.' He was smiling and she liked the understanding in his eyes. 'But reality and my office beckons. And I need to do a shop, Josh will be home tomorrow too, and he won't be impressed by the state of the fridge.'

'I'll collect Edwin from the hospital then if you're working.'

'Are you sure? That's kind of you.'

Ben grinned. 'I've got his wellies so he should be happy enough to see me.'

Once Daisy was back at her desk the next morning she didn't feel for once as though she'd never been away. Her mind was still full of Edwin and she couldn't forget how she and Ben had spent the past days together and everything they'd done. But each new morning was another one closer to his leaving and she was dreading the race being over and, gone with it, the anchor holding him in Thorndale.

Henry arrived, bringing her coffee and getting her back up to speed. The meeting with Jon and Annie Beresford was arranged for the week after next, another dull thud reminding her of Ben's leaving. She also had received enquiries from two new potential clients, and it seemed her business was growing. This didn't please her in the way it normally would, and she was still thinking about Ben when she closed her office and drove to Edwin's farm.

He was sitting in an old armchair in the yard near the back door, the dogs at his feet as he rubbed their ears with hands speckled with age and bent with use. His usual uniform was back: overalls over the top of ancient trousers and cap firmly wedged on what was left of his wild grey hair.

'I see you got your wellies back.' Daisy was smiling as she crossed the yard, pointing to his feet.

Edwin snorted. 'Told Ben not to bother comin' back if 'e lost 'em. Ah reckon there's a good ten years left in 'em yet. Reckon they'll outlive us.'

Daisy dragged an empty bucket towards him and upended it, sitting down. 'How are you? You look better here than in that hospital bed.'

'Why does everyone keep askin' us that?' Edwin was irritable and Daisy knew he didn't mean it. 'Am reet, it was just a faint cos us bloods aren't reet, that's all. They've given us pills, like everyone else. Tekkin stuff now to keep us upright.'

'Probably better than the alternative.'

To her astonishment, a sudden rush of tears filled Edwin's eyes. 'Thought Ah might nivver see this place again,' he told her quietly. 'Or us dogs or t'sheep.' He was shaking his head, trying to hide what he didn't want her to see. 'Don't know what Ah would've done wi'out Ben, 'e was grand.' He gave Daisy a sideways glance. 'An' you, lass.'

'Don't suppose you've told him that, though, have you?'

'Ah've told 'im a few things 'e needed to 'ear.' Edwin's mischievous glint was returning as his gaze went to the shopping bag at her feet. ''Ave you brought us some of that lasagne Ah like?'

She laughed, standing up. 'Yes, I'll leave two in the fridge and put the rest in the freezer. You can't microwave it, though, they're in foil containers. Stick them in the oven for about half an hour, okay.'

'Reet lass, they'll be grand wi' a plate o'chips.' Edwin grabbed her hand as she passed him. 'Thanks.'

When she returned from the house, she sat with him a while longer in the evening sun, its warmth diminishing, telling him firmly that she was taking him to the GP next week and he had to go. He reluctantly agreed, giving her a look that was sort of accepting.

His farming pals were popping in and out too, and Daisy knew between them they would be able to keep an eye on him, praying his health would stand up so he could stay at home for as long as possible. Neither she nor Edwin needed to say it but she also knew they were not looking forward to Ben leaving at the end of next week.

She drove home and was met by the delicious and very welcome smell of fish and chips, and a bear hug from Josh, who looked relaxed and very tanned after his holiday in France. He seemed to have grown and filled out, his hair blonde from the sun, and she couldn't shake the realisation that he'd gone away as a boy and come home more like a young man, so grown up. His phone was propped on the table and he was keeping an eye on it as they ate. He chatted about his holiday and the fun he'd had, even with young sisters pestering him.

He asked about her week off and she told him some of what she'd done. He was wide eyed about her riding again, telling her at once she should keep it up. They went their separate ways after eating, Josh heading out to see Mia and Daisy setting about making a large pan of soup for Edwin to freeze.

Chapter Twenty-One

The week rushed by for Daisy and she saw little of Ben, even though both of them were at the farm checking on Edwin every day. Ben went in the mornings, she was there after work, and they only spoke a couple of times and usually about Edwin.

She spent Wednesday afternoon with Gwen and the rest of the RDA team at the riding school, but Ben wasn't there, and it was another disappointment. Daisy wondered whether he was avoiding her on purpose, distancing himself from the place and the people he was soon to leave. She was missing their days together already; the past few had felt flat, with Edwin falling ill and the triathlon so close.

Nina had invited Daisy to stay over for the wine tasting on Friday, her enthusiasm for the evening spilling through her messages and, Daisy guessed, in the excitement she was feeling about the role she had assumed as matchmaker. Nina's own upcoming race was far enough away for her to at least taste the wine and she asked Daisy to arrive around six so they could have supper with Ben first.

Josh had already gone to his dad's when Daisy arrived at Nina and Scott's cottage fifteen minutes early. There was no sign of the red Land Rover and she hadn't seen Ben all day, other than a quick glimpse this morning as she was leaving for work. It was a beautiful evening and the light was only just beginning to gather into dusk as she knocked and stepped inside, calling hello.

Originally a tiny cottage on the edge of a farm, Nina and Scott had extended it to create a bright, open space, letting in the best of the south-facing light. They'd kept the cosy sitting room at the front of the house and lived mostly in the extension, a terrace leading off it with glorious views of the hills beyond. Daisy remembered how the sad and small space had looked when her friends had bought the house and could never see it without marvelling at the transformation.

Nina was in the kitchen and she hurried over to meet Daisy with a hug, reaching for Daisy's bag as they separated. 'I'll take this through,' she said with a knowing smile and Daisy resisted the impulse to roll her eyes.

The guest bedroom was a mini suite they'd created behind the kitchen to accommodate Nina's mother, who couldn't manage the stairs when she came to visit. Daisy helped herself to a glass of the Prosecco she found in the fridge and topped up Nina's sparkling water. Nina was quickly back, and Daisy watched as she began to put ingredients together.

'Can I help?'

'No, it'll be ready in no time; it's only Scott's quick paella. Ben should be here any minute.' Nina indicated the glasses further along the island. 'The wine merchants brought everything earlier so we're good to go as soon as Ben is.'

'Where's Scott?'

'In the shower: he was late leaving a job. He'll be down any minute.' Nina looked at Daisy, her smile widening. 'So, you and Ben. What's happened this week?'

Daisy didn't get time to say 'nothing' before there was a knock at the door, and she felt a spark of anticipation at the realisation Ben had arrived.

'You get it.' Nina paused slicing chorizo, the knife suspended above the chopping board. 'Don't forget to kiss him hello. This is supper with friends now, not some stilted conversation about the race or Edwin. It'd look odd if you didn't, Daisy.'

Daisy was glad she'd chosen a dress for tonight as she crossed the floor. Off-the-shoulder in palest pink and falling to her knees, it was emblazoned with roses and she'd paired it with shocking pink heels that felt elegant and sexy. Her hand went to her hair, tousling it quickly and then she pulled back the door. Her mouth dropped in surprise and a few moments passed before she realised she was gaping and shut it quickly.

In the hours since she had glimpsed Ben this morning, looking much as he ever had, he had changed. Gone were the usual cycle or running kits, or the battered combat shorts and T-shirts he wore in between training. In their place a different set of clothes adorning a quite different man had emerged and she already loved the transformation.

In order to deliver his promise of the wine tasting, Ben had chosen a classic white Oxford shirt and dark navy trousers with brogues. The stylish cut of his clothes emphasised his lean and muscular frame, and the simple colour combination highlighted his sun-tanned face and stunning green eyes.

But it was his hair that had changed him the most – from the informal, borderline-scruffy guy she was familiar with, into the sophisticated man before her now. The length she loved was gone, though still long enough to be swept up and back, making his face appear narrower. His beard was shorter too, emphasising the firm shape and strength of his jaw. So this, then, was the New York banker and Daisy felt quite sure she would invest everything she owned in a moment should he but ask.

'Hey.' He was smiling, and there was an awkward moment as she reached up and he bent down, their faces bumping as they each tried to kiss the other. 'Sorry.'

'It's fine.' Daisy stepped back. 'Come in.' She was thinking of the touch of his beard, his mouth skimming her cheek, the appreciation she was sure she'd seen in his eyes as he took in her dress, the scent of the warm and woody cologne he wore, different from the sharp lemon one she knew he preferred for showering.

Scott bounded down the stairs, coming over to hug Daisy. She returned to Nina as the two men shook hands and chatted for a few moments before joining them. Scott reached for a beer from the fridge and Nina poured Ben a glass of water after he refused a beer.

'I'm hoping you're going to convince me to appreciate wine in a way I haven't before.' Scott knocked the top of his bottle. 'Nina's always telling me my taste in drink is terrible.'

'Only because you're still drinking the same stuff you always have when there's so much choice out there.' Nina gave him a smile and he dropped a kiss on her temple, their easy intimacy somehow emphasising the lack of Daisy and Ben's all the more.

Ben had pulled out a stool next to Daisy and they were both watching the other couple as they put the meal together. Scott cooked whilst Nina set the table outside and they asked Ben about the tasting to come.

'So the theme is Old World versus New World wines. We've got two whites, both Chardonnays but one is from Burgundy and the other New Zealand. Same idea with the red, which are Cabernet Sauvignons from Sicily and Australia. And a vintage champagne to finish.'

'Sounds brilliant, we're so looking forward to trying everything.' Nina topped up drinks as Scott carried the pan outside and set it down, Daisy and Ben following with plates.

The conversation turned inevitably to the race as they ate, as well as the village and everything being done to save the community bus. Nina wanted to hear Josh's latest news and whether Daisy had taken on the new clients who had enquired about her business. Daisy was aware of Ben listening as she confirmed she hadn't, and Nina wanted to know why not.

'Because I don't think I'll have enough time to give them, Nina. Henry's business keeps me busy and if I take on the Thorndale estate then there's no room for more. Once Josh is settled in college I'm going to have to think about what comes next.'

'Oh?' Nina was on to that comment at once, as Daisy had known she would be. 'Looking for a business partner, you mean? Or something else?'

'I'm not sure, I haven't thought it through yet. Enough of that, I'm not interested in talking shop tonight.' Daisy turned to Ben, giving him a merry smile that was just a little forced. 'When can we try the wine?'

'Now, if you like?' Ben was still watching her.

'Perfect.' Nina stood up. 'Give me and Scott a few minutes to clear up and then you two can sort out the tasting.'

Scott looked surprised but stood too, disappearing into the kitchen with Nina. A pause followed, enveloping Daisy in daring as she decided to follow Nina's lead and see where it might take her. 'Nina seems to be trying to match make,' she remarked. 'Maybe we should play along, pretend it is a date this time.'

She waited for an agreement, to see if he would offer something beyond his silence and nothing followed. She felt frustration and then disappointment as she looked across the garden, blinking back the hurt.

'Daisy?' Ben's fingers were light on her arm, a sudden urgency in his voice. 'Something's come…'

'Right, all set.' Nina was looking between them as she re-emerged in the garden, Scott behind her. 'We're all yours, Ben.'

Ben stood first. They all knew he could manage perfectly well by himself but Daisy followed him into the kitchen anyway, watching as he took a bottle of wine from the fridge.

'Would you pass me the glasses please?' He pointed to the tray Nina had left ready and Daisy carried it across, standing next to him at the island as she put it down.

Her glance moved to his shirt, her eye caught by something. 'Your collar is twisted.'

She lifted her hands, her fingers skimming the firmness of his shoulders as she reached for his collar, straightening it slowly. His eyes were on hers, darkening with a sudden desire he didn't attempt to hide as they moved to her mouth, and her lips parted in expectation. One hand reached for hers, trapping it against his shoulder as the other went to her neck.

'What were you going to say, Ben? Before Nina came outside?' Daisy's voice was low, wanting to be sure, as she took half a step towards him.

He hesitated. 'It's complicated.' His thumb was tracing a lazy circle on her neck, her pulse thudding beneath it.

'That's it? What's complicated, exactly?' She heard the frustration in her voice, the hurried question as time seemed to be running away from them ever faster.

'More than you know.'

'Is it really, though?' She couldn't think beyond this moment, didn't care what would happen next week when he left. There was only now and the look in his eyes and she closed the last scrap of space between them. 'You could stay here tonight. I'm not driving back.'

She saw the alteration at once, felt it as his hand fell away from her. Saw the silent apology, the awful realisation that she had been wrong yet again slamming into her with a speed that left her horrified. She spun away from him, into the garden and back to wherever it was they had been before. Ben followed with the wine a few moments later and she sat mute, trying to convey an ease to Nina while knowing she was failing utterly.

She heard everything Ben said as he took them through the wine tasting and remembered none of it. She copied the others, went through the motions, her senses still sharpened after the moments with him in the kitchen. He talked about identifying colour, opacity and viscosity, and the three types of aroma, and she felt his words bouncing through her mind, reverberating with misery.

Ben's appearance shouldn't matter but somehow it did, this smartened, sexy man belonging more now to the city he had come from than this small village he had happened upon outside her house that day. She wanted the whole evening to be over and Ben gone, far away from her and Thorndale, knowing she would regret her crazy wish the moment he left.

Scott was oblivious as he tried everything with enthusiasm and Daisy knew Nina understood at least how she was feeling, if not why. Daisy smiled, nodded, tasted the wine, not wanting to spoil Nina's gift to her as they tried to guess the Old World variety versus the New, correctly identifying the red and failing on the white. When the tasting was over, Nina offered coffee after Scott had thanked Ben, declaring a newfound liking for red wine if not white.

'Actually, Nina, I should get going.' Ben offered an explanation for standing so quickly and a hand to Scott across the table. 'Thanks anyway. I'm heading over early to the race HQ tomorrow and I haven't got all my kit together yet.' He hesitated and Daisy sensed his glance flicking over her before returning to Nina. 'Thanks for buying the promise, I hope you've enjoyed it.'

'Of course we have. Thank you, it's been brilliant. I'm sorry you have to go so soon.' Nina came around the table to gather him into a quick hug. 'All the best, make sure you go through those dynamic stretches we talked about. I'll see you Thursday, yeah? But call if you need me before, I could re-arrange something and fit you in on Monday.'

'Thanks, Nina, I'll sort out the appointment after the race. And thanks for all you've done for me, it's really helped. My shoulder's much better.'

'My pleasure, I'm glad if it's made a difference and kept you on target.' Nina was looking at Daisy now. 'Daisy, you'll see Ben out, won't you?'

Daisy hadn't intended doing anything of the sort but complied anyway, aware of Ben following her through the house. She pulled back the door, a cheeriness in her voice that even to her sounded forced. 'Good luck, Ben, hope the race goes really well. Night.'

He gave her a final, unfathomable stare before walking away and she banged the door behind him. Always she was on the brink of letting him see how she felt, what she wanted, and time and again he held back, trying to make her understand his reticence without ever using words enough to explain.

The door sprang open again, making her jump as Ben rushed back in. Suddenly she was in his arms and he was holding her tightly, his voice a murmur against her hair. 'Daisy, I'm sorry. I didn't mean to hurt you, that's the last thing I want. The race...' Ben drew back to look at her. 'Will you come on Sunday, to watch? I know I have no right to ask, I just know I want to see you there when it's over.'

His eyes searched hers, hopeful and afraid at the same time, and for a crazy moment she wanted to ask him not to go back to New York, to stay in Thorndale and allow himself to carry on healing where she would still be able to see him every day. But she knew she couldn't ask – he had a job and a life back in New York, and she wasn't sure her heart could take another rejection from this man.

She swallowed down her frustration, refusing to let hurt and disappointment from before spoil what little time they had left together. They were friends, clearly all he wanted, and she cared about him far too much to reject that, if there was nothing else. 'I thought I might come to watch if I won't be in the way.'

'You're never in the way, Daisy, except in the right way.'

His voice was rushed and it pulled her in, leaning closer until there was no further she could go, resisting still the desire to trace the contours of the muscles she felt beneath her fingers. Her head tucked easily beneath his jaw and then he dropped a quick kiss on it.

'I'm aiming to finish around two, obviously I don't expect you to hang around all day.' Some of the briskness was back as Ben let her go. 'So, if you want to be there...'

'Stay safe,' she called, her voice following him down the path as he strode away. He lifted a hand and was gone. No matter whether he was in the cottage all day or not, before now she had known he would always return, the lights twinkling at her through the dusk. Tomorrow was different, he had already told her about the B&B he had booked close to the race HQ. She would be alone again, the cottage empty and giving a glimpse of the days to come.

Scott made himself scarce when Daisy returned to the garden, leaving her with Nina. Her friend hugged her tightly, firing up the patio heater to keep them warm as they talked long into the night.

Chapter Twenty-Two

Whatever time Ben was planning to finish on Sunday, Daisy wanted to be there to see as much of him as she could. She left home very early so she could be at the start of the race, near the southern end of Ullswater. The field leading to the shore and serving as race HQ was packed, the bikes cordoned off to keep the public away from the transition area.

Competitors were streaming down to the edge and she saw safety officials in kayaks already on the lake, ready to intervene should they be needed. She had no hope of spotting Ben in the crowd of mostly black wetsuits topped with green or blue swimming caps as they waded into the water. A flood of nerves spilled through her stomach, surprising her.

She wasn't worried about him, not really. He had worked hard for this day and all she dreaded was what would come after. The race was underway now and she stayed until everyone was in the lake, knowing she had seen him start even if she hadn't been able to identify him in the mass of athletes.

Following the swim she knew the competitors had to cycle thirty-eight miles, returning to leave their bikes in the transition area and setting out to run up and down Helvellyn, reaching a height of over three thousand feet across nine miles.

Running and cycling were all very well, but this? This was something else. Much as Daisy admired the athletes' commitment, knowing the reason driving Ben on made her wonder what might come next for him. Would he ever be able to stand still again? Would he always be pushing, aiming for the next thing to consume him, to keep his mind free of the horror he had experienced that awful night in New York?

Before long, the first competitors were in the transition area, discarding their wetsuits and leaping onto their bikes. She watched, spotting Ben tearing off his swimming cap and goggles, not too far behind the leaders, his hair making it easier for her to identify him. She ran to the edge of the field, clapping him as he shot past on his bike, head down, helmet on.

She went in search of something to eat, finding a table in a cafe and settling down to wait. It was going to be a long morning and after an hour and second peppermint tea, she headed back to the race HQ. It was quiet with the athletes gone, officials stamping their feet to keep warm. The weather was changing, the scent and feel of autumn in the air, and it was another unwelcome reminder of Ben's departure.

Some of the bikes were back, the leaders already on their way up Helvellyn, an enormous test of stamina and fitness after the swim and cycle they had just completed. Daisy hovered for a bit, but it was pointless trying to guess when Ben might set out on his run so she found another coffee shop instead.

Eventually she saw the first runners passing through the village, mud spattered, wet and still pushing on. She went to stand outside with other spectators, clapping them through. She didn't linger in case she missed Ben at the finish and returned to the race HQ in its now muddy field.

The atmosphere was a huge contrast to the festival feel of the Mud'n'Mire event a few weeks ago, when she had first seen Ben race. This was a much more subdued affair as the leaders crossed the finish line, raising a hand in triumph or falling to the ground, exhausted and spent.

Volunteers were on hand to remove tags and hand out drinks and food, and some finishers were happy to hug supporters whilst others strolled away on their own. There was a commentator making announcements, but it was very low-key and all the more serious for it.

Daisy waited, her attention constantly straying back to the road fifty yards away. Eventually she thought she saw Ben and stretched on tiptoe, unwilling to move and lose her place. Then she knew it was him, watching as he ran steadily between the metal barriers onto the field.

Seconds later he was over the finish line and she saw him looking around, tugging a small rucksack off as he accepted a drink. She moved towards him, suddenly uncertain, Friday night still in her mind. But then he spotted her, a huge grin lighting up his face and she laughed, thrilled to see his exhilaration in his achievement.

He marched over, the rucksack falling to the ground and then she was in his arms as they hugged, Ben lifting her up jubilantly. She laughingly protested, trying to make him put her down in case he hurt himself after the race he had just run.

'Done.' He couldn't keep the triumph from his voice as he set her back on her feet. He was wet and covered in mud, transferring some of it to her waterproof jacket, his soaking hair pushed back from his face. 'I did it, Daisy. I really did it.'

'Congratulations, you've earned it. I know how many miles you've put in to do this. Well done, Ben, you must be so pleased.'

She was saying all the right things, she meant them – she felt so proud of his achievement – but she was desperate to know what was coming next, if he were leaving on Saturday in six days, or would there be perhaps a day or two more for them? But now wasn't the right time and she wanted to watch him enjoying his triumph for as long as he could.

He checked his watch, pursing his lips. 'Time's not bad, four hours twenty, which is about where I'd hoped to be, probably enough for a top forty finish. Hell, Daisy, it was hard work. Harder than I thought, and the mountain was so tough.'

Adrenaline was slowly dissipating as they made their way to the exit, Ben nodding at other finishers, strangers who had shared this experience with him and knew what it had taken to achieve it in a way she did not. Rain was steadily falling, and she didn't want him to get cold.

'Where are you staying?'

Ben opened a bottle of sports hydration fluid. 'Just down the road, opposite the car park. I'm going to head back there now and cool down, then eat and shower.'

'Right, good, I'll leave you to it then. Congratulations again, I'm so happy you did it.'

'Daisy? Do you have to go? I wondered if you'd like to find a nice pub that serves good food. Not The Coach. What do you think?'

She would have accepted anything that meant more time in his company. 'Sounds perfect, I know a great place not too far from here.'

Merriment gleamed in his eyes through the grime on his skin and the wet hair falling onto his face. 'Do you mind waiting whilst I shower? I won't be too long, you can wait at the B&B if you like.'

'The cafe's fine. Do you want to come with me, and I'll drop you back here later, save you having to bring your car to the pub as well?'

Ben looked confused for a moment and shook his head. 'I'll bring Edwina to the pub with us. I'm not staying in the B&B tonight; I'm coming home. I paid for two nights so I could keep the room until after the race.'

Home. His simple use of the word lit her from the inside until she remembered it was only temporary. But still, he'd said home and Daisy was glad he was coming back for whatever remained of his stay in the cottage.

'Don't you want to wait for the results?'

But Ben was already hurrying away, and she marvelled at his energy after the race he'd just completed. 'Nah.' He turned to give her a quick grin. 'I haven't won, and it'll be ages until the last competitor's back. I'd rather go to the pub with you.'

Ben was back within forty minutes, striding down the street towards her, changed into jeans and a hoodie. He looked effortlessly handsome and she swallowed as she dumped the last of her takeaway tea into a bin.

'Hope I haven't kept you hanging around too long.'

'No, you were quicker than I expected. Let's go, it's about half an hour from here.'

Ben followed in Edwina as Daisy led the way to the pub, eventually turning off to follow a steep pass before dropping into a tiny hamlet where a traditional Tudor pub sat just past a small church. Surrounded by tall hedges and rolling fields below high fells, many people missed it if they didn't know just where to find it.

They'd arrived after the usual rush for Sunday lunch and Ben nabbed a quiet corner table whilst Daisy went to the bar. She ordered two pints of ale, aware of him watching her as she carried them to the table and sat down. She handed him a drink and they clinked glasses.

'Cheers. Here's to completing crazy triathlons, may your knees never fail you.'

Ben laughed, acknowledging her comment with a lift of his brows as they drank. 'Thanks, Daisy. No doubt I'll be sore tomorrow.'

'You need to have that session with Nina. Maybe don't leave it until Thursday.'

He didn't answer at once, suddenly awkward. 'Probably a good idea.' He looked away, taking in the details of the pub. 'It's nice here. Different to The Coach.'

They were sitting on the opposite side of the room from the welcome glow of a log fire and Daisy was glad of it on this misty, wet day promising autumn chills and lower light.

'The beer is good.' He looked back at her as she laughed. 'What?'

'You're drinking Responsibly,' she told him, enjoying the confusion spilling into his expression.

'Yeah, well, probably just the one pint as I'm driving and it's not ideal for hydration after a race. But I'm ready for it.'

'That's just it: you can have another, if you like. As you're drinking Responsibly.'

He was still confused, puzzling over her comment and then he grinned. 'That's what it's called? The beer?'

'It's very low alcohol so we're fine with it. But if you want the alcoholic version you'll have to drink Irresponsibly.'

'Clever. I like it. Anyway this is good, but I still prefer the Nickel.'

'So have you got another race or event in mind, now that this one is over? Something at home?'

'Home?'

'New York.'

'No, nothing yet.' Ben paused, some of the wariness returning. 'I'll have to see how training fits in with work; I won't have anything like the time I've had here.'

Daisy didn't want him to see that she was dreading his leaving – he seemed so at home now in Thorndale, and she couldn't help but wonder how he would cope with being back in New York. 'Are you looking forward to going back?'

'I have to find out if I still have what it takes to do my job, if I can pick up what was good about my life there before. I know I've learned a way of coping over these past months that I won't be able to achieve so easily once I'm there.' Ben lifted an arm, gesturing to their surroundings, before his gaze came back to hers. 'But I'm not quite sure I'm ready to give up all of this yet.'

This was the moment to confirm that he was planning to leave on Saturday, the end of the six weeks he had paid for. But Daisy didn't voice her thoughts, didn't want to hear how few days they had left, the final date of their time together. She wanted only to draw out this afternoon and enjoy every minute.

'It's so lovely, what you're doing for Edwin.' She changed the subject instead. 'He'd probably never tell you himself but he's loving having you around the farm. He even told me for someone who sits, and I quote "on his arse" all day in his job, you're quite a good worker, which is high praise indeed.'

'It's been great, spending time with him and I'm happy if it's been useful.' Ben leant closer to her across the table.

Daisy was remembering their ride and how she had confessed her fear to him, until he had soothed away the fright and shown her a way forward. Her arms were resting on the table and she watched as his hand inched across until his fingertips touched hers. She slid her fingers under his, expecting him to withdraw, to decide they were treading beyond where he was comfortable. Slowly he stroked her hand with a thumb roughened from working outdoors and it was desire then that plunged through her stomach.

'Daisy, I...' He halted, one shoulder rising. 'Doesn't matter. I might have to change the date with Nina, that's all. Shall I get us another drink and bring menus?'

Daisy agreed, missing him the moment he moved. When he came back to the table with another beer for him and the red wine she'd requested, she was elated to note he was still smiling with the intimacy of moments ago, not lost to the time he had been away from her.

Their food soon arrived and Ben told her about the race, how challenging he'd found it. Whenever her eyes met his she saw an urgency there now, reminding her of their first days when he hadn't known how to stand still, hadn't known how to become a part of the place he'd chosen to stay in before he'd even realised he needed it.

'I'm glad you came today.' His voice was low, drawing her in. 'You were the only person I wanted to see when it was over.'

She reached out to slide her fingers between his, felt them tighten around hers.

'A woman like you deserves more than me, Daisy, more than the little I have to give.' Ben's smile was bruised, lost. 'You really have no idea how wonderful you are, do you? I'm not just talking about battling for the bus, or your business and Josh, but the way you look out for Edwin and cook lunch on Sundays because other people look forward to it. Advising Nina when she was setting up her business and supporting her when she thought about giving up, helping her find a way to go on.'

'She told you about that?'

'Yes, and that if it weren't for you and Scott she'd probably have left, tried to start again somewhere else. And you do it all with such love.' Ben paused, their hands still entwined, his gaze troubled. 'I'm so far from everything you are. My relationship ended because I shut down, didn't want Juliana or anyone around me.

'She tried to reach me, to get through and I pushed her away time and again until it was finally over. She didn't suffer fools and there were only so many times she was prepared to try, and I don't blame her. We were getting serious, thinking of a future, and I broke all of that.'

Someone arrived to clear their plates and bring more drinks. Daisy thanked them, trying not to be impatient. Her voice was low as she leaned towards him, not wanting to miss a word. 'Your illness did that, Ben, not you. Not the person you are really.'

He released her hand as he sighed, and she missed its warmth the moment he withdrew it. 'I knew I wasn't coping, and everything seemed frantic somehow, like I had to live in the moment at a hundred miles an hour or I'd fall, I had to keep on running. We were good together, we suited the life we'd built but I felt I didn't deserve anything good, after Aaron and she was right to tell me to go.'

Daisy reached for his hand again, offering her compassion and more, desperate to make him understand. 'Ben, you can't go on thinking you don't deserve happiness and holding back from anything that might bring it. You made a mistake; you weren't well. It's always devastating but it's understandable you weren't thinking clearly after everything you saw.'

'All the time I've known you, Daisy, you've been trying to show me a way forward without even knowing you were doing it. Giving me moments to hold on to, slowly bringing me back.' The weight in his eyes was trapping her, holding her still. 'But what if it happens again, my illness, and I can't trust my own self? How can I offer that to someone else?'

Daisy felt the tears again for everything he'd lost and the man he had become, a reduced version of himself, one who didn't seek happiness or believe he deserved it. She saw now how he'd struggled to accept the kindness of strangers and the simple care they'd given him, asking nothing, gathering around him and helping him move forward, just as he'd done for her.

'I've got something for you.' She reached for a package in her bag and handed it to him. 'For when you're back in New York. It's about a boy and the animals he meets along his way, but mostly it's about love, kindness and forgiveness.'

Ben took it, tearing the tissue gently as he opened her gift. She watched him reading through the introduction, flipped through a few pages, his gaze moving over the beautifully drawn images and exquisite written words.

'How is it you know me so completely, Daisy?' His voice was soft as he raised his head, tears hovering in his eyes. 'It's perfect. Thank you.'

'Because I know you're brave and wonderful and loving, and I have to hope when you read the words in the book, you'll let yourself believe it someday.' She had nothing more to offer here beyond the love she knew was spilling from her eyes, blinking back the tears before they fell. 'I'd like to think it will remind you of hope and happiness, and help you learn to forgive yourself.'

Ben's smile was suddenly lost in the breath that caught in his throat. 'I've been happy here, with you.'

'You have?' Daisy felt a rush of joy followed by sadness. More than anything she wanted him to be well, to heal, and they both knew he would be doing that far from here, from her. 'Even though I shouted at you for not wanting my homemade brownies?'

'Well, maybe not then.' The familiarity of their teasing was something in those first days she had never imagined sharing with him. 'I think it must have been after I met Edwin and he started shouting at me instead.'

'He's much better at it than me, and he only really shouts at the people he cares about. But I'm so pleased, Ben, really. Thorndale is a good place.' She was lost in his eyes, not pushing her away, drawing her ever closer. 'Shall we go home?'

Chapter Twenty-Three

Ben nodded at once, his fingers reaching for Daisy's hand, drifting across her skin as he followed her out of the pub. They emerged into rain, still holding hands as they ran to the cars through the darkness. Daisy skidded to a halt with a horrified gasp, her free hand going to her mouth.

'I can't drive! I'd completely forgotten about it and I've had more than one glass of wine. I know we've been there ages, but I can't risk it.'

'That's okay.' Ben pointed to Edwin's old Land Rover. 'I'll drive us. We can leave your car here and I'll run you back tomorrow to pick it up.'

'But we're about forty minutes from home and I've got a meeting first thing with a client. I can't believe I've done this, I'm so sorry.'

He was still smiling as he opened the door. 'Come on, we're getting wet.'

She jumped inside, shivering and not from the cold as Ben joined her. They drove home in silence, Daisy's mind whirling with everything Ben had told her. She wondered if he was thinking, too, about their conversation. When they finally pulled into her drive, she drew in a deep breath, not ready for the evening to be over.

'Would you like to come in?'

He'd been in the house so many times before but this time they both knew it was different. She saw the pause, a coming apology in his eyes and couldn't believe she was wrong, and had misjudged him again, after everything that had gone before in the pub. She fumbled at once for the door, shocked and ready to escape as his voice finally reached her through the silence.

'It's not that I wouldn't like to,' he said, letting go of her hand to pat her arm awkwardly as he lowered his tone into a desperate plea. 'Maybe it's best if I don't. There's something…'

'Forget it.' Utterly humiliated, Daisy leapt out and ran across the courtyard. She heard the car door slam as she unlocked the house and rushed inside. Fuming, beyond livid, certain she hadn't imagined the intimacy they'd shared in the pub, she leaned on the door, trying to slow the adrenaline racing through her body with slow, deep breaths.

But acceptance wasn't going to come easily, and she yanked the door open again and marched back into the courtyard. She was so angry, she could barely drag her thoughts into place, but she wasn't prepared to settle for another rebuff. She was going to find out why, whatever it took to learn it from him.

Shock made her stop still as she saw Ben – not in the cottage as she had expected, but leaning against the garden table, head down, the lengths of his choppy chestnut hair hiding his face. He straightened and lifted his head. Stunned by the look of anguish and regret on his face, her anger dissolved, her words a whisper carried to him on the breeze.

'Don't you want me, Ben? Have I really got it so wrong?'

A despairing sigh followed as tears gathered in her eyes. She needed an answer, she was going to make him spell it out and then she could begin to put him aside once she knew the truth. But those thoughts were forgotten as he crossed the courtyard in a few, rapid strides. He halted right in front of her, staring into her face with an intensity she had never seen before, his real emotions finally revealed.

'I've wanted you since the moment you sat me down in the kitchen after the accident,' he said roughly, one hand going to her shoulder. 'I only came back and took the cottage because I hoped to see you again, even though I never expected to be able to do anything about it. I feel as though I'm home when I'm with you, Daisy, and I would've showered under a bucket to be near you. And trying to pretend I felt differently all these weeks has been almost unbearable.'

'But why,' Daisy whispered, a tear snaking from one eye and trailing down her cheek. Ben saw and brushed it away, his touch tender and belying the fire in his words. 'Why the pretence?'

'Because I wasn't sure what I could offer you would be enough, for either of us. I can't stay here, and I didn't want to hurt you or start something that had to end. That's why, Daisy. Never because I don't want you or care about you. I thought you were better off without me, after everything that's happened.'

Her hands reached up, pulling his head down as she tangled her fingers in his messy hair, dragging his mouth onto hers. His arms went around her, one tightening across her back to pull her against him as the other held her face, his touch on her skin so gentle.

It was barely enough, and she slipped an arm around his neck, trying to support herself without halting their kiss. She was backing up and he followed, still crushing her against him, still kissing, still exploring and offering more until she was pressed up against the house and they could go no further.

Never before had she felt like this. Desire raced across her skin, leaving her breathless. She knew it was undoubtedly the kiss of a lifetime and one that had been promised since those first days, when she had understood him without ever having known him and he her, and now no other would do.

His hoodie was a barrier and she tugged at it impatiently. He let her go long enough to wrench it off, letting it fall to the floor at their feet and leaving him in a T shirt and jeans. His gaze went to her face, slowly falling to follow his fingers trailing over the neckline of her top and she gasped, dragging in a breath.

She wanted every button gone, wanted to yank it apart and watch his eyes follow and he kissed her again, holding her steady against the cool wall with the length of his body against hers. His lips moved to her neck, following a pattern already traced by his fingers and his hands trailed onto her shoulders, gently holding her as he lifted his head to stare into her eyes, hazy with desire.

'Daisy, you need to know before this goes any further that I'm leaving for New York tomorrow.'

Daisy's mind buzzed with utter confusion as she tried to make sense of Ben's words and she blinked, her arms still around him as his grip on her tightened. She repeated them silently as his meaning began to dawn and she gasped again, her hands falling away. Ice seemed to be sliding through her veins now, the chill of his statement blasting away the heat that had scorched her moments ago.

'Tomorrow? Not Saturday?'

'Yes. I'm so sorry, I didn't know how to tell you.'

'So is this finally happening because you felt sorry for me? "Poor old Daisy, always on her own, may as well give her what she wants before I go". Were you just going to post the keys through the door on your way out? Just leave, without saying goodbye. Was that your plan, until I ruined it?'

Ben was still trying to hold her, to make her understand and she couldn't pretend that this could continue, that she could make just this one night last for the rest of her life. Her world had shifted again, becoming two parts, the one before this moment and everything that would come after when he had gone.

'Daisy, please, let me explain.'

'Just get away from me, Ben, you've said it all before. Don't share, don't get involved, keep your distance. It's what you've been doing since the beginning and I'm the fool here for thinking it might be different.'

She hurried inside the house, slamming the door and yelling her last words to him through the beat he was hammering on it. 'I wish you'd never come here.' Her voice fell, and she had no idea if he could still hear, even though the banging had stopped. 'I wish I'd never met you.'

Sleep eventually came when she was all cried out, her tears soaking the pillow. She was restless, waking time and again, slowly understanding that reality was worse than her imagination as she remembered the events of last night.

She had forgotten to set an alarm and didn't need it anyway, waking before five and unable to sleep again. She got up and showered, moving through the silent house, her movements stilted and sad. Today was Monday and Ben was leaving. Today. This morning, probably.

She had a meeting to go to and for a moment she considered cancelling, telling the client she couldn't make it. But her business would still be there when Ben wasn't, and she knew she might as well get on with it. She plugged her phone in to charge so she could call a taxi to take her back to the pub.

Daisy was in the kitchen, making a cup of tea she knew she probably wouldn't drink when she heard the outside door being unlocked. There was a single tap on the door from the passageway and then Ben was in the kitchen. Of course, he still had his keys and as usual she hadn't bothered to lock the door.

She faced him warily from behind the width of the old table. It was little consolation to notice he looked terrible too, his eyes puffy and fraught. He seemed to be limping as well, no doubt a payoff from the triathlon. Good, she hoped it really hurt. Like her heart.

'We should get going,' Ben said, his voice unnaturally bright as he indicated the door. 'I was hoping we could talk on the way.'

'Are you mad? Why would I go anywhere with you?' Her voice dripped ice and her look was cold as she stared at him. 'Anyway, you've got a flight to catch and I don't want to delay you.'

'It doesn't leave until this evening and whatever you think of me, we need to talk. And you need your car so you may as well just come.'

Despite everything ending so badly last night, she still wanted every last moment with him. She reluctantly gathered her things, Ben waiting outside as she locked up. The village was still quiet at this hour and they were silent until he began to speak, the miles behind them steadily increasing.

'Daisy, I didn't know until Friday that I needed to leave today. I have to go on a course, and it was all confirmed at the end of last week. I tried to put it off so I could stay for these last few days, but they want me there on Thursday. After everything the company has done for me, I didn't feel I was in a position to refuse and ask for more time.'

He paused and still she stared ahead, unwilling to add anything to make him feel better. 'I didn't know how to tell you without us going back to where we were before, when I was only meant to be a paying guest. I knew the moment you agreed to rent me the cottage that it was so much more for me, and I thought us being friends was the best I could hope for.'

Daisy knew he'd never been just a guest, not for her. From those first moments after the accident she'd felt her heart reaching out to him, wanting to offer what care she could. And now her heart would be broken, scattered into pieces he would leave behind.

'I knew if I told you I had to leave it would spoil the weekend and it was selfish of me, to want to enjoy those last couple of days and not think about leaving you. How you found out wasn't right, but I thought you should know before we went any further and assumed I'd not told you just so I could take you to bed. I'm so sorry, Daisy. I never meant to mislead you, and I certainly didn't want what happened between us last night to stop.'

'Thank you for explaining,' she said, her voice a quiet murmur amidst the din of the noisy old engine. It was a glorious day, the sun rising slowly over the hills, but its beauty couldn't lift her in the way it normally would. Her heart felt leaden, as thought it was encased in something solid, something unpleasant that weighed her whole body down. 'But it doesn't change where we are now, or that you're leaving and I won't see you again.'

Tears filled her eyes again at the thought, she couldn't imagine how her business would ever be enough now that Josh was starting college and wouldn't be with her during the week. And she couldn't imagine herself dating anybody else, not after these weeks with Ben. Her life stretched before her, separated from his by the wide gulf of the ocean between them.

'I don't want this to be the end,' he said quietly, reaching for her hand. They were in the car park now and he pulled up next to her Land Rover, cutting the engine and enveloping them in a sudden silence.

He shifted in his seat to look at her as she stared ahead. 'I'm serious, Daisy. I thought I could leave and let you go, that it would be for the best, but I can't. Not after everything I did to push you away and still you turned up to support me. I tried so hard not to make my leaving even tougher, but I don't want this to be the end of everything, of us, unless you do?'

She raised her shoulders, knowing the question in his eyes was reflected in hers. 'You know I don't. But what else can it be? You'll be too far away, and I have to be here. There's never really been an "us", just a few lovely weeks I'll always be glad we shared.'

'We can call, FaceTime, whatever. And you could come out, you and Josh, and I can fly back here whenever we want.'

'Don't, Ben, please.' Her smile was bereft and her heart breaking, having to say the words to make him leave her behind. 'I can't live that life, I don't want to be the one at the end of the phone waiting for you to call and always wondering why not when you don't. Thorndale isn't your real life, you belong in New York.'

Her hand reached up to touch his cheek, feeling the graze of his beard against her palm. The gesture brought another sharp reminder from last night, the memory of his mouth on hers and how his hands had roamed hungrily over her body, thrilling her with his touch.

'If we've helped you to heal then I'm glad, but you were always going to leave, and I've let myself ignore that.' Her hand fell away before his could join it and she stared ahead. Her fingers were on the door, about to open it, when he spoke.

'So that's it, then? No point in trying, is that what you're saying? Or is it that you don't want to take another risk?'

'On what exactly?' Her voice rose in frustration and she spun back to look at him. He was slumped in his seat, shoulders low and radiating despair.

'Love, that's what. Just good old fashioned, horribly inconvenient, falling in love.'

She stared at him, her eyes widening even as her mouth fell open in utter shock. 'You don't mean it,' she whispered, her lips forming words her mind couldn't follow. 'You couldn't possibly.'

'Don't I?' Ben's grin was ironic and the laugh that followed didn't sound any cheerier. 'I'll take it back if you can say truthfully you don't care about me. But it won't change how I feel.'

She hadn't ever dared let herself name what she felt for him. There hadn't seemed any point, whenever she'd thought they were growing closer he'd push her away again, bruising her with his brusqueness. And now she understood that it had been a shield for him too, a way to try and frustrate the inevitable that had overtaken them anyway, with all its difficulties and separations to come.

'Shall I take it back?'

She shook her head slowly. 'But what can we do?'

'Not give up before we've even tried, for a start.' He raised her hand to his lips, brushing her skin with his beard as he kissed her fingers. 'Can we at least call, make plans?'

She shook her head again and his eyes narrowed as he watched. 'No calls. I mean it, Ben, I don't want to be sat around at midnight wondering when you'll finish work, what party you're at or which city you're heading to next. Let's message, only when we feel like it, when we have something to say. I'm not making any promises and I don't want you too, either.'

'And then what? For a month, six, what? What do we do next?'

'Two months today, we see how we feel. Who knows, when we're not bumping into each other every day we'll probably be glad we didn't make some silly promise to keep something going that was never meant to be.'

'Is that what you truly believe?'

Not for me, she wanted to say but she didn't. She wanted him not to leave more than anything but that wasn't possible, and she understood he needed the chance to see what remained of the life he had before.

'If everything between us has changed by then, we'll know. Do you agree, Ben? No phone calls, no video calls, just emails or messages.'

He nodded reluctantly, quickly checking his watch and she got out of the car. So it had begun. The separation, the life that was coming after the summer and she would not hold him back or plead for more. They had two months to decide, and it would have to be enough.

He followed her to the car, waiting whilst she threw her bag inside and turned to face him. He tried to smile but it was lost in a sudden rush of tears filling his eyes and she stepped into his arms, resting her head on his shoulder as they held one another.

'Two months,' he murmured, lifting her chin with a finger. 'Two months to prove nothing has changed and what we feel is worth taking a risk on.'

Chapter Twenty-Four

'You've done what?' Nina gaped at Daisy, astonished. 'The guy as good as tells you he's in love with you and you tell him to sod off for two months and that you'll message? Then what? Are you going to compile all your love notes into a spreadsheet and email them to him for comparison? See who's got the most?'

'You make it sound ridiculous.' Daisy didn't bother to hide her huffiness at Nina's incredulous response. They were having a coffee to catch up, or as Nina was now referring to it, coffee to tell Daisy to sort out her life.

It was Saturday lunchtime, Ben had only been gone for five days and Daisy was glued to her phone, constantly checking for anything new. She missed him in a way she hadn't imagined possible. She had always known he was there, in the little house at the bottom of the garden and these past few mornings she'd hated seeing it from her bedroom window, its silence somehow shouting his absence.

Ben's leaving on Monday had coincided with Josh's return the same evening and he'd spent his last day at home with Daisy before college began. She had found the process of moving quite a lot of his stuff to his dad's house on Wednesday almost unbearable.

She'd always known that university beckoned for Josh and that she'd cope when the time came, but it felt as though she'd handed her heart over twice already this week when she'd left him at Mark's two days after Ben had left. She'd done her best not to cry when she'd hugged Josh goodbye, and he'd promised to let her know how he got on over those first few days.

He'd returned late on Friday and wasn't yet up when Daisy had left the house to see Nina. Mrs Timms was agog, trying and failing not to listen every time she appeared at their table to whisk away an empty cup or scoop up non-existent crumbs.

'That's because it is ridiculous, D! It's obvious, to me at least, probably not to Ben, how you feel about him and yet you're happy to bury yourself here and watch him leave.'

'I didn't have any choice, Nina. His job is in New York and mine is here. And then there's Josh, I can't just leave him. And you were the one who warned me to be careful.'

'Oh don't give me Josh, Daisy. You and Mark have done a wonderful job but take a good look at him. He's making a great life for himself and I don't think he'll fall apart if you get on a plane and go visit Ben for a bit, do you?'

'Be careful you don't use him as an excuse to keep standing still; he doesn't need you looking over his shoulder every minute. I know your career is important to you and rightly so, but you can be an accountant anywhere, even in New York.'

'Don't hold back, will you.' Daisy couldn't keep the sarcasm or hurt from her voice. 'Is that what you think of me? Am I really so dull and predictable?'

Nina reached across the table to grasp her hand. 'Of course you're not, you're an amazingly creative, loving, beautiful woman and so many other things. Yes, it's a bit shit that Ben lives four thousand miles away but you're not going to turn into the world's worst mum just because you've finally met someone who rocks your world.

'You need to let yourself find out what happens next. Take the risk, Daisy, and go. Have fun with him, find out how you both really feel. You'll always wonder what might have happened if you don't. And I only wanted you not to be hurt but it's too late to worry about that now.'

'I know. I didn't want to fall in love with him, Nina, I really didn't. I can't bear to think of him meeting some girl across a crowded airport lounge and before you know it he's joined the mile-high club, if he's not already in it, and then he's going to tell me all the reasons why it could never work between us.'

Nina shrugged. 'You've still got to risk it. For all you know, *you* could be his mile-high girl.'

Daisy burst out laughing at that and Nina made her excuses, ready to dash off to train as usual after her morning clinic. She hugged Daisy tightly and Daisy sniffed, thankful for Nina's practical and loving advice, despite her protestations.

Mrs Timms reappeared, and Daisy ordered another drink. She'd promised to pick up some shopping for Edwin and decided to head into town after the coffee, pulling out her phone to check for new messages.

'I take it you've heard, then, Daisy? Isn't it marvellous?'

She looked up, trying to feign interest in whatever scrap of information the older woman wanted to share. The cafe was at the heart of any news and Mrs Timms usually the first to impart it. 'What's that then, Mrs T?'

'Apparently a "mystery benefactor" has donated ten thousand pounds to the community bus fund to keep it running; it was just confirmed this morning. I thought you'd have known.'

Daisy stared up at her, the phone clattering to the table. 'I haven't looked at my emails yet.' Her thoughts were chasing one another through her mind and her smile was suddenly incredulous.

'I think we can all guess who it might be.' Mrs Timms set down Daisy's second flat white, dropping a kind hand onto her shoulder. 'I told him he shouldn't be leaving you here and going back to that great big city. Nothing he'll find there he hasn't got here.'

So the Thorndale community and its funny little bus, so much a lifeline to all who depended on it, had truly come to mean something to him. Daisy knew the money was enough to finalise the purchase of the new bus and keep the scheme running for another two years at least and she reached for her phone.

Edwin was strangely quiet when she called in with his shopping later and she made them a cup of tea. They sat around the small kitchen table, still set for two, as though his wife had just popped out and would be back soon. Daisy was always gently trying to persuade him to change it, but he stubbornly resisted every effort, stopping short of setting out a second knife and fork.

They talked about the dogs and which farmers were in line for the new puppies, due in two weeks, and made plans to bring the horses down to a field closer to the yard where there was better shelter away from the worst of the coming winter weather. He'd been to his GP appointment and they were keeping an eye, sending him for more blood tests in a couple of weeks.

When she asked him for the third time if he was all right, he eventually confessed he was fine, just a bit weary and, more surprisingly, he admitted to missing Ben and his help around the yard. Even he was referring to the red Land Rover as Edwina now and Daisy hated seeing it sitting idle in the barn once again. She didn't know whether to laugh or cry when he grumpily told her that Ben had left it with a tank full of fuel and he'd drained nearly all of it out in case someone tried to pinch the vehicle.

She took the keys Ben had left when she returned home and wandered down to the cottage with her phone. It was utterly silent, not a thing out of place, almost as though he had never been here. She went into the bedroom, already cleaned and ready for new guests, guests Daisy didn't want. All those nights he had slept here when she was but a short distance away, thinking about him. How much time they had spent apart whilst they'd ignored what they really felt and could have been together before the end?

She pulled the duvet back and climbed into the bed, wondering which side he had slept on, whether he had imagined her with him here, as she was doing now. She reached for her phone, took a picture, half of the bed in the frame, and sent it.

I miss you x

She checked the time. It was around eleven a.m. in New York and she had no idea how he was spending his first weekend back in the city. Would he meet with friends for brunch, bump into his ex, spend it training? She didn't know and she was still lying on the bed when his reply came. She drew in a breath, a sad whisper filling the silence for a second.

I didn't spend a night there without wishing you were with me. I miss you too x

Ben's first message had arrived on Wednesday, not even forty-eight hours after he'd left, whilst she was in her office, trying to keep her mind on work. She hadn't recognised the number and had stared at the photograph of a stunning apartment lobby, wide glass doors framing a uniformed doorman and opening onto a huge minimalist space lit by natural light. Ben had attached all his new contact details and a short message.

> New building, still prefer the cottage. Am I allowed to say I miss you?

Daisy had enlarged the picture, shrunk it back to normal, tried to make whatever sense she could of his new surroundings, trying not to compare its obvious luxury to the simple cottage he had left.

> Not buying that, looks incredible x

The next day it had been a picture of a small park, a dramatic waterfall spilling down granite rocks and framing lush planting and a small cafe tucked between trees. It was beautiful in its simplicity, and she couldn't begin to see how he could consider a life beyond this exceptional city.

Friday was the kickboxing studio in his building followed by a view of his apartment, all white, grey and impersonal. She knew the apartment belonged to his company and he was staying there whilst he searched for somewhere new.

She hadn't quite known what to send Ben, at first. He didn't need to know Henry had asked her out for dinner or that she'd turned down another potential client, unsure whether she wanted the additional business. She didn't feel photos of the village he now knew well compared with his images of New York and it was only on her early walks each morning before work, no longer needing to make sure Josh was out of bed and onto the school bus, that she found inspiration.

She captured a sunrise, later now as autumn sidled closer, over one of Edwin's fields scattered with sheep and glinting with dew. The terrace outside the cottage, leaves from the trees falling to linger on the chairs where they had sat in the sunshine. The latest image of Nina's hacking jacket as Daisy scrambled to finish it, and a new horse recently arrived at the RDA, its coat as fluffy as a blanket.

The weeks began to move on until their first month was up and she knew nothing had changed if the messages still flying across the Atlantic and all that they revealed were a means of measurement. Ben was settling in at work, she had viewed two more houses and was getting used to Josh coming home at weekends instead, spending every spare moment between studying and the band with Mia.

Nina had been right, as usual. Josh was successfully forging a new path with support from his parents when he needed it and an idea had dropped into Daisy's mind after that first month. Her future was already changing, and without a new home of her own yet and Josh at college, she knew she had a big decision to make. The meeting with Annie and Jon Beresford had gone really well and Daisy had accepted their invitation to take on their business, with support from another member of staff based on the estate.

She had been riding again, booking one of the RDA ponies until she felt ready to try a different horse. He was a sensible bay gelding called Oscar who was quiet but required a little more skill. She'd soon graduated to gentle hacks close to the yard, with Gwen on top of her ancient cob for company. When she'd shared this with Ben his replies had been full of praise and support, and she loved him all the more for it.

She'd been gathering information and making plans before she called Nina to talk over her idea. Nina had been delighted, cheering Daisy on and telling her at once she must go. She spent a couple more days rearranging client appointments, working late into the night to get ahead and securing Josh's support. He'd given her a big hug and made her promise to send pictures.

She'd never travelled on her own, always going on family holidays before, and it was only her absolute determination to see it through that kept nerves at bay whenever doubts crept in. Mike told her it was about time and Edwin had been mostly silent, but she knew from the glint in his eye and the sharp nod of his head that he was pleased. Connie promised to keep an eye on Mrs Hodges, Mrs Timms had offered approval and more besides, and Daisy was on her way.

–

Three days later, as she stepped off her third flight since she'd left home twenty-four hours earlier, she was exhausted and doubting her own sense. Customs seemed to take forever with serious officials scrutinising everything and she was nervous as she eventually retrieved her suitcase and dragged it into arrivals, looking around for her lift.

She soon found it, staring up at her driver, Beau, who was very tall and tanned with wide, wide shoulders, lifting her case into his truck as though it weighed nothing. She had expected the chill outside, and she blinked at the sight of the Rockies soaring high above. The Yorkshire Dales and Cumbrian fells were the backdrop to her life, but these mountains were so different again, reaching far into the sky, snow-capped and serious, hewn into hard angles and ridges.

Beau pulled out onto the highway and Daisy felt the first blast of excitement racing through her. She had arrived: she was actually here in Big Sky country in Montana, and she'd never flown so far in her life. She'd done it alone, had left her routine and familiarity behind and set out on something new. They drove past parking lots and diners, and she nearly squealed when she saw her first ranch, a wooden sign swinging in the wind, advertising the Dancing Spirit, aware of Beau grinning beside her.

Soon they were heading along a private avenue of trees turning copper and gold between post and rail paddocks, beneath a giant sign confirming they'd arrived at the Triple C ranch. Daisy was wide eyed as they drove up to the Main Lodge, a large two-storey building with a wide sweep of grass sitting in front of a huge belt of pine trees.

Beau retrieved her case and she hopped down from the truck, hardly able to believe she had made it so far and followed him inside. Wood panelling, colourful rugs and stone walls greeted her, and she loved it, staring around in wonder, her tiredness temporarily forgotten.

Once she'd checked in and been shown to her room, she went straight to the windows, exhilarated by the view. The ranch lay before her, a giant lake beyond, a jumble of buildings and corrals with wooden fencing and horses grazing. She saw actual, real cowboys in their leather chaps over jeans and wide Stetsons, yet another reminder of Ben and she laughed as she turned away to check out her room.

A queen-sized bed sat close to the curved windows and she resisted the temptation to lie down and allow jet lag to do its work, inviting though it looked. The decor was plain and simple, but attractive and she loved the huge shower and bath big enough for two. Daisy set about unpacking and settling in. She couldn't wait to go and explore, and every time she thought of riding here her stomach fluttered with nervous excitement.

She took a couple of photos and sent them to the family group and Nina, checking her last message from Ben. It had arrived on Friday, before she had left home, a picture of the Alice in Wonderland sculpture in Central Park and a hurried line he'd dashed off between meetings. He was working long hours and had been away a couple of times on business and she bit back her worries about his health. He'd given her nothing to suggest he wasn't coping, and she was certain he missed her.

He was spending what little spare time he had in the gym in his building or running in Central Park, unwilling to lose all of the fitness he had gained in the summer. She had replied, giving away nothing of her plans or any clue that she would be leaving England very soon to be somewhere closer to him. Under the same sky, at least.

She hadn't told him about her trip because she wanted to prove to herself that she could get on a plane, leave everything behind and move her life somewhere else, even if only for a short time. Nina had been astonished that she hadn't made plans to see Ben in New York but Daisy knew she had to do this first.

She needed to prove to herself she could do more than just fly to him, that she could take herself to somewhere new, alone. She'd chosen Montana because he'd been here, had begun to heal here and she wanted to see what he had seen. She was still uncertain at times when she rode at home and if she could do it here, if she could overcome what had always held her back, then she knew she would be able to step out of everything that kept her feeling safe and go find him.

Chapter Twenty-Five

Dinner was a huge, informal affair with all of the just-arrived guests gathering together and talking excitedly as they made introductions and shared their hopes for the days ahead. The food was glorious, plentiful and home-cooked. After a couple of hours, Daisy pleaded jet lag and returned to her room. It was already three a.m. in England and she was exhausted. She fell into bed and was asleep in minutes.

She didn't need to set an alarm and was awake at four a.m., Mountain Standard Time, which she thought wasn't bad, given it was eleven at home. She tried to sleep again but it was impossible, instead getting up to shower, returning to bed with her kindle until seven o'clock.

She made her way back to the dining room, following the smell of fresh coffee, her usual quest for tea abandoned by the fabulous aroma drifting through the open doors. Breakfast was amazing, with endless choice, but she managed only scrambled eggs, fresh fruit and coffee, more nervous about the horse orientation than she wanted to admit.

She needn't have worried. The moment Rusty, a narrow little chestnut with a wide, white blaze down his face, was led across to her, she loved him. She'd described her riding as intermediate and knew she could swap if she felt he was too much for her, if he needed a more confident rider.

There was a two-hour ride planned for this afternoon after a morning getting to know their horses whilst they were assessed by the ranch staff, and then this evening they would all ride a wagon out to the lake and enjoy dinner outdoors.

It felt strange at first, and she tried to settle into the deeper Western trail saddle with its longer stirrups and higher pommel. But Rusty seemed happy and so was she as they practised in the huge outdoor arena, trying not to get in the other riders' way. The first day disappeared in a blur of busyness and adventure and again she crashed into bed in the evening, shattered and sore.

But the next day she was up in time to do it all over again, starting with chores and saddling before breakfast and then an all-day ride, heading close to the border with Canada alongside a stunning blue-green lake with wide sandy beaches and stopping for a picnic lunch, not lingering too long in the cool of an American fall. She took photos of everything she saw, sending them each night to the family and Nina, but not to Ben.

She waited another two days to message Ben, until she was halfway through the week and completely exhilarated by everything she was experiencing, despite the tiredness, falling into bed every night after dinner and the evening activities with aching thighs and a wind-burned face.

But it was a tiredness that came from exercise, from pushing herself and knowing she was up to the challenge, that she wasn't merely coping here but thriving, the thought of not quite knowing what lay ahead a thrill rather than a threat. But the days were hurrying by and she didn't have too much longer before time would be gone.

She wanted something new to show Ben, something no one else had received so far. Her group had ridden into the mountains, climbing a ridgeline above trees and stopping to look out across unbroken prairies, the vast, green land disappearing far beyond what her eyes could distinguish, the majesty of the Rockies soaring behind them.

She was sitting on Rusty, confident now, comfortable with her horse, coming to understand the way he moved and adapting her body to follow. She reached for her phone and snapped the scene before them, including Rusty's long chestnut ears in the shot so Ben would know what she was doing. She clicked on the image and loaded it, making sure to tag the ranch's location, and tapped out a few words to accompany it.

So this is what a Montana sky looks like.

She pressed send and hoped it had gone. A risk, a declaration, her heart, all captured in a photograph and the words she'd sent him. That evening dinner was in the dining room and then there was to be singing around a campfire, but Daisy pleaded exhaustion and crashed into bed.

She slept more fitfully, trying not to stare at her phone but doing it anyway, double checking her message had sent. The morning came and with it a lesson in roping skills before a shorter trail ride in the afternoon. She had heard nothing from Ben, pushing the doubts from her mind as she unsaddled Rusty after the trail ride and headed back to the lodge.

She would have noticed Ben even if she hadn't been looking for him. Sitting on one of the wooden benches scattered about the front lawn, he was both totally out of place in his crumpled city suit and completely at home in the mountain wilderness surrounding them.

'You came.' Two small words, confirming the hope that had been inside her since she had decided to come here, to find what he had found.

Daisy's heart missed a beat, not in surprise but longing as he stood up. It had been a month, a little more, since they had last seen one another and she drank him in, the messy chestnut hair, shorter than before, the beard the same, his eyes somehow weary and bright all at once.

His lips parted in a wry smile as he walked towards her. 'You said calls were off limits,' he reminded her. 'Not visits. And you did tag the location so I'm guessing you wanted me to find you.'

She laughed, allowing joy to bubble up inside her as he reached for her hand. She'd missed his touch, missed the way his skin felt on hers and how he made her feel, saw everything he knew she was. She wanted to smooth away the tiredness and show him all the ways she cared.

'Does this mean the two months is up?'

'If you want them to be,' she said simply. His grip on her hand tightened as a sudden rush of relief filled his expression. 'I thought it was the sensible choice,' and her laugh was a quick sound that became almost a sob.

'I thought you should have your freedom, that once you were home again, you'd realise whatever you felt about me belonged in Thorndale and not in your real life. I thought you wouldn't want me, and I didn't want to begin something so far away that would only lead to an end.'

'Let me tell you what I've learned about real life, Daisy.' Ben's voice was a murmur and still she heard it above the people bustling to and from the lodge, staring curiously at them. 'Banks and boardrooms were my world for a long time but the moment I met you, a much better life found me.' He took half a step nearer, stroking her cheek with his thumb, smoothing away the questions she hadn't yet voiced.

'My real life found me sitting in The Coach waiting to walk home with you. Watching you being brave enough to get on that pony and ride again. Eating fish and chips in the sun, standing still to bake bread together and trying to keep my hands off you whilst we watched an old movie in the dark. Swimming naked in the tarn.'

'I still can't believe I did that!'

'We are so going to do that again.' His voice was low, speaking to life the words already in his eyes, his smile becoming more sensual. 'A better life found me wrangling sheep with Edwin, hoping he might have good things to say about me to you and racking my brains to come up with a promise I could give you for the auction before I had to leave. Trying to teach you to line dance like a pro.'

'That was you, wasn't it? The donation?'

Ben nodded. 'I did it for everyone, Daisy, but mostly I was thinking of you. You've shown me a way back to life and I want no other, as long as it's with you. I want you to know you can lean on me when you need to and I'll always be there for you, no more separations.

'It seems everyone in the village thought I was crazy to go back, and that's all because of you. Mike gave me a lecture and Edwin called me every kind of bloody fool for leaving. He thinks the world of you. Even Mrs Timms had a go: I thought she was going to poison my coffee, she was so cross. But I needed to try, to know I could do my job again, that I was better than I had been since Aaron died. And if I knew that, then I could offer you a future.'

Daisy lifted a hand to his face, touching him gently, lost in the love she felt for him.

'Do you remember what you said to me, about my head knowing the truth and eventually my heart would catch up?'

She nodded as he took a deep breath. She reached for his hand, pressing it to her lips, able, finally, to touch him, to reach out and find him waiting, wanting her beside him.

Ben kissed her fingers, and she lowered her arm so he could continue. 'I knew my heart had caught up the moment you stood on the doorstep offering me brownies with this incredible joy and warmth, and I was lost and found all at once. If you'll have me, I want to spend the rest of my days sharing my life with you and showing you how much I love you.'

'But what about your job? New York? You know I can't...'

He pointed at his suit with his free hand. 'It turns out I don't need this any longer.' His smile widened into a laugh at her confusion. 'I went to the airport last night after I got your message, straight from the office after quitting my job.'

'What? But what about your company, everything they've done for you?' That first rush of elation was followed by doubt and questions as she tried to image how a future for them might look, where they might be.

'The company knew as well as I did that it was a risk, having me back, but they were good enough to offer. My heart wasn't there anymore, Daisy, it was about four thousand miles away in this funny little village where this extraordinary woman, who I happen to be in love with, lives her life.'

'I've come a long way since February, a journey I never imagined having to make, and it's taken time and more to get here. Time I'm grateful to have had to think about what's next for me, next for us hopefully, and how I can live a life that makes a difference.

'I loved the city, I still do in a way, but I don't want to be there.' Ben stepped forward, finally closing the space between them, his words a whisper calling straight to her heart. 'I want to be where you are, Daisy. Back in England, so we can be close to Josh, see my family and get to know my new niece or nephew. And my parents can't wait to meet you.'

'Seriously? You've told them about us?' Daisy was astonished, wondering what he might have said to the family who loved him, had wanted him close too.

'Didn't have to. My mum insisted on weekly video calls since I went back to work and she knew. I think she guessed how I felt about you the moment I told her about staying in the cottage.' Ben drew Daisy into his arms, held her against him as he murmured against her hair. 'There is a slight problem, though. You still haven't said you love me.'

'How could you doubt it?' She heard the tease in his voice, wanting him to be certain she adored him. 'I've always loved you,' she whispered. 'Even before I knew you.'

He kissed her, their arms tight around each other, a reawakening of the fire that had found them before, promising everything. From the first she had understood him without ever knowing him; she had known they needed one another without speaking a word. She tipped her head back, lifting her hand to touch his face again, tracing her love onto his skin, feeling the rough scrape of his beard against her fingers as he spoke.

'You know my family still have horses on the farm? When we go down to see them, I'm going to show you all the places I rode as a kid. And there's a foal they've bred that's just waiting for a good home.'

Ben started to laugh and she giggled, loving how the new happiness suited him. 'She's mine, ours really, and I'm thinking we should call her Edwina. That Land Rover's not going to last forever.'

'Oh, Edwin will love that. He won't say so, though, I can just imagine the swearing.'

'Me too. He'll say she's fit for nowt if she doesn't work, eating up good hay that could be feeding cattle and sheep. Anyway, enough of Edwin. I've got other things on my mind.'

Ben slid his arm across her shoulders, pulling her tightly against his side as they headed towards the lodge. 'I've got an idea to share with you.'

Epilogue

'Are you quite sure we're allowed to do this?'

'Absolutely.' Ben reached across to smooth Daisy's cheek with a finger. 'You've got dirt on your face.' He leant forwards, dropping a kiss there and she laughed as she kissed him back, his hands reaching beneath her layers of clothing to warm himself.

'You're freezing!' She jumped, wriggling nearer anyway, trying to keep him close. 'There's so much to do.' She pointed to the chaos surrounding them and he pulled back with a smile that promised time later. 'So much stuff.'

'Edwin said we'd know what to save when we found it.'

'It just feels strange, that's all, after so many years. I keep expecting him to appear and roar at us.'

'He definitely won't be doing that. I dropped him off at the Mart this morning and with the promise of a free lunch and a lift back later to have a look, he was happy to let us get on with it.'

Daisy and Ben were in one of the barns on the farm and after a couple of hours hard work, they'd already cleared a lot of stuff into the yard, the red Land Rover doubling up as a truck to cart stuff away for recycling, rehoming or dumping. There would be a sale soon to auction off the items that would be no longer needed on Low Gill farm, some had been donated to a museum in town already.

It was dirty work and Edwin had helped from time to time, marvelling at the items they unearthed, sharing his stories of life on the place he had been born and imprinting his memories into theirs. Strangely they did know what to keep when they saw it. The silage knife he had lost twenty years ago and had been overjoyed to find, the broken sheep shears sent away to be mended, a pair of antique hay rakes that were going back on the stone walls and a set of harness from the days when horses had worked on the farm.

After Ben had joined Daisy on the ranch in Montana back in October they had finished the week together, riding out every day and enjoying the incredible experiences the spectacular West had to offer. They'd moved on to New York and he had shown her the city and all that he loved about it.

She had understood he was still coming to terms with what he'd witnessed that terrible night and he had been ready to leave when her holiday was over. They'd returned home to Thorndale and moved into the cottage he had rented from her all those months ago, no more messages required.

Josh had been happy to see them, though wrapped up in Mia and the band, he'd barely noticed Daisy's absence and she was thankful. Mike had wanted to know if both she and Ben would be interested in working in the pub and they'd told him regretfully no, they had other plans.

Mrs Timms had pursed her lips when Ben had popped into the cafe but she'd given him a free coffee so he'd known she was pleased to see him and had surprised her by scooting around the counter to lift her off her feet in a big hug. She'd told everyone afterwards she'd not felt arms like it in many a year, giving Daisy more knowing looks whenever she appeared now.

Edwin had given Ben a long, dark glare when they'd gone to see him and made Daisy cry when he'd thumped Ben on the back, his huge fists spelling out the affection he'd never put into words. There was a conversation to be had and they'd taken him out for lunch to his favourite place, the cafe at the local Auction Mart, who provided good, honest platefuls of home cooking piled high enough for hungry farmers.

Over a mountain of steak and kidney pie and chips, they'd outlined their idea. Edwin had taken to it at once, shaking his head in something Daisy had felt was close to relief, eventually admitting he wasn't sure he could manage another winter alone on the farm.

And so it was agreed. Daisy and Ben were to buy the farm from Edwin, and they had helped him begin looking for a new home immediately. Edwin had his criteria, which included not much to do with the house and everything to do with location and what was outside the actual building.

They'd quickly found a stone-built bungalow on the fringes of the village, which was old fashioned enough to suit him inside but had a small barn, the necessary shed for the vintage tractor and a few tools. Most thrillingly of all for Edwin, there was a two-acre field surrounding the property that was already stock proof so the dogs and a few sheep could make the move with him.

Theirs wouldn't be a typical Dales farm in the future, though. Back in October on the ranch Ben had shared with Daisy his idea and she'd loved it at once. He wanted to bring more horses onto the farm and begin offering equine-assisted therapy programmes, allowing the animals to use their sensitivity, intelligence and empathetic behaviour to improve and promote mental health and wellbeing.

There were months of planning and rebuilding ahead, of making the farm suitable, training, and searching for the right horses, and they didn't expect to be ready to begin before the summer. Daisy and Ben were also riding regularly after Edwin had informed them with a glint that the farm came with his two horses. She and Ben had gradually brought the grey gelding and chestnut mare back into routine riding work.

Flint was becoming everything Daisy wanted, steady enough to plod around the village and yet alert enough to have a canter across the hills when she felt like it. She had hopes he might be their very first therapy horse, he was so laid back and intuitive.

Lark was sharper and suited Ben more, and Daisy doubted she'd be going anywhere near their visitors. They'd also recently acquired a beautifully bred native Dales pony with a foal about to be weaned and planned to develop a small herd to graze the hills, to play their part in keeping the breed going into the future.

The foal bred by Ben's parents, Edwina, would be almost a yearling when she arrived in the spring, coinciding with a visit Ben's parents were making. Daisy had taken to his family at once, and they to her, the two mums bonding over more than the love they shared for their boys, no matter their sons' ages. She also knew Ben's mum appreciated the love and support he'd found with Daisy, and she and his father had offered to help with the new business in any way they could.

Ben had sold his house in London and they were helping Edwin settle into his new home, where he marvelled at modern central heating and the benefits of Wi-Fi. He also spent a fair bit of time on eBay trying to buy old farm implements that thankfully he was usually outbid on, declaring them too expensive.

Daisy's parents had returned from Canada in November, thrilled to welcome another addition to the family. They were making plans to sell their family home and look for somewhere smaller so they could travel between their two daughters and their families.

Ben had also completed his volunteer training and was driving the new community bus for an afternoon every other week, getting used to sharing his news with the passengers who climbed aboard with cheerfulness and stoic attitudes to knees that refused to bend properly and the chill winter weather. They liked to ask after him and Daisy and find out how their plans were coming along.

She'd teased him no end about that as they'd laughed together, and she loved him all the more for becoming part of her home, recognising its strengths and living with its limitations. There were still occasional days when those last moments with Aaron found him, but Daisy knew he had learned a way of coping and he would reach out to her as they supported one another.

Ben was still training but it was more relaxed now, a means of keeping fit rather than recovery. Daisy had started swimming with him, but he'd been utterly unable to persuade her to come running and she intended to cheer him on from the side-lines again at the next Mud'n'Mire race in the summer. He'd been admitted to Nina's running group and he and Scott had discovered a mutual love of whisky when Ben had taken a temporary finance job at a local distillery.

'Hey, come here.' Ben lunged after something near his feet, trying to catch the squirming mass and toppling back onto a pile of loose haylage. 'You've got a job to do.'

Daisy threw him a glance and he stuck out a foot, tripping her so she landed beside him on the hay, laughing as she gave up trying to escape. She leaned over to kiss him, loving how his eyes narrowed as her lips hovered over his, brushing them slowly.

His hat had slipped, and she pulled it off, revealing the long hair, darkened by winter, that he'd grown back since they'd come home. She squealed as something landed on her and fell on top of him. Ben reached out, clinging on to a handful of black and white fur, and Daisy wriggled away.

'Got you.' He sat up triumphantly, holding the puppy in his arms, who promptly tried to nip his nose. 'Ow, you little monkey!'

Daisy was still laughing as she watched them. The puppy had been a gift from Edwin, a beautiful working collie he'd kept from the last litter likely ever to be bred on the farm, telling them the place still needed a dog whose pedigree name began with Low Gill. They'd fallen in love with her at once, naming her Hope, and she was at their side in everything they did, bringing joy and trouble in nearly equal measure.

Ben gently settled her onto his knee and looked at Daisy, suddenly nervous. 'Hope has something for you.' He lifted the puppy across, and Daisy took her, cuddling the warm body against her chest.

'What do you mean?' Her tone was suspicious. 'I'm sure it's not my turn to clean her up if she's been rolling in the muck heap again.'

'Nope, not that.' Ben pointed to her collar and Daisy reached down, finding a small box attached to it. Her fingers recognised the shape and her eyes, wide and astonished, flew back to Ben's as she tugged it free.

'Open it.'

She did, and gasped as she found an exquisite antique emerald and diamond ring nestling inside. Ben reached for her left hand and she let the puppy escape so the little dog could jump up and down in the hay next to them. He took the box and slipped the ring out, looking up at Daisy with the gorgeous smile she adored and a question in his eyes.

'Hope wants to know if you'll marry me.'

Daisy reached down to place her hand against his cheek, her eyes giving him her answer long before her words. 'Tell her yes,' she whispered. He grinned delightedly as he tugged her towards him for a kiss, and they both looked down as he slid the ring onto her finger.

'We mustn't lose it, Edwin will disown me. It came from his grandmother and we found it in a toolbox in the barn last summer, family legend has it she lost it during haymaking. He told me then I was a bigger fool than he already thought if it wasn't sitting on your finger before the year was out.'

'Hopefully, he's only half right as it's still January, but I wanted to wait until the farm was ours.' Ben was looking at Daisy, his love, hope and promise for the future shining out of the green eyes she had always understood and loved. 'This ring belongs here, just like we do.'

Acknowledgements

The idea for this book came out walking one day when I noticed a house with a small building at the bottom of the garden. The character of Ben popped into my head when I imagined him passing through a place he knew nothing about. What might happen if he stayed and who might he meet? Daisy's compassion and kindness were inspired by the family and friends in my life who share their love and laughter so willingly. Thank you.

My family and I had a lovely time at the Total Warrior event at Shap in the Cumbrian fells in the name of research. It was great fun and a lot of effort for the competitors, and I still can't quite shake the idea that I might bump into Ben there one day. The Helvellyn triathlon is an extraordinary race and I never travel the Kirkstone Pass without marvelling at the training required to complete it. The day spent at the finish to watch these amazing athletes was so helpful.

If you're travelling north on the M6, maybe jump off if you can at Junction 39 and head for Shap. You'll find a small place with history and heart, stories of a drowned village and the people reinterred there to make way for it; award-winning fish and chips not to be missed, an old abbey tucked away beyond the village beside a river. This place is a favourite and I'm looking forward to exploring again in the future.

Horses have long been a love in my life and I must thank the brilliant volunteers at the Formby and Southport group of the Riding for the Disabled Association. They answered all my questions and were so helpful when I visited, and any mistakes I've made in describing these lessons are my own. The RDA is a wonderful organisation and the people who work so tirelessly to keep it going are inspiring.

Thank you to Susan Yearwood, Emily Bedford and the team at Canelo, and Katrina Power for continuing to support and publish my writing. One book was the dream, number three is above and beyond! Thank you.

Thank you to book bloggers for championing authors and spreading the word amongst readers. It makes such a difference and I very much appreciate the opportunities to write articles and be included on blogs. Thank you again to all the readers discovering my books and enjoying my characters.

Thank you to Catherine, who took part in a Facebook event and suggested the name of Scott for my competitive, rugby-playing stonemason. It was a great choice and I think it really suits him.

It wasn't difficult to imagine a delightful teenage boy who is capable, loving and empathetic. Thank you, Fin, you continue to be a total superstar, and I love you for that and everything else. Your dad is teaching you well.

My mother-in-law Irene is an enthusiastic supporter of my writing and the dedication is so true. I hope you know how much your encouragement means to me and the number of times I've leapt when you've told me to jump. I will look after the ladle well.

To my husband Stewart, for everything you do and all we share, thank you. We've always been a team and I so appreciate how you step in and take on my part of the load as well as your own to enable me to write for longer when I need to.

A very special horse came into my life many years ago and at age thirty-two he continues to be a joy to everyone around him. He's taken those of us blessed enough to share his journey to places we never imagined and looked after us along the way. Daisy and Ben find a love of these wonderful animals drawing them closer, and I can easily picture their future surrounded by more.